RESONANT

RESONANT

Robert Leet

ROBERTLEET.COM

Permission can be obtained from www.robertleet.com
ISBN: 978-0-9995953-3-6

Published by RobertLeet.com

Cover design & interior formatting: Bea Reis Custodio
Cymatic images: Le5gualkee

Introduction

I wrote and published my first novel a few years ago. Since I have not mastered the art of marketing yet, l cannot say it has been widely read. However, because many of my readers claimed to enjoy my scribblings, I decided I would try my hand at another. My first book, *Timewise*, tackled a subject the physicist Richard Feynman called the only inscrutable problem in quantum physics, namely making sense of the two-slit experiment. For my second book I thought I would explore another interesting issue in science, namely how reality arranges itself in levels of scale that are strangely divorced from each other. From small to large we have the various scientific fields of quantum physics, relativistic physics, Newtonian physics, chemistry, biology, environmental science, planetary physics and astrophysics. Of course, they all blend together seamlessly if one looks closely enough, but the fact is one can spend one's scientific career as a biologist, for instance, without understanding the intricacies of plate tectonics, even though our entire biological existence depends very much on the heat and chemical transfer systems of our planet, which are largely driven by those shifting geological mechanisms.

Unfortunately, although I am a diligent worker and have managed to ply my trade as a structural engineer with enough success to sustain myself up to this point, I found writing is a much different endeavor. In short, I developed writer's block and have been unable to create more than half a dozen pages of my new work.

My frustration turned to delight a few months ago when I received a small metal box full of melted plastic, ashes and a sheaf of paper in the mail, along with the following note:

Mr. Leet,

I am called Miguel. I am working in construction all the time, and last week find the box I am sending you. I saw it while I repair a chimney fire in a house in Cambridge, Massachusetts. I think who put it there took out the medicine cabinet so he could hide it behind the wall, but the bathroom is near the chimney and it burned bad in the fire. But some of it is OK, as you will see.

I send it to you for two reasons. My girlfriend read your novel and so I try to read it too. I need to know English better so I can go to school here. I begin to study science at the Universidad Nacional Autónoma de Nicaragua, but I must leave there when they shoot the students. That is the second reason I send this to you. I do not have the right papers, I cannot let anyone know who I am. You understand sometimes it is better things stay hidden, so you will understand.

I like your book and how it sees quantum problems. It is important to understand how people think makes the scientific attitude. Humans exist by figuring out the future, and that is what we want from science, too.

Your story remind me of a paragraph from a great Mexican author: "Pensé que el universo era un vasto sistema de señales, una conversación entre seres inmensos. Mis actos, el serrucho del grillo, el parpadeo de la estrella, no eran sino pausas y sílabas, frases dispersas de aquel diálogo. ¿Cual sería esa palabra de la cual yo era una sílaba? ¿Quien dice esa palabra y a quién se la dice?"

Anyhow I like your book and think you will know what to do with this.

Understandably, Miguel did not put a return address on his package, so I have had no way to get more information about the manuscript.

The box he sent me is an old-fashioned light-gauge steel box that might be found in mid-twentieth century offices to store or transport papers. It had a cheap lock that had been pried open by the time I received it. The box was approximately ten inches by twelve inches by six inches deep. It was covered with black soot when I received it, inside and out. Inside was a handwritten manuscript, or at least part of one, along with some remaining ashes and small lumps of melted plastic, as I noted above. It appears from what the author tells us that the better part of what was in the box burned. As you will see, the manuscript appears to have been written in 1991. It's a shame the writer did not choose a small heat resistant safe in which to store his papers.

In his note Miguel — assuming that's his real name — mentions the manuscript contains information that someone apparently wanted hidden. Specifically, the question is whether the identities of the people involved in this story should be unmasked, as a few of them were allegedly subject to persecution by a government agent, and in fact may have actually broken some national security laws. In the course of editing what was saved, I have changed the names of everyone mentioned and a few other details as well. I have also reconstructed much of the last two pages of this narrative myself, as they were partially burned, along with the other documents referred to herein. I suppose with enough resolve and resources, the true identities of some of the people involved could be discovered, but as the events described took place nearly thirty years ago, I doubt there is much danger of any harm befalling anyone still living. Besides, this tome solves my problem of not being able to write anything on my own, so I feel compelled to publish it.

Before I go on, I feel I would be remiss if I did not address the lines of Spanish in Miguel's note. After considerable research, I discovered they are from a short story by the Mexican Nobel Prize poet, Octavio Paz. Loosely translated (I'm afraid my English is not as good as Paz's Spanish) they are:

> *I imagined that the universe was a vast system of signals, a conversation between immense beings. My actions, the sawing of a cricket, the twinkling of a star, are no more than pauses and syllables, scattered phrases in their dialogue. What is this word of which I am a syllable? Who says this word, and to whom is it addressed?*

If any reader happens recognize some of these events despite my subterfuge and thinks they might know any of the people involved, I would greatly appreciate hearing about them. It would be interesting to contact them to see if they remember events the same way "Joe Tenatt" did. Without further ado, I present his manuscript.

1

I would like to get to the point quickly because I do not know how much time I will be given, but unfortunately my point is more of a saga, a saga through a vast landscape with obscure landmarks, much like the prairies where I grew up. So, because the path I want to take you down is circuitous, I will need to be patient. I hope I have time.

My name is Joseph Tenatt. I'm a problem solver, and my milieu is mathematics. You might say I'm a mathematician, but mathematics requires stamina and a good memory, so it is a young person's game and I am far from young. Still, I've acquired some knowledge and a favorable reputation over time, and am often yet called upon to point others in the right direction or even recommend a working mathematician whose talents might be suited for a job at hand.

I've lived in Cambridge, Massachusetts, since I caught the bus out of Draper, South Dakota, to attend Boston University as an undergraduate. If I had been considered of sound health I would have been conscripted for the war, but I have Tourette's and the head of our local draft board, who was also my high school's basketball coach, was so unnerved by my twitches and random guffaws he did not think I should be allowed anywhere near the military. I had already learned to live with a certain amount of rejection and decided I might help our country in other ways.

I left Draper full of hopes and ignorance and wonder. I remember staring out of the bus window for hours the first day of my trip onto the familiar and friendly fields of wheat, imagining they were waving hello to me, or goodbye, as the bus rushed past. The wheat fields of the Great Plains were soon replaced by the sterner corn sentries of the Midwest. The fields no longer waved, they only watched in stillness as I passed through their territories. They in turn were eventually replaced by the massive, uncaring forests of the Northeast. These forests have been here since the ice age, and though they have been cut down many times by humans, they just grow back in their own time, unbowed. Here even the roads could no longer travel directly from point to point as I was used to in South Dakota, but gave way to the rough dictates of the eastern terrain.

Perhaps I have grown used to a disinterested universe, maybe I have fewer hopes today than I did then. Certainly the form of my ignorance has changed, but I think the wonder I experienced when I was young has not left. It just moves at a slower pace, as do I.

I've since also obtained degrees at Harvard and Northeastern, and taught at both of those schools as well as MIT, Tufts, Lesley, Brandeis and a few more. I've worked as a research mathematician in many of the private and semi-private concerns scattered throughout the area in medicine, defense, technology and manufacturing. To an outsider this may sound impressive, and they are all fine institutions where I feel I did credible service, but the fact of the matter is I have never stayed too long in any one setting. I've bounced from one job to another as a matter of choice, both my own and my disparate employers'. I feel I didn't become so much unwelcome as bored anytime I decided to move on.

I live in the same second floor condominium I once shared with my wife, in an old house on the Somerville side of Cambridge. The area is an old working class neighborhood full of boxy wooden two-story houses that were built close to the streets as a matter of economy because they were meant for factory workers, but in today's atmosphere it sometimes appears to me they are willfully crowding forward to better catch the latest local gossip. They are slowly being converted into upscale condos for folks who cannot afford more expensive neighborhoods of Greater Boston, but many are still unrefurbished places for students and even poorer immigrants from outside the United States. My place is in between, which means my home is comfortable and I can afford it.

My wife passed nearly fifteen years ago, much too soon. Breast cancer. I guess I live as if she only died yesterday, though the grief has attenuated some. I think the only new piece of furniture in my apartment is my easy chair. It is just about the only piece of furniture I use, in fact, as I eat, read and sleep on it. The only other change is the addition of a microwave. And my two cats, Cleo and Ranger.

My wife, Georgiana, and I had a Jack Russell terrier. We called him Spike, and he was the love of her life, as she was of mine. When she passed I was left with Spike and we soothed each other for several years, but then he also died. I was too broken-hearted to get another dog and too lonely to live alone, so I got Cleo, a ravishing Calico. Then Ranger showed up at my door, half-starved and looking miserable as only a feral tom cat or fox with mange can. He is entirely black, with long, and now lustrous, fur and eyes as yellow as the center disks of daisies. It took him a few weeks to get used to being inside, but he never asks to leave the apartment anymore. Cleo and I nursed him back to health and the three of us get on quite well. Cleo likes to sit on the left armrest of my chair, Ranger on top of the back. They occasionally take turns purring in my lap.

Tadeusz and Marta Witkowski live in the unit below mine. Teddy is a professor of particle physics at Northeastern, and a good violinist, as am I. Marta teaches music theory at the New England Conservatory and is an excellent cellist, a far more accomplished musician than either Teddy or myself.

The Witkowskis escaped with their two young children from Soviet controlled Poland in a small dinghy they managed to navigate from the East German coast to Denmark. I like to think we are all refugees from an alien world, but my monotonous bus trip through the American Midwest has little in common with their harrowing and occasionally ludicrous journey across the Baltic Sea in a leaky boat with a fitful outboard motor. We all love Mozart, though, and I spend more evenings as part of a musical trio in their cozy apartment than I do in my own abode. Marta has created a piece of Szczecin in their flat, from the Old World furniture, intricate wall tapestries and brightly painted ceiling, to the delicate fine china and delicious otherworldly aromas of her Polish cooking.

Teddy has a broad, pale, calm face, and his voice is usually quiet as well. There are evenings when I'm not sure he has spoken at all, but when he does, his words are usually infused with meaning that, like poetry, can come back to me days later from new directions. Marta is also free of pretense, but she is as elegant as Teddy is plain. Her speech is more voluble than Teddy's, as is her visage, but even so there are few excesses in her speech, just wisdom and warmth.

To an outsider we likely appear as three intellectuals who have forgone physical health for the rigors of our mental pursuits, but to me the Witkowskis are more like a couple of laughing Buddhas who have come to understand what is important and what is not. I wouldn't tell them this, but I consider myself their student in the meaning of life.

As I mentioned, I've had a long, peripatetic career in math, so I'm unusually suited to matching younger colleagues to appropriate employment.

Sometimes I'm hired and even get paid for my efforts, often I merely pass a few names to an acquaintance over a stein of beer. I don't need much in the way of income as I own my place and my violin, and can walk most anywhere I want to go. I'm happy to just keep stirring the coals.

The path I wish to lead you down began with a call from an old friend, Major Clive Bernard. I'm sure Clive was a real major at some point, but I met him at the Lincoln Labs in Lexington in conjunction with work we did on information theory and artificial intelligence. We were part of a team working on autonomous vehicles, but as with so much of the work I have done, the team disbanded when the money ran out. It may have been picked up later by another team, but I will likely never know. Clive and I both had peripheral roles. His expertise was in what types of obstacles such a vehicle would likely encounter, and to a lesser extent what kind of intelligence information would be needed from it. I developed mathematical algorithms for the computer programmers.

Clive and I gravitated toward each other because we clearly did not belong to the social scene of the rest of our team. Our humor was too pointed and our social graces too coarse to be included in their camaraderie. I believe he is now associated with the CIA, but he claimed to be working for DARPA when we met on the occasion in question. DARPA, the Defense Advanced Research Project Agency, was created to ensure the United States military always has an eye on the most recent scientific research. It has had a finger in just about every new technology since the fifties, and allegedly a bunch of stuff that never made it. I've even heard stories DARPA has worked on paranormal phenomena, but I doubt you could get anyone to officially admit it.

Clive and I have a good relationship, probably because when I ask him about his ongoing endeavors I know his answers will be meaningless, but I do not mind being lied to — I prefer just to observe the context. In turn, Clive appreciates my acceptance.

Clive had called me up and asked me to meet him at Huxley's Coffee. That was a sure sign he wanted me to come, as I feel about Huxley's Coffee as Ben Franklin did about beer — it might be the best proof God exists and loves me. Huxley's is almost as famous in Cambridge for its ambiance as for its coffee. The pastries, though also excellent, come in third. It's located in a kind of basement in an old three-story brick building not far from Harvard Square. One needs to descend half a flight of worn stone steps from the sidewalk to reach the entrance, which graciously has the name stenciled on the door glass. No sign is visible from the sidewalk, but the place is almost always busy, so more advertising is not needed. The coffee bar guards the entrance, and there is a potpourri of rooms arranged like small caves further inside, each filled with large and small tables of no discernible pattern with similarly unmatched chairs clustered around them.

It was July, but it had been raining for days and was just the kind of weather fit for a hot drink. I entered alone and ordered a cappuccino, but when I went to pay the barista waved me off. "Major Barnard has taken care of it," she said with no uncertainty. She looked like a high school student and was cute enough to be a cheerleader, but was just as likely getting her PhD in world affairs. It was typical of Clive to have taken care of my check in advance.

I wandered through the collection of dark rooms until I spotted Clive at a small table in a short hallway between two larger rooms. It was also typical of Clive to pick a spot that wouldn't have neighbors sitting nearby.

"It's been a dog's age, Joey," Clive said when he saw me. He is the only person in my life who calls me Joey, he has never called me anything else. He rose from his seat as I approached his table and extended his massive right hand. He grabbed my hand in his, then covered it with his equally large left. His blue eyes stared directly into mine and he grinned as if were the happiest moment of his life. I couldn't decide if he reminded me more of JFK or Burt Lancaster. Maybe Lancaster playing JFK as a war hero.

"It's been a few years. How are you, Clive?"

"Great! I'm great. How the hell are you?" If you did not know Clive Bernard you could be offended when he greeted a convenience store cashier he had never met before with the same exuberance as he did you, but that would be a mistake. As I said before, with Clive you watch the context.

"I woke up this morning, so I'm doing fine." I don't usually share Clive's exuberant manner. I'm not an unhappy person, but I guess I just don't have his energy.

We chatted about a few old friends, and a little about world politics. He told me he had just returned from Southeast Asia.

"Were you in the Philippines when Marcos was kicked out?" I enjoyed asking Clive pointed questions about his activities to see how he wouldn't answer them.

"That is highly classified information Joey. More than a few of Marcos' cronies would love to know that. Some of his friends are pretty sore losers."

"Did Imelda really have that many shoes?"

"Not sure, everything was packed by the time we started moving their stuff out of there. But there was a shitload of cartons in their rooms."

This was typical of Clive — to let me know more than any news source but never give me anything specific. He filled me in on what would happen for the next six months in the Middle East. "We're concerned some of the remaining American hostages in Iran might not last much longer. Frankly, I think Ollie and Bob are screwing this thing up." Clive paused for a second, then continued, "I should have been there last year, but what can one man do?" He was as nonchalant as if he had told me the sun would shine the next day.

After ordering another of Huxley's heavenly cappuccinos and biscotti for each of us, Clive got around to business.

"I'm looking for a mathematician, Joey."

"Not me, I hope."

"No, you old war dog, you and I are past our prime. I need someone young." It was amusing being put in the same class as Clive physically. He is at least twenty years my junior and built like a linebacker. I'm built like a retired professor whose most physically challenging activity is rosining a violin bow. "I need a mathematician who's a musician, or vice versa, with no personal life. A good mathematician."

"That shouldn't be too hard. Most mathematicians have no personal life," I joked. "We're all a little too crazy for that."

Clive ignored my humor. "And can pass a strict security clearance."

"What's this all about?"

Clive engulfed me in his broad smile. "You know I can't tell you that. Let's just say I'm working for the navy, so it involves long tours on a crowded ship."

"So this person can't get seasick either."

"Most people get over that." Clive treated my irony the same way I treated his exuberance — he tuned it out.

"I'll think about it. What's the pay? How long is the tour?"

"Tell you the truth, Joey, the pay's lousy and the work can never be put on a resume. I'm looking for an adventurer."

"That should help me whittle it down. Too bad I'm too old, it sounds like my kind of project."

"It would have been, Joey, it would have been. That's why I thought you could help me find someone suitable."

I promised him I would think about it.

"Don't think too long, Joey. The ship's due to sail." He surrounded me with his smile again. "Of course, I can't tell you when."

I filled my thermos with coffee on Clive's dime before I left Huxley's. I knew it would be the only payment I received, even if I found the perfect match for his project. On the plus side I didn't feel any obligation to start calling around for a music lover looking for a chance not to play for months at a time.

I related my conversation to Teddy and Marta that evening during a break from a Brahms trio.

"Code-breaking," Marta said.

"What?" I asked.

"He's looking for a code-breaker. The best code-breakers are mathematicians who are also musicians. The British found that out during World War II."

I agreed she could be right, but we were more interested in mastering one of Brahms's convoluted passages at the moment.

It must have been a few weeks later when an old neighbor of ours, Jeannie Mellon, dropped by the Witkowskis' while we were practicing. I say *old* in the sense she had once been a neighbor. Jeannie has thick, long auburn hair and lively hazel eyes. She was in her late twenties at the time, and though she isn't really plump, she is more round and rosy than svelte. She is the kind of person who would consider herself rude if she were less than cheerful. However, she is a serious and accomplished cellist and was just beginning her musical career. In fact, she had been a student of Marta's and had often played with us when she lived nearby. Then she moved across the Charles River to Brookline and we no longer saw much of her. On this occasion she brought her fiancé, Matt, to invite us to their wedding.

At some point in the evening I turned to Matt. "I don't imagine I have to tell you you're a very lucky man." Matt was professionally neat, polite, clean shaven and attentive to the Witkowskis and me, but I also saw he was quietly and comfortably self-possessed. He managed to be simultaneously reserved and yet relaxed among a group of people he had just met.

"No sir, you don't. That's why I proposed to her."

"You proposed!" Jeannie broke in. We all laughed. Matt's skin wasn't black enough to hide his blush.

"Well, with a little prodding," he admitted. "Jeannie was pretty insistent."

We all turned to hear Jeannie's explanation. "I guess I just didn't want to end up like Sonya." It was her turn to blush.

"Sonya?" I asked.

"You know her, Sonya Perez. Her boyfriend dumped her a couple of months ago. They had moved in together at his place, and one day without warning he told her she had to move out. She was devastated, still hasn't gotten over it. I guess I wanted to pre-empt that from happening to me."

"Not to worry," Matt said. "I would never do that, I just wasn't sure you felt the same way."

I did know Sonya Perez and wasn't surprised Jeannie did too. She had taken a graduate math seminar I taught one spring at MIT called Applying Pure Mathematics. When I first saw her in class I thought she might be lost, there weren't that many female mathematicians then, but I soon found out she was a brilliant mathematician and we collaborated on a project when the seminar was over, I think for developing some sort of bomb-sniffing robot. I learned she was also a musician, a flautist, so we often played together at Magazine Beach on the Charles River during lunch break. Sometimes we felt we were playing to help the scullers rowing up and down the Charles keep time; sometimes we felt it was their smooth rhythmical strokes that kept time for us.

"What's she doing now?" I asked Jeannie.

"Trying to find her feet. She had thought she wanted to apply for a professorship at some college up in Maine because Reynard, her boyfriend, wanted to move there, but that's not in the cards now. You should talk to her, she's very fond of you, you know."

"And I of her. I'll give her a call."

2

I did call Sonya shortly after talking to Jeannie. She agreed to meet me at a local pub later that week. I arrived there about half an hour early and had already downed a pint of red ale and was working on my second when she arrived. I had a mug of her porter ready. I hadn't seen her in over a year, but she looked the same as I remembered. She was what we would have called "pert" when I was growing up, but now I guess I will settle by saying she was energetic, friendly and smart. She had startling brown eyes, startling because of the way they danced when she spoke. It was as if she telegraphed her message with them as well as by enunciating her words. She wore a kind of spiked pixie haircut, not because she mussed with it, but because her straight black hair was too thick to lie flat. I stood to greet her, not knowing if I should offer to shake her hand or not, but she short-circuited my approach by giving me a warm hug. It was enough to make me wish I were young again.

"Sonya, you're looking good. I'm so glad you agreed to meet me."

"Of course I agreed. I should have called you myself. How have you been, Joe?"

We had established a first-name basis when we played Haydn and

Mozart together. I sat down and pushed her beer across the table. We exchanged a few pleasantries and both ordered another round. I didn't want to open any wounds, but I did want to find out how she was holding up.

"I hear you almost took a teaching job in Portland. You'd be good."

"Maybe, but I get the feeling most math professors spend their careers teaching freshman algebra and sophomore calculus. Not sure that sounds very rewarding."

"It has its good side. Every once in a while you introduce someone to their life's love. What are you doing now?"

Sonya turned a little red when I asked her that question, then grinned sheepishly. "I'm an adjunct professor at Simmons. But it's just temporary, until I find something else."

"What do you have in mind?"

She reddened a little more. "Nothing yet, just looking."

It was obvious she didn't want to talk about her breakup, but I didn't really care about it either. "I know a position that might interest you." I told her about Clive Bernard.

"I'd be glad to talk to him. Do you have his phone number?"

"I'll let him know. He'll get in touch with you."

Before we parted I invited her to come to the Witkowskis' any evening to play with us, and we agreed to keep in touch.

I called Clive the next day and gave him Sonya's number. "I knew you'd come through, Joey." I didn't bother explaining I was doing it for Sonya, he knew that.

I didn't hear from either Sonya or Clive again that year, but I did run into Jeannie months later, a few weeks before her betrothal. It was a wonderful crisp autumn day full of the bright dying leaves that remind us how beautiful life is on its way out. Sometimes I need that.

"Joseph," she said, "I'm so glad I ran into you. I wanted to ask you a couple of things."

"Ask away."

"Do you know what happened to Sonya? I invited her to our wedding, she said she'd come, but now I can't get hold of her."

I was sure Sonya was on a secret ship somewhere far away, but I didn't explain that to her friend. "I'm sure she's fine," I said.

"I hope you're right. I was worried about her, but she was a little more cheerful last time I saw her. She even made a joke about trading Bangor, Maine for the bounding main. Do you think she went to Europe?"

"I've no idea." I'm a poor liar and I thought it best to change the subject, so I asked her about her other question.

"It's about my wedding too. My father passed away several years ago. Would you be willing to stand in for him at the ceremony?"

"I'd love to, but I might not be able to."

"Why not? You're coming to the wedding aren't you?"

"Of course, but when push comes to shove, my dear, I might not be able to give you away."

"I'll have to trust you to do your duty. There's a rehearsal tomorrow evening at the Twelfth Baptist Church, eight o'clock. It's Matt's family church, so that's where the wedding is going to be. Please come." I went, and I behaved myself at the wedding as well.

One late spring evening months later Sonya herself knocked on the Witkowski's door, flute in hand, while we were playing. There might be something more fun than a cello, two violins and a flute, but I've no idea what it could be.

We played a piece by Mozart, of course, then Bach. It didn't matter what instruments any piece was written for, we all understood the music well enough to make it work. Marta was of the opinion that European classical music, properly understood, required a strong dose of improvisation. "In his day, Mozart was known as much for his impromptu creativity as his written compositions," she told me once when she was trying to coax me to add more to my playing. If required, Marta moved to her piano to create a backbone for the rest of us to hang our offerings on.

When we had finished a particularly lovely and intricate Bach fugue, Sonya said, "Sometimes I think if I knew I was going to die imminently I would just pick up my flute and play until the end came, no regrets."

Teddy and Marta exchanged glances and then they both beamed at Sonya.

Teddy said, "Speaking from experience, I think that would be a wise choice."

"What kind of experience? You don't look dead," Sonya said.

"He's talking about the experience of imminent death, my dear," explained Marta.

"During our escape from the Iron Curtain ... I'm sure you've heard that tale, haven't you?" said Teddy.

"In your little motor boat? Of course."

"Keep in mind the quality of East German motors wasn't what you would expect in West Germany. And the one we had was pretty well worn out anyway. So of course it quit on us. We had no idea where we were, what the currents were, what the weather was going to be. We didn't know anything except we had a couple of sandwiches and two gallons of water. Janek and Lena were too young to be frightened, but they were getting restless. So we unpacked our violins — naturally Marta didn't bring her cello — and played. It was the only rational course." Teddy smiled sweetly when he had finished.

"Did someone hear you?" Sonya asked.

"No, no, no" Marta broke in. "No one heard. That's not why we played."

"A Danish fishing boat eventually happened upon us," said Teddy. "That's why it never advanced past imminent death for us. But for two days we didn't think anyone would find us, we just played because there was nothing else to do. And now that death does not seem so imminent, there still isn't anything better to do, so let's play some more!" Teddy tucked his violin under his chin and led us back into Mozart.

Later, as Sonya left the apartment, she asked if she could stop by my place the next day. "Of course," I said, "You can spend the night if you need to."

"No, I'll come by in the afternoon."

She arrived the next day carrying two brown paper bags with grocery items sticking out of the top — I remember celery and lettuce, a box of crackers, and mayonnaise. "Are you going to cook us a meal?" I asked. I thought she might have missed home cooking while at sea.

"You wouldn't want to eat anything I made." Sonya proceeded to set the top few items aside and then pulled a pile of cassettes out of the bottom of one of the bags. "No one can know I brought this stuff to you. It's part of my mission, which is technically unclassified, but which we were told to consider sensitive and not talk about to anyone outside our team." She looked at me for a second as if she was lost, then continued, "But I need your help."

"What's your mission?"

"We're listening to whales, trying to figure out what they're saying. The navy has been accused of devastating their populations with low frequency sonar, so we're supposed to study what they are saying to each other as part of the navy's response. But there are some back channel pressures being applied, I feel there are some very important actors who don't want us to succeed."

"Why not? The whales aren't our enemy."

"I'm not entirely sure the navy sees it that way. Maybe the higher-ups think if we show how intelligent whales are, it will put even more pressure on them to stop their current practices."

"But everyone knows how smart all cetaceans are."

"Everyone knows they're smart, but I'm not sure anyone else knows *how* smart they are."

"What have you found?" I asked.

"I've so much to say all at once, I don't know where to start. Gerry and I think they have a fully developed language."

"Who's Gerry?"

"Gerry Watkins is the other half of my team, or actually another fourth. He's the sound technician, and a lot more. He's a real genius. I want you to meet him, but he wants to make sure you're on board before he risks exposing himself."

"You make it sound dangerous."

"Like I said, our entire project is secretive, so even talking to you could get me in trouble, but I feel there's something more going on. I'm sure we can't be the first crew to explore the whales' language. The navy's given us too much background information to start with, but I haven't been able to locate any records of previous crews or scientific documentation to explain how they know what they know. I don't know if there are other research crews out there now, and if not now, what happened to the others who came before us."

"Why do you think there were previous crews? Why did they want a mathematician instead of a linguist? The navy is secretive about everything, why do you think this is any different?"

As I questioned her, Sonya seemed to get more agitated. "I told you I don't even know where to begin, but let me start with the last question. As I said, Gerry is an electronics whiz. Of course we bunk in separate quarters, I think I'm one of only three women on board, all of us supposedly civilian researchers."

"Supposedly?"

"Yeah, well Joanne DiLeonardo seems to be on the up and up, she is a linguist, she's trying to discover if there is a whale language, and if it exists, trying to decipher it. She is amazing, brilliant, I've never met anyone like her. I think she is the solidest member of our group, emotionally. She really has her feet on the ground, but that doesn't prevent her from letting her imagination explore the clouds, if you know what I mean. Kathy, however, Kathy Woods, is supposed to be a biologist, but I don't think she knows her stuff at all. I know I sound a little paranoid."

"Yes, you do. That can't be the reason you're so suspicious."

"No, no, not at all. Like I was saying, Gerry is good. So one day while he was testing some transmitters and receivers in his bunk, he realized he was getting some outside interference. He searched around and found an electronic bug in his room, under his bed. He masked it, and realized there was still interference, though a little less than before. He found another bug in his equipment tool box. When he took the box outside, the interference in his room disappeared."

"That is strange."

"Then he found another one in one of my pens, one that I had brought with me from shore. He isn't allowed into my quarters, so he taught me how to do a surreptitious search. I detected a bug in the room I share with Kathy and Joanne, and another in Joanne's equipment."

"How about Kathy?"

"Kathy tries to be super friendly in our room or at mess, but she is pretty standoffish when it comes to work, so I can't get to her stuff. Maybe it's just her personality."

"Okay, the navy is spying on you. Why do you think there were crews before yours?"

First of all, they gave me some very clear, and I must say accurate, ideas of some of the things I should look for."

"Like what?" Sonya's story was getting more interesting.

"At this point it seems whales, at least humpback whales, not only have a language, but Gerry and I think they possess some knowledge of geometry, a mathematical language they use to describe their journeys, either journeys they have taken or ones they plan to take, or both. Your second question is on point — if we were the first researchers, why would they hire a mathematician right off the bat? But we don't know how the navy obtained its ideas."

"Do you only study humpbacks?"

"So far. They appear to have the richest vocabulary, as it were. Anyway, I … we, Gerry and I, don't know how it works yet. Gerry attaches transmitters to the humpbacks we are studying so we can record and listen to their conversations. We are looking for patterns that will let us decode their system."

"Marta was right!"

"What does she know about us?"

"Nothing about you, but she predicted the navy was looking for a code-breaker when I described my conversation with Clive. She says musically gifted mathematicians are the best at that game. But why are you coming to me?"

"To go back to my story, I'm sure the navy has been doing this a long time, and yet they aren't giving us any information from their previous research. I want to continue, but I'm afraid, too. I want someone on the outside to know what is happening, and to help us."

"How can I help? I don't know anything about naval intelligence or whales." Actually, I knew a fair bit about naval intelligence, but it was true I knew very little about whales.

"For one, I want you to keep these." She pointed to the two paper bags she had brought. "This bag has copies of recordings of the whales. That one has copies of Gerry's notations of how they move." She reached in and pulled out a few narrow three ring binders. "The gray notebooks have very detailed notes of what they do while we record their singing — at least I call it singing because that's what it sounds like. There is a separate gray binder for each whale. The brown notebook is less detailed but shows the movements of pods as a whole, 24/7."

"So how did you get all this stuff off the ship?"

Sonya chuckled a little, and her magic eyes lit up for the first time. "The actual notebooks I bought here. I transcribed the notes onto toilet paper to get them off the ship, and then fixed them up for you yesterday and this morning. The tape I copied one day on board when I took some sick time and no one was around. If anyone knew what I did I wouldn't be here. The situation is a little ridiculous. On the one hand, the consequences for showing you this information might be pretty stiff, at least that's what we've been told, but the actual security on board is pretty loose. I'm not sure the captain thinks it's that important. I suspect the secrecy starts higher up."

"Why don't you put this on a computer?"

"They say they can't maintain a minicomputer for us on board, but I'm sure they use them to manage the ship. We copy all this raw data to headquarters, where I bet there's a team of navy mathematicians and programmers with mainframes doing what I'm doing alone, by hand. It might be more paranoia, but I get the feeling the Navy wanted civilians on board to show they weren't hiding anything. And frankly, it's very easy to isolate a few women on a navy ship."

"Are you sure the humpbacks have a mathematical language?"

"I'm pretty sure. I often sit with Gerry while he monitors the whales singing in real time. They even appear to use gestures while they sing."

"But surely the whales can't see each other under water! Especially during their deep dives."

"I don't know, they do have huge eyes. In any case, they are incredible listeners. It's all pretty amazing. Here, you need to watch this." She handed me a small film canister. "We were able to make films of us watching the movements of a humpback while listening to him. This is a portion of one of those films I snipped off."

"How's that?"

"We positioned our camera so you can watch Gerry's lie detector contraption while listening to the whales. It's kind of crude, but it's the best we can do with the equipment we have."

"Lie detector?"

"Yeah. Don't ask me where he dug that up, it's almost an antique. The navy sure didn't give it to him. He's rigged it up to record the whale's movements. You need to see it to understand."

Sonya looked hurriedly at her watch. "I have to go, but Gerry wants to meet you. Can you see us Sunday?"

3

It may seem I have a lot of meetings with people at coffee shops and pubs, and it's true. One of the wonderful features of Cambridge is the variety of gathering places it contains. As I've mentioned, I've lived here since I arrived as a teenager and seldom leave the metropolitan area. Hell, some years I never even cross the Charles River to go to Boston. I can't drive — in fact I can no longer even ride my bicycle because I've lost my sense of balance — but among the restaurants, the independent and student run theaters, and the plethora of concerts nearby, I feel I can tour the world at my leisure. The other half of the story is my apartment is pretty shabby, and, besides, Cleo and Ranger don't appreciate guests, especially men. When I replaced my recliner I asked my neighbor Rico to help me carry my old one to the curb. I didn't see Ranger for a couple of days after that, so I try to keep visits to a minimum.

Arranging a meeting with Gerry was another thing altogether. Gerry wanted to meet at an outdoor cafe on Newbury Street on Sunday. Sonya told me to arrive at 11 am, order a coffee and read the *Boston Globe* until he and Sonya arrived. And to have a couple of extra chairs at my table. Gerry was banking on the other tables being full so they would have to ask to sit at mine. I had doubts about the actual cover his ritual would provide, as well as the wisdom of meeting someone so paranoid, but I agreed for Sonya's sake. I also had doubts the weather would cooperate with us, but it turned out to be bright, sunny and fresh — especially enchanting because of the relief it brought from a long cold gray spring. Spring is the most subtle season in New England. Some years it doesn't seem it will ever come, but at its best it brings the first hope to the annual struggle of light versus darkness and warmth versus cold.

I arrived on schedule and immediately saw there was more than madness to Gerry's plan. The area was busy, as he expected, and most of the tables were occupied. It seemed the warmth had melted winter's angst for the entire city. Gerry could have taken two hours to arrive and I would have been happy.

"Are these seats taken?" a tall lanky man finally asked me, motioning to the empty chairs at my table with his free elbow. He was awkwardly holding a newspaper under his arm while balancing two coffees in that hand and two lunch plates in the other. His face was so sallow, and his eyes so puffy and sad I first assumed he was just another of Boston's lost denizens, but he was wearing the telltale T-shirt with a Cheshire Cat grin and the accompanying words "The Cat's Meow" below. It was Gerry Watkins.

"No, not at all. Please, sit down." He did and proceeded to unfold his paper and ignore me. I continued to read my paper as well but I also tried to inconspicuously examine my new acquaintance. As I said, he didn't look particularly healthy. His skin was pale with pale red blotches here and there, and more than a few pimples. His arms weren't exactly skinny, but I could imagine his muscles were steel wires, not flesh. There was a tenseness in his demeanor that was certainly in accord with Sonya's brief description. He was trying to size me up as well, so I eventually quit looking at him at all so as not to increase his wariness.

In a few minutes Sonya arrived. "Sorry about that, there was a long line at the loo," she said to Gerry as she sat down. Sonya picked at her sandwich but didn't pick up the paper. The three of us sat together in silence for several minutes, then Sonya let out a small laugh. Gerry and I both looked up in unison.

"You guys are reading the same article. What are the chances?" Of course the chances were 100 percent if Gerry wanted to talk, zero otherwise. We talked about the article awhile, then engaged in other small talk.

Finally Gerry said, "So, Sonya filled you in a little on our situation?"

"She told me you guys were bugged."

"Bugged, lied to and handcuffed."

"Handcuffed?" I said.

"Figuratively. The US Navy is one of the most sophisticated institutions in the world, and they give Sonya a pad of paper, and I have to jerry-rig an old lie detector I happen to own to collect data."

"Why do you think they're doing that?"

"I think they need us to try but want us to fail. Nothing else makes sense." Gerry was blunter than Sonya, but they seemed to agree on the basic situation. He described his apparatus in more detail than Sonya, and expanded on his ire at being spied on.

After a half hour or so Gerry stood up suddenly and said to Sonya, "Let's go." He had never really relaxed, but I assumed I had passed his muster, or

I doubt he would have spoken to me at all. I trusted Sonya's judgement, so I took their concerns seriously. But even though I sympathized with them, Gerry seemed unusually angry. I felt he might be one of those unhappy individuals who would be bitter and morose regardless of his situation. On the one hand I felt sorry for him if that were the case, but I also had a twinge of jealousy when Gerry lightly put his hand on Sonya's butt as they walked away.

As I folded my *Globe* and prepared to leave, I glanced around at the rest of the sidewalk tables. Any one of them could be hosting a conversation as full of meaning and doubt as ours, or as mundane as hoping against hope the Red Sox would finally break the curse and win it all that year. In any case, Gerry's cynicism had piqued my curiosity even more than Sonya's earnestness.

Sonya had left me a great deal of information in Gerry's notebooks, so much that I didn't even try to make heads or tails of it at first, I just took my cassette player out and listened to the whales "singing" for hours on end. The songs were so beautiful, so unhuman-like, and yet so intelligent sounding, I could see why Sonya thought they had a real language. It occurred to me maybe she just wanted whales to have a language. After listening to the cassettes for many evenings, so did I.

One day I borrowed a projector from Rico and watched the film of Gerry monitoring a whale's movements with its song playing simultaneously. He had developed a method of attaching his transmitters, which were the size of small bricks, to the back of a humpback with what were essentially three inch long harpoons, four per receiver. He couldn't launch the devices with a harpoon gun, so he had to get the sailors to maneuver a small life boat close to a whale by guessing where it would breach, at the risk of their boat being crushed by one of the behemoths as it launched itself from the sea, then jamb the prongs into the thick fat of a male humpback using a stout pole. Sometimes one of his bricks would stay attached to the blubber for a year or more, for thousands of miles. Evidently his instruments could transmit data up to a hundred miles, and they also had the capability of storing a few weeks' worth of data when the whale was out of range of the ship. If he got back into range, Gerry could signal a receiver to transmit its information to him.

Gerry had hooked up the transmitters to a polygraph. One of the needles measured the vertical path of the whale, another the horizontal, and a third would record either the intensity or pitch of its voice. He told me during our meeting he was still working on recording both inputs together. He set up his camera so one could simultaneously see the whale in front of the ship and his detector. I could see why Sonya was impressed with his ability — when they were closely following a whale and recording it in real time, the effect was profound. After watching the three graphs for a while I almost felt I was actually watching the whale move in his machine as well as in the ocean. And with the sound of the whales singing there was a multi-dimensional experience that was uncanny. The film Sonya gave me was less than half an hour long, but I would spend whole days playing it over and over. I wanted to show it to Teddy and Marta, but as Sonya had warned me the project was sensitive, I was reluctant to get them involved. The truth is I could see no reason anything I was looking at should be secret or important, so I arranged a meeting with Clive to find out what he knew.

Clive and I met at Huxley's again, and he gave me his typical overwhelming greeting. I mentioned events had unfolded in Iran just as he predicted.

"Yeah, I expected better from Bob, but Ollie has never had the best judgement. I shouldn't have said anything, but for some reason I trust you not to embarrass me by blabbing too much. I must have decided to trust you after we worked together on the Lincoln Lab thing."

"You going back to the Mideast?"

"No, I've bigger fish to fry now."

"India, China?"

"Bigger."

"What's bigger than that, World War III?"

Clive grinned at me. "Let's not get melodramatic. Sometimes diplomacy works."

I knew I wasn't going to get more out of him by pursuing my inquiries, besides I had something more important to me on my mind. "Clive, I'm concerned about my friend, Sonya."

"Not to worry if you haven't heard from her, I'm sure she's fine."

"I have heard from her. It's what she said that concerns me."

Clive's grin disappeared. "She talked to you about her mission? I don't think she's supposed to do that."

I had an uneasy feeling I may have said the wrong thing to the wrong person, but I decided I had to go ahead. "She thinks she's being set up to fail, that the navy has had previous missions doing the same work they will not share with her or her project members. She also found out, or Gerry did, that they are bugging their rooms and their personal equipment, and they think one of the team members is a spy, that is, is spying on them."

"Who's Gerry?"

I was digging a pretty deep and slippery hole for myself, so I kept going. "One of her team members."

"She revealed a team member's name?"

"More than that, I met him." I decided to almost level with Clive, hoping I hadn't put my friend and her companion in danger. I say almost level, because I didn't tell Clive I actually had some of the information they had gathered.

Clive sat there for several minutes, but his mind was clearly far away. Finally he turned to me. "First, I want to apologize if I solicited you to put an acquaintance in danger. I'm used to that type of situation, but I had no idea this could be one. Second, it is extremely dangerous for anyone to reveal anything about a secret naval mission, and your friends may be too naive to know the kind of trouble they may be getting into by talking to you."

"That may be so. I certainly realize the danger I could be putting them into by talking to you, but I've decided to trust our relationship because I feel they could be in more danger if we don't help them."

"That brings me to my third point. It would be easy enough for me to find out a little something, maybe even a big something, about their situation. Once. But if it is as serious as you say, the difficult part will be for me to avoid tipping my hand. Once I do I will be useless to you and I might really screw things up for your friends. And for the same reason, you shouldn't call me again. I've never met this Gerry guy, I had nothing to do with his placement, but I was taken with Sonya. She's a very sweet kid."

"So what do you recommend?"

"Are you still in touch with them?"

"No, they're at sea again. I don't know what to expect, maybe this thing will just blow over." I did not think anything would blow over.

Clive was silent again for a moment, then he looked directly at me. "I will look into it, but it might take a while. In the meantime I don't want you to do anything stupid."

"Like what?"

"Like anything at all. There is nothing you can do to help them at the moment, and a lot you can do to make things worse."

I left Clive, shaken. I was more worried than ever because he was worried. I decided to take him at his word and not do anything until I heard from him. Nothing except continue to listen to the whale recordings and examine Gerry's logs. It had been a while since I had engaged my mathematical mind, and I rather relished the challenge.

For several weeks after my meetings with Sonya, Gerry and Clive, I did nothing but listen to the sounds of the cetaceans Sonya had given me. At first I listened as I would to Bach or Mozart, as if it were music, but the music of an alien being, instead of just a superior human such as Johann Bach or Wolfgang Mozart. Gradually I began to think of the sounds differently, to imagine a true language. Now, I know there are those who would say all music is a language, a language of the heart or the soul. I don't disagree, but in this case I'm talking about a language of the mind. Some languages do sound more musical to me than others, for instance French or Hawaiian. I've only heard one or two conversations in Hawaiian, and though I couldn't understand it I was truly mesmerized. But Hawaiian is soft to my ears, full of vowels that could come from the gentle lapping of small waves on a quiet beach. Humpbacks bellow and grunt, whistle and whinny, hiss and click — their songs are full of the effort of living in the ocean, of swimming thousands of miles every year, of repeatedly diving unfathomable depths, of finding the means to sustain their massive bodies, and, it seemed to me, of something more, of communicating feelings and ideas among themselves.

4

Sonya had raised the possibility the humpbacks were either recalling a previous voyage or discussing a future one. I considered both could be true, but I decided to look for evidence they were planning their future travels and then see if I could detect patterns in their sounds that presaged the path the pod subsequently took. Biologists generally believe the sounds are mating calls because they are mainly produced by the dominant males during mating season. I reasoned the dominant males could also be the ones shaping a pod's voyages, and the calls might be travel instructions.

It didn't take me long to imagine I had found types of correspondence between the whales' songs and travels, but then the patterns would disappear. I soon went back to just listening to Gerry's recordings without trying to make something more of them. To be honest, they were so interesting they didn't need to have meaning.

One of my favorite pastimes in retirement is to walk along Massachusetts Avenue in Cambridge. On many days it looks like an ordinary small town business district, but on some days, as it is the direct route between MIT and Harvard, it feels vibrant with some sort of unseen energy, as if having so many capable and inquisitive minds crowded together creates a separate intellectual being. This seems to be especially true in the summer when the undergrads go home, the pace of the city relaxes, and all that's left are serious grad students desperate to finish an experiment or thesis. One day as I was absently enjoying my afternoon stroll, I was greeted by the familiar and exuberant voice of Clive Bernard.

"Hey, Joey. How are you? Care for lunch? The hamburgers here are pretty good." We were standing in front of the Plough and Stars, a local pub. It was mid-afternoon, so the place was nearly empty. I don't usually eat regular meals during the day, unless you call two cups of coffee and a piece of toast with butter a regular breakfast, but I knew Clive hadn't just happened upon me. He wanted to talk.

We talked about the weather, we talked about local politics, Clive waxed ecstatic about some Estonian or Latvian folk dancers he had seen the week before. Then a pensive look slowly covered his face.

"It's funny how you can find the damnedest things in the strangest places. There must be a lesson there somewhere, like to be on the lookout for treasures even when you throw out the trash."

I thanked Clive for the burger and beer and continued my stroll. It was midsummer, the day was so clear and hot and calm it approached perfection, as if I had merged with the Earth's atmosphere, as if my metabolism so closely matched the weather we had flowed together and were a single entity, a long delicious warm breath of life. It was a day to savor, but I couldn't enjoy it because I was thinking about Clive. I knew he would leave me something in my garbage can. I also knew he might have found something serious about Sonya to make him act so obtuse. Of course, it's also true he had come to love being obtuse just because it was fun.

My first instinct was to go rummage in the outside trash can that evening, but I realized Clive would know my regular habits and proceed accordingly. It was only Wednesday, and Monday morning was when our street brought our bins out to the curb. He wouldn't leave me anything until then. I was forced to wait.

Needless to say, I was anxious to find a treasure Monday when I went to retrieve my trash can, but it looked empty. I figured I would need to wait another week, then I noticed there was a wadded up Snickers wrapper at the bottom of the barrel. I don't eat candy bars, but Clive does. I dragged the bin back to our rear porch and grabbed the wrapper. When I arrived at my apartment I unfolded it. Written on the inside of the wrapper were the capital letters MITLSA. Under that was a string of numbers. They looked like Library of Congress catalogue numbers, so I surmised the capital letters stood for MIT Library Storage Annex, the building where MIT keeps the papers and journals that are so obscure and little used the institute doesn't want to waste shelf space to house them in its regular libraries. I still had library privileges at MIT, so I visited the LSA the next morning.

The item Clive referenced on the candy wrapper was a bibliography of navy research papers for the year 1970, nearly 120 pages of one and two line citations in small print. After several hours I realized I was no longer paying attention to what I was scanning. I was able to check the volume out, and spent the next several days looking for something relevant. Finally, on the third time through the tiny script, I noticed an article entitled "Tracking Tonal Variations in Megaptera novaeangliae" in the *Journal of American*

Marine Biology. The journal was only briefly published, and was primarily used for military researchers to communicate with each other. Of course MIT had the journal, at the LSA.

The article was written by a marine biologist named James Farrity who spent two years on a naval research vessel tracking humpback whales all over the world. It documented variations and therefore also similarities of the humpback sounds in different populations by use of sonography, a method of depicting sounds on paper. If nothing else, the article was proof Sonya's voyage wasn't the first of its kind. The author was a postdoctoral scholar at Woods Hole Oceanographic Institute at the time, so I at least had a lead to track him down.

I called Woods Hole several times, and finally was able to ascertain that a Dr. James Farrity had worked at the Institute for several years, and then moved to Humboldt State University in Arcata, California. A few calls there and I was informed he had left Humboldt for the University of Maine. I finally contacted him at his office in Orono.

"I remember that trip," he said, "It was kind of fun but I'm not sure anything came of it — just a couple of pretty dry articles. I wanted to publish the actual sounds, but the navy wasn't interested in funding anything more. They took all the original tapes, but I had made copies of everything, which I think I still have somewhere. Why are you interested in whales?"

I was prepared for his question. "I belong to an amateur string quartet, and we want to do an arrangement mimicking whale's songs."

"Interesting. How did you get my name?"

"I just started asking around at Woods Hole and your name came up. I'm not sure how."

"Well, they're not really songs, I mean I don't think the whales are just entertaining each other."

"What are they doing?"

"I'm not sure what they're saying, but I think they're communicating ideas, I think they have a language."

"That's amazing. Why didn't the navy follow up?"

"I think they may have. They sent a couple of ensigns out to California years ago to see if I had copies of my work, they claimed they had lost the originals. I was kind of pissed off at them so I denied having anything. Then a year or two later another biologist got in touch with me, a Harvey

Jenkins or Jensen or something. We had a kind of strange conversation. He wasn't sure I existed at first, but our stories were pretty similar, and he was frustrated the navy wouldn't let him pursue his work. He seemed a little out of control, frankly, so I tried to cut him off. I mean I wasn't rude to him or anything, I just didn't want to get involved with his anger."

"Would you let me have copies of your tapes?" I didn't want to push Farrity, but I was dying to hear his recordings.

"To tell you the truth I'm not sure they're still playable, but I have no use for them. If I can find them you can have the whole lot, and my notes to boot."

"Do you have them in Orono?"

"I don't know where they are. I have a storage locker here at the University, they may be in my attic at home. They may even be at our cottage in Truro. I'll look around and call you back."

I had become paranoid enough that I didn't want to give Farrity my phone number, but I didn't want to set him on edge either, so I relented.

While I waited for him to call me back, I attempted to find this Jenkins or Jensen person. I had developed a friendly relationship with one of the secretaries at Woods Hole, the one who located Farrity for me, so I decided to give her a try again. Her name was Betty Murphy, I think she was bored with her normal routine of filing papers and running errands for the professional staff, and took my requests as a challenge of her prowess of knowing everything that went on at the Institute. I imagined her as the kind of woman who could work at a place for decades without really being noticed, then pull a Lady Murasaki and write an extensive and compelling memoir of all the famous and near famous people she had observed. At first she said she didn't have a record of anyone by the name Jenkins or Jensen at her Institute, but she said she'd dig around. She called me back the next day.

"I couldn't find either Harvey Jenkins or Harvey Jensen anywhere. The closest I could find was a Harold Jennison. He earned his PhD at Scripps, you know, in San Diego. I don't know if he's your guy or not, that's all I could find."

I called Scripps Institute of Oceanography and had the same difficulties I originally had with Woods Hole. Finally I found someone willing to help me out. They once did have a researcher named Harold Jennison, the records indicated he did some work with the navy, but he was killed in a motorcycle accident shortly afterwards and they didn't know what his work with the navy entailed. I was beginning to think Jennison was going to be a dead end.

I didn't dare call Clive again, I didn't want to compromise his usefulness, so I just hoped Dr. Farrity would call me back and I listened to Sonya's whales a lot in the meantime. He called me less than a week after our first conversation, though it seemed much longer to me.

"I've found at least some of the recordings, and a bunch of my notes as well in my attic. I'm going to be in Bristol for a few weeks. If you want to drive up here when I get back, I'll unload everything on you. I'm never going to look at any of that stuff again. Better bring a van or pickup though, there are quite a few boxes."

"By the way, could the scientist who called you have been named Harold Jennison?" I asked.

"Could be. Have you found him?"

"Unfortunately, he died in a motorcycle crash a few years ago."

"Too bad. He was a piece of work, he was sure the navy had a plot to cover up his work, and mine too. You know, he said he was going to come to Arcata to show me something he said would prove his theory. Might be the same guy."

I thanked Farrity for his help and promised to get back to him, but now I needed a driver. I didn't want to ask Teddy or Marta. They were both terrible drivers, like me they went almost everywhere on the MBTA, the subway system. Besides, all they had was a little Fiat, and clearly it wasn't up to the task. They kept it in the tiny garage in our backyard, and basically only went out on Sundays to get out of the city, especially in the fall when they'd go mushroom hunting in western Massachusetts. I went with them once — it was a beautiful trip to some beautiful woods, but I swore I'd never get in their car again. I love Marta, but her driving terrified me. Besides, I didn't want to get my friends involved with my little mystery. I couldn't tell if Clive's caution was due to a real danger, a matter of habit, or just because he wanted to mess around with my head. It could be parts of all three, but I had to assume there was danger. But I did mention to Marta I wanted to pick up some material in Maine.

"Why don't you ask Jeannie? Matt has a large van. He sets up music venues, you know, provides the speakers and all that stuff. He's very good, the conservatory even uses him on occasions when we have a performance off campus."

I called Jeannie that day, and she agreed to help me out. I chafed at the wait, but there wasn't much I could do but wait. I decided to fill the time by informing myself about what was known about whales. After a little research I was directed to a biologist at Tufts, a Dr. Agnes Denton. She agreed to see me the day after I called her.

Dr. Denton was in her fifties, she had the lean physique of an athlete to whom extra weight would be a detriment, and the slightly severe look of an athlete no longer young. Her hair was short and bleached quite blonde, her face looked like it had absorbed years of sunlight. I was grateful she spared a little time for me, but I could tell by her attitude when she shook my hand she was a doer, and was not likely to want to spend all afternoon chatting.

The walls of Dr. Denton's office were covered with magnificent pictures of whales, all sorts of whales — breaching whales, spouting whales, nursing whales, solitary whales, pods of whales. There were blue whales, right whales, humpbacks, killer whales, as well as pictures of dolphins and porpoises. Every picture was framed, every picture was beautiful. As I looked at the pictures I understood her athleticism. At the least I suspected she was an accomplished scuba diver as well as photographer.

"Did you take all of these?" I asked.

"Every one. It's what I do."

"Do you study their vocalizations as well?"

"I study everything I can think of. They are amazing creatures, worthy of our attention and admiration."

"And protection?"

"Absolutely, if only we would."

"What effect do you think the navy's sub-sonar communication has on whales?"

Denton studied me for a while before she answered. "If someone dropped a trash can outside your window once in a while you would hardly notice it. But if a gang of idiots banged on all the cans in your neighborhood 24/7 it might drive you mad. We may be doing that to some of the whales with all of our noises, the navy's included."

"What do you think their vocalizations, their songs, are for?"

"Not sure. The navy has been recording them since the sixties, so I've been listening to them for nearly thirty years. I can make out patterns, I can see changes in those patterns over the years. I believe it's a form of music to be sure, their jazz, it's very sexy actually, but I really don't know."

"Do you think it could be a language?"

"I'm just not certain. There's no proof of that, and only the adult males sing."

"How about a form of mathematics, a geometrical language?"

"I think that's highly unlikely. I mean I love whales and all, but they're still only whales."

"Maybe they're smarter than we think."

Agnes Denton gave me a bemused look. I had the feeling she had had this conversation before and didn't want to have it again. "Maybe, maybe not. The Inuit claim the whales talk to them."

"The Inuit?"

"Well some Inuit. They say the whales size up the whale hunters, test them to see if they are worthy."

"Worthy? And if the hunters are worthy they allow themselves to be killed?"

"Something like that. In a way it makes sense — it would take a lot to go hunt a whale in a sealskin kayak with a wood and bone harpoon." Dr. Denton flashed me her bemused look again, then said, "Maybe you should talk to Florence Miller."

"Who is Florence Miller?"

"Well, she's someone who thinks whales are very intelligent, supremely intelligent, if you will. If you go over to the campus center, I'll bet there's a flier of hers on the Happenings bulletin board. I'll bet she's giving a talk somewhere tonight. If not tonight, tomorrow night."

I could tell Dr. Denton was trying to end our conversation, so I thanked her for her time and headed to the Tufts Campus Center. As she predicted, I found a flier concerning Florence Miller. She was scheduled to give a talk at the Somerville Library the next night on "The Ramifications of the Horizontal Alignment of Chakras in Four-Legged Animals." I had no idea what a chakra was, nor was I particularly interested in land animals with legs, but on the recommendation of Dr. Denton I decided to attend.

I arrived at the library about ten minutes early, hoping I could have a quick word with Ms. Miller, only to find the library was closing. The speech

I wanted to hear was being given at the west branch of the library, a forty-five minute walk. I arrived as she was giving her concluding remarks, which I didn't understand. The audience was sparse, and they left quickly, so I was able to corral her as she left the building alone.

"Ms. Miller, my name is Joe Tenatt. I want to ask you a few questions about whales. I understand you agree they are very intelligent."

"Of course, I love whales. They are some of the most highly evolved life forms on the planet! Are you going my way? We can talk as we walk, I never ride in cars. They destroy one's balance."

I told her I didn't drive and would walk in whatever direction she wanted. Upon hearing this she declared, "Call me Flora. We must be fellow voyagers. I can tell by looking at you. Your Muladhara and Svadishthana are quite strong. Interestingly, your Manipura and Anahata are quiet, but your Vishuddha emits a definite glow."

I told her I had no idea what she was talking about.

"Didn't you attend my lecture?"

"I went to the wrong library. I arrived at the end of your talk."

"And you've never studied Tantric Yoga?"

"I've never studied any yoga."

We were walking down Elm Street, which was well lit at night. Flora was heading across the river to Jamaica Plain. It was more or less on my way home, though I didn't want to go that far. When I explained my ignorance of all things yoga she suggested we go down a side street. She was dressed in a soft, tight fitting ankle length skirt and a loose long sleeved blouse, and she was almost a foot shorter than me. She didn't strike me as someone who would mug me, so I agreed. When we came to an unlit spot she stopped to stare at me.

"Extraordinary! I guess your lack of study explains why your Sahasrara and Ajna are so dark, but you show incredible promise for enlightenment if you apply yourself."

"I would like to ask you about whales."

"It's too bad you missed my lecture, but I will go over the main points, then we can explore how they pertain to whales. Do you know anything about chakras?"

I didn't, and didn't think I wanted to learn. "No."

"Chakras are the junctures of our physical body and our subtle body. Normally the Muladhara is considered the base and lowest of the major chakras, and Ajna the highest. Practitioners interested in enlightenment and becoming one with the universe need to work their way through the hierarchy to attain fulfillment. That is why I'm amazed you already have such considerable energy, however sporadic, in three of the chakras, evidently without practice. Very commendable."

"I see," I said. I didn't.

"It is easy to see why yogis have developed the idea of a hierarchy, as the pattern in humans is apparently from low to high. In most animals, however, the same progression would be from back to front, so it is much harder to theorize that one chakra is higher or more important than another. In fact, I have discovered animals tend to develop their chakras in unison, which is why they are more spiritually developed than humans."

"How did you discover this?"

"Scientifically, through careful observation."

"And whales?"

"Whales are special. I think it is because their swimming motion mimics the pulsation of Kundalini."

"Kundalini?"

"Kundalini is the spiritual energy that enervates the chakras. When all the chakras are open Kundalini can easily pass up and down the subtle body, or back and forth in most animals, horizontal animals."

"So fish must be similar."

"The motion of fishes is side to side. I think this asymmetrical movement forms a much weaker passage of Kundalini, they aren't nearly as spiritually powerful as whales and dolphins."

I was beginning to realize Dr. Denton pointed me toward Flora because she felt my questions were ridiculous and wanted to get rid of me. I couldn't imagine she would be interested in chakras. Nevertheless I persisted. "Do you think whales have a language?"

"A language? They emanate truth, I never thought they needed a language. What kind of language?"

"A mathematical language."

We had wound our way onto Mass Ave, which was only slightly out of my way. When I mentioned the possibility of a mathematical language, Flora looked at me intently, then gently shook her head. "You're a wonder. I cannot possibly see why whales would need mathematics. As a spiritual scientist I regard mathematics as antithetical to my studies, and I am sure whales would feel the same. What could they do with mathematics?"

"I think it might help them navigate."

"I think it would help them get lost."

"Lost? How so?"

"Spiritually lost, like the human race."

"Don't you think mathematics, and science in general, can help us get out of our messes?"

"Do you seriously consider that possible, or are you playing with me? What is your game, anyway? You must realize science is helping us deplete the very oceans we are talking about, destroying the ecosystem whales have helped create."

"Whales eat a lot of seafood, too."

"Whales eat to create balance in their world. We destroy balance. You can't compare the two."

"I understand the Inuit claim to communicate with whales."

Flora stopped in her tracks. I felt I could feel her eyes burning through the back of my head. "You can't believe everything you hear, Joe. The Inuit evidently believe the whales allow themselves to be slaughtered by worthy hunters. I would be the first to admit Inuit whale hunters are worthy, perhaps they tell themselves the whales give themselves up to increase their courage or their stature. But I cannot see why such a superior being as a whale would allow humans to kill it. It makes no sense to me."

I was a little surprised by Flora's fervor. I wasn't sure I disagreed with my new friend's conclusions, but I wasn't really interested in her approach, either. We had reached a good place for me to say good-bye.

"Well, it was interesting meeting you, Joe. You know, I give private lessons in yoga, if you ever decide to refurbish your chakras."

We bowed and shook hands. I told her I'd think about it.

5

The trip to Orono took over seven hours because we picked a brilliant autumn Friday when the northbound Interstate traffic was packed with leafers looking to capture the irradiant glory of fall before it evaporated into gray winter. Even worse, Matt's van had a manual transmission and a stiff clutch. We briefly talked about taking side roads, but quickly realized in Maine that would make our trip even more arduous. Several hours of freeway stop-and-go traffic just about wore Jeannie out, but she remained cheerful the whole way, apologizing every time she jerked the vehicle forward. When we finally arrived at our destination she had to do a few calisthenics to get her legs going again, but she was young and recovered quickly.

James Farrity lived in a huge Greek Revival era house built by one of the early Maine lumber barons. The mansion and grounds reminded me of a plantation, they were so vast and ordered. He lived about half an hour west of the campus, but he had given us good directions so we had no problem finding his place. He came out to meet us as soon as we arrived. He had a vigorous stride and a strong, friendly handshake. Farrity was about the same height as me, but about ten years younger and certainly in better physical condition, though that's not necessarily saying much. The grounds around his place were well manicured, it was apparent he put a lot of energy into his efforts.

"Good to meet you, Dr. Tenatt.

"Good to meet you, Dr. Farrity, but let's stick to first names."

"Agreed."

"And this is my chauffeur du jour, Jeannie Mellon."

"And good to meet you, Jeannie." He paused as he studied her. "Haven't we met before, I'm sure I know that name, and your face is familiar."

"I don't think we've met, but I was up here last spring with the Old Town Quartet."

"Of course! Marvelous concert. I especially loved the Haydn pieces. But I thought it was a local group."

Jeannie looked confused for a minute, then grinned when she understood Farrity's misapprehension. "You mean the name, 'Old Town'? The group was supposed to be temporary. One of the violinists was from this area, it was his idea."

I was embarrassed I had never seen Jeannie perform, but I knew how good she was from playing with her. "Do you play?" I asked Farrity.

"I wish I could. I've heard musicians claim everyone has some musical ability, but I'm proof that's not true. Anyway, let's go exploring."

He led us to his attic, which was crammed with piles of stuff haphazardly stacked everywhere. It looked like there could have been some items from the year the house was first built, and then some from every year since. The attic was definitely not maintained with the same order as Farrity imposed on his yard. I concluded he wasn't obsessive-compulsive, just disciplined when he wanted to be.

"I looked in a couple of these boxes last week, I think this whole pile is what you're looking for." He pointed to over a dozen medium sized cardboard boxes. We eventually carried fourteen heavy boxes down to the van. It was a cool day, but the attic was quite warm. I was sweating profusely by the time we were done, and thankful we didn't have to carry the boxes up the stairs.

It was already late afternoon, but Farrity offered us some hot tea before we left. We sat around his back deck table as if it were summer, except we were bundled in hooded sweatshirts to ward off the early autumn evening chill. Farrity's house was on a rise, so we were able to look over a large pond onto the endless Maine autumnal forests. It would be imprudent of me to try to describe a New England fall day, to paint with words the thousands of shades of reds, oranges, yellows and greens celebrating under a deep blue sky. If you've seen it, my description would fall flat. If you have not, it wouldn't help you understand.

"Quite the spread," I said.

"It's beautiful," Jeannie agreed.

"They say at one time Bangor was the largest lumber port in the world, so there was plenty of wealth around here in those days. Not as much going on now, so even a professor can afford an old palace. I must say I love it here, keeps me busy in my spare time."

The trip back was at least three hours quicker, and much easier on Jeannie, than the trip out, for which we were both thankful.

"So, what is all this stuff?" Jeannie asked as we headed home. "Do you want to bring it all to your place?"

"I guess so." I hadn't thought much about what I was going to do with Farrity's records, and I hadn't spoken to Jeannie about my concerns for Sonya's safety. I decided the least I could do was let her know what she was transporting. "These are Dr. Farrity's research records, including a lot of tape recordings of whales he made years ago." I felt I had to offer an explanation, so I made up a story. "I heard some short snippets of whales on the radio and they reminded me of someone like Sun Ra or Pat Metheny. When I heard there was someone up in Maine with a bunch of recordings I called him up and asked for some copies. He felt they were too fragile to copy, so he just gave them all to me."

"And what do you plan to do with them?"

"I guess I'll get an old reel-to-reel recorder and see if I can play any of them."

"How old are they?"

"At least fifteen years, maybe more."

"And they've been in his attic all this time?"

"Not the whole time, probably ten years. Not sure where they were before that."

"Don't you dare try to play them!"

"Why not?" I wondered if she had figured out what I was doing.

"Because you don't know what you're doing. Let's get Matt to look at them. He'll know how to rescue them."

"I thought he was into setting up the equipment for musical performances. What does he know about restoring old audio tapes?"

"As much as anyone, maybe more. You may not know this, but Matt and a couple of friends started up a company selling stereo equipment as undergraduates. When they graduated he sold his share to his partners for several million dollars. He didn't see the growth potential, because other, bigger firms were moving into their niche market."

"What was that?"

"Selling stereos to undergraduates, mostly guys looking to get laid. Anyway, he knows as much about sound and electronics as anyone. If your tapes are salvageable, he's the one who can do it."

"I can't afford to pay him much."

"Wouldn't matter if you could, he still wouldn't accept anything from you. After all, you're the man who gave me to him."

We took our cargo to Jeannie and Matt's place and unloaded all of it, even the paper records. They owned a large house, another mansion really, not unlike Farrity's, and it had plenty of extra room. Matt came home as we were carrying the boxes into their living room, or at least what was originally an ornate living room. In fact it looked more like the central loading dock of a warehouse. Jeannie explained the situation to him, so he gingerly opened one of the reel containers and studied it carefully. It struck me he gave it the same attention he would a rare, precious recording of Enrico Caruso.

"O, yeah, these are brittle. Give me some time, I'll make them sound as though you're out on the ocean."

I remembered Sonya's tapes, which really didn't sound very good on my cheap machine. "I have some more recent cassettes. Do you think you could make them sound better, too?"

"No doubt. What are all the notebooks?"

I explained they were the notes that went along with the recordings.

"Bring everything you have over here, I'll collate it all for you. Might as well know what you're listening to."

His remark was prescient, but I didn't reply.

When Jeannie drove me home I handed her the two bags Sonya had given me, without the groceries. I was glad for Matt's expert help, but I no longer had the whales to listen to. I felt I had lost some friends.

After a few days of insufferable silence, I had an idea. I sauntered over to Harvard's reference library and began looking for any articles by Harold Jennison. I wasn't sure what his specialty was, except he was a biologist. I no longer had library privileges at Harvard and couldn't bring any of these tomes home, so I basically spent a week at the university searching everywhere I could think of for anything he might have written. I finally found an article entitled "Urban Effluent Consumption by *Sardinops caeruleus*" by Roger Reckow and Harold Jennison. My hope that I could locate a co-author had paid off.

It turned out Dr. Reckow was a well-known, much published researcher who was based at the University of Miami. I was able to contact him, but he came across as rather too busy to spend much time with me.

"Yes, I remember working with Hank on a paper or two. He was knowledgeable enough, I liked his effort, but he was a bit of a hothead, quick to take a slight. He was the junior author in any collaboration we had."

He said this as if it was important for me to understand their relationship.

"Did you work for the navy with him?"

"Every serious marine biologist works with the navy at some time or another."

The way he put it, it did make my question sound lame. I tried again, "I mean, did you go on any extended research voyages together?"

Reckow paused. "No, not that I recall, but I think we quit working together because he took a gig on a navy vessel. Why don't you ask him?"

"Dr. Jennison died in a motorcycle accident several years ago."

"I see. That's unfortunate, I'm sorry to hear that. You know, if you want to know anything about him, you should talk to his old girlfriend. She was quite a chick, he was totally in love with her, but she was from a different world."

"How do you mean, a different world? Do you know how I could get in touch with her?"

"She was a real hippie, had a little farm up in the Coast Mountains, grew organic artichokes and stuff like that. I remember her name, it was Carolyn Truesdale. Her farm was called 'Shanty Shanty' I think. Just outside San Luis Obispo, I'm pretty sure, never went there myself, but I met her in San Diego once. Very colorful. Look, I have to go, hope I've been some help."

San Luis Obispo is a long way from Cambridge. I couldn't see myself searching for a hippie farm three thousand miles away, but I decided to call the San Luis Obispo Chamber of Commerce just to see if they'd heard of this woman or her farm.

"You mean '*Shanti Shanti*', not 'Shanty Shanty'," the voice on the line explained. "'Shanti' means 'peace' in Sanskrit. Of course I've heard of Carolyn Truesdale, her crops are famous. She sells them to high end restaurants in L.A. and San Francisco. Even to a couple of places around here."

"Do you have her phone number?"

"Well, let's just say Carolyn is a little eccentric. She refuses to talk on a phone. I wouldn't be surprised if she hasn't left her farm in a decade. I'm friends with her sister, so I've heard a little gossip. I could give you the farm number, but the staff probably won't admit she exists. Why do you want to talk to her?"

"I'm interested in an old boyfriend, some research he did on humpback whales."

"Oh, I see." There was a noticeable pause. "I think her boyfriend is dead."

"I heard he died in a motorcycle accident, but I can't locate any family members. I was just wondering if there were any whale recordings around."

"Why do you want recordings of whales?" she said.

I dragged out the story of making music, it seemed to have worked on Farrity.

"Well, I think you're going to have to go up to the farm yourself and see if she'll talk to you. She might, she might not. Come to the Chamber of Commerce if you're ever in town and ask for Marylin, I'll show you how to get there." She paused long enough that I assumed she was about to hang up, then added, "If you ever make a recording of your whale music I'd love to hear it."

6

The day after my conversations with Dr. Reckow and Marylin, I grabbed the MBTA to Brookline to see how Matt was doing with my tapes. He was in his large garage packing and loading equipment, but immediately quit his labors and led me through his Victorian estate to a back room.

"This is a great house. It has so much room, and so many rooms," he said. As I followed him down a meandering hall I saw he had electronic equipment in all of them.

"It looks like you're using them all."

"Jeannie and I live on the second floor, her music studio is on the third in the old servants' quarters, and I have the first. It's perfect. Here we are, I call this the whale room." Matt went to the far wall and opened what appeared to be a walk-in cooler like restaurants use. There were all my tapes and notes.

"This is a controlled atmospheric environment. I've managed to get sound off the first part of a tape, but it's a time-consuming process. You're going to have to leave all the masters with me or they'll get even worse over time. It's hard for me to imagine someone leaving these beautiful tapes in an attic for years. Unforgivable."

"Can you make me copies, to listen to at home?"

Matt gave me a sidelong look. "Listen to this." He took a new reel from one of the shelves and we left the cooler. He inserted the reel into a tape player and started it. I was dumbfounded by the sound. He had promised me I would think I was at sea when he was done, but he had understated his ability. I felt I could get seasick listening to the whales.

"I could make a cassette copy for you, but it wouldn't sound like this."

"You think I should listen to them here?"

"We love this project. Jeannie thought she might give composing music based on these tapes a go. You could come and go as you want, we'll give you a key. What are you doing with this anyway?"

I wasn't ready to tell him what I was doing, but I couldn't keep lying to my friends either. "I'm not sure, trying to understand what the whales are doing."

"Good idea. We want to help."

It took Matt several months to record all of my music onto playable tapes, and then we worked together matching the recordings to the notes. I tried to do some of the collating by myself but I wasn't nearly as adept as he with his electronic equipment. His business was burgeoning and he had little free time, so I was all the more thankful for his aid. He had hired a couple of workers to help with the concerts, which worried me at first — I wanted to be as secretive as possible about my project and didn't relish having the extra eyes around. I quickly realized Matt's assistants were too busy with their own tasks to pay much attention to an eccentric like myself, and I came to enjoy playing up the resident genius mathematician role.

Eventually I dragged a cot into the room so I could lie down while I listened. One of the first discoveries I made was all the whales in a group made some sounds, not just the adult males, but the females and calves were much quieter. It was known that whale pods aren't permanent. I thought to myself maybe they had to constantly reintroduce themselves to each other.

Gerry's attitude had rubbed off on me — I was still a little paranoid, so I would take roundabout routes to Matt and Jeannie's place on Corey Hill, but I never had the feeling I was being followed and I began to relax a little.

One day when I returned to my apartment I couldn't find my cats. I've heard cats can hear their people from a block or more away. I don't know if that is true, but I do know Cleo always greeted me at the door, and Ranger would saunter in as soon as I closed it behind me, so naturally I was concerned. I headed down stairs to see if Marta or Teddy knew anything.

Marta answered the door and before I could speak, she said, "I have one of your cats." She looked at me as if she had just unveiled the deepest secrets of my soul. Cleo entered the room and began rubbing on my leg while purring. When Marta and I sat down, Cleo jumped on my lap.

"How did you get her? Why is she down here?"

"Someone broke into your apartment."

"It didn't look broken into."

"They were pros, Joe. I didn't hear them, and I was home the whole time."

"So how do you know anyone was up there?"

"When they opened the door, they must have spooked the cats. This one came to my door and started scratching at it. I went to see what was going on and I saw two men coming down the stairs. I asked them what they were doing, which startled them. They pretended they couldn't understand me.

One of them started speaking Russian. I speak Russian fluently, I studied in Moscow for years, so I asked them what they were doing again, in Russian. I think that shook them. One of them muttered they were lost, still in Russian, and they started coming toward me. I pulled this out." She showed me a revolver she had in her apron pocket. "At that point they took off pretty quick, and I went upstairs to make sure your door was shut."

I was having a hard time comprehending what Marta was telling me. "Why were Russians breaking into my apartment?"

"They weren't Russians, they only spoke Russian. They were Americans."

"How do you know?"

"I speak Russian without an accent, I grew up speaking Polish and Russian. I can tell an American accent when I hear it. So the question is why are professional American burglars who speak Russian well and don't want to be identified breaking into your apartment?"

I wanted to change the subject. "Do you always carry a gun?" I asked.

"Of course. I grew up in the Soviet Union, I know what it is to be defenseless. Thank America for the Second Amendment and the Detective Special!" She held her pistol up and smiled.

I was speechless for a while. I learned to shoot a rifle growing up. My dad would drive us away from town and we would pick off prairie dogs with a twenty-two, but I hadn't even thought of having a gun of any sort since leaving South Dakota. "You could have been shot, Marta."

"I had the draw, and I don't back down. That's why I'm in this country. I would have gotten at least one of them."

I was beginning to realize I had to tell Marta and Teddy my story. I wanted to keep them out of this for their safety, but now I needed to tell them for the same reason. "I'm going upstairs to see if I can find Ranger and see what kind of mess my visitors made. When Teddy comes home I'd like to take you both out for pizza and beer."

I went to my apartment with Cleo. As soon as I let her down Ranger came skulking out of his hiding place and started rubbing against my leg, just as Cleo had done earlier. I searched through my apartment and concluded Marta had been right, the burglars were pros; they had left no trace of their visit, aside from the tell-tale cats. I was sure they were looking for anything Sonya could have given me. It was only luck I had brought her cassettes and notebooks to Matt's place, but I realized I didn't know how much my visitors knew. Maybe they were only suspicious because Sonya had visited me and Gerry had disabled one of their bugs, but maybe they had been following me and had tapped my phone and knew a whole lot more. Maybe they were raiding Matt's even then. All I could do was wait. That's what Clive had told me to do in the first place, and it seemed appropriate at the moment.

Teddy came up to get me that evening, and the three of us walked several blocks to the Spring Hill House of Pizza. It was just after Christmas, the time winter begins to turn truly frigid. We were hidden in our thick winter parkas. In order to be heard we would have needed to stop and stand face to face. Instead, we went side by side in silence. Like me, Marta and Teddy would walk throughout the year when they could, but there was a considerable drop-off in the number of fellow pedestrians on the street during the coldest months. We appeared to be completely alone that day. I looked behind us occasionally, just to check if we were being trailed. I took one last look as we entered the restaurant, and still no one was in sight. We ordered our dinner and beer and talked shop for a while. It was a slow evening, and when I was sure no one had followed us into the restaurant, I began to tell the Witkowskis my story. As I spoke I realized both of them had more relevant experience than I with a hostile government spying on its own citizens. I expected them to tell me how naive I was.

"So that's what you were listening to, whales. We could hear it downstairs, it's beautiful!" Marta said.

"I hope I haven't put Matt in danger," I said, trying to redirect the conversation.

"Don't get worked up before you know. We are as smart as the government, even if we are small. Of course the navy is dangerous. Its mission is to kill. But look, they have already made a mistake, and we don't know that you have. We have to be patient."

As Marta explained this to me, Teddy nodded in agreement. Finally he spoke. "We," motioning to himself and his wife, "have known both Hitler and Stalin. We have learned not to panic, but to wait. This you must learn."

"What I don't understand," I said, "is why they thought I might have something worth breaking into my apartment for. They can't know I gave Sonya's number to Clive Bernard. Remember, I told you he was looking for a mathematician?"

"Yes, and I told you he wanted a decoder," said Marta.

"And you were right. Anyway, I know Clive would never let anyone know where he got that number. He was shocked Sonya said anything to me about her project. And Sonya visited us over six months ago. Remember, she brought her flute one evening, and came back to see me the next day."

"Is that the only time you have seen her?"

"Then, and then a couple of days later I met her and one of her fellow researchers, a guy named Gerry, over on Newbury Street."

"Could someone have seen you then?" asked Teddy.

"Well, we ate outside. But Gerry was very careful. It seems unlikely." I sat there lost in the confusion of my memories for a while, then suddenly remembered how Gerry left so quickly. "Maybe Gerry saw something, or someone. He got up and grabbed Sonya and they left very quickly. At the time I figured it was just his awkwardness, but maybe he felt we were spied on. But why wait half a year to bust into my place? Why not the next day?"

"I will tell you again, you must be patient," said Teddy. "You can go crazy spinning in circles of your own making. When you don't know something, admit it and wait."

As I climbed up my stairs after dinner I listened to the steps creak beneath my feet. I had lived in this apartment for over thirty years, and the creaking had become a comfort, a sign I was home, and yet I had never paid close attention to the sound before. This time the old steps seemed louder than usual because of the comment Marta had made about my intruders being professionals. I was impressed by how two large men could climb my stairs without making a sound, but I was more impressed by my amazing neighbors, who took this all in, who understood better than I the reality of a surreptitious government, yet were more interested in the beauty of my humpback tapes than in the danger at hand. I understood I could trust them. I needed to trust them.

I didn't panic, I did wait. I knew I could never call Clive again; any move would have to come from him. I didn't go to Jeannie's and Matt's either. After a few days Jeannie called me. "Matt's worried about you because you haven't been here for a while. Are you alright?"

I almost panicked. I didn't know if my phone was tapped, and did not want Jeannie to mention the whale tapes. "I'm busy now, but I'm fine. Can you meet me at the McDonald's on Kenmore Square tomorrow for lunch?"

"McDonald's?"

"Please. I have a surprise for you."

There was a long pause, then Jeannie relented. "Okay, see you tomorrow."

I had fully adopted Gerry's paranoia, and some of his habits as well. It took me over two hours to wend my way to McDonald's, and I arrived there at least thirty minutes before Jeannie. I knew she was puzzled by my request, but of course she had no idea how serious I was.

I was sitting facing the door and saw her enter. She spotted me almost as quickly and called out, "Hi Joe, what's the big deal?"

"We'll get to that. Do you want to order anything?"

Jeannie scrunched up her nose. "There's nothing here I want."

"Good, then let's go for a walk." I left my coffee cup, mostly full, on the table and guided her down Commonwealth Avenue. It was cold, a thick winter fog shrouded Boston. Usually cold humid weather ignored my winter clothes and gripped my body in a naked, icy hug the way a merely crisp frigid day could never manage, but I was so agitated by having to introduce Jeannie to my danger I ignored the discomfort. I began to explain the situation, starting with Sonya's and Gerry's fears, my research into possible previous similar voyages, and the break-in. We finally sat down on a frosted bench on the boulevard.

"So, you see, I may have put you in some peril. You haven't seen anything suspicious the last few days?"

"Nothing."

"In any case, it might be best if I took all those tapes, no reason to get you involved."

"Joe, you're forgetting Sonya is my friend, too. If there is anything on those tapes that can help her, we need Matt's expertise." I wasn't expecting this response, so we both sat in silence for several minutes.

Finally I spoke up. "I appreciate your offer, but you had better talk to Matt first. If he wants to stay involved, then I suggest the three of us, and the Witkowskis as well, have a meeting to discuss how to proceed. Marta and Teddy have a more sophisticated background than any of us in how to live with a dangerous government. They may look like rather harmless typical European intellectuals, but they practically rowed that boat across the Baltic to escape from the Soviet Union. They have an acute understanding of what we're facing."

"This is turning into a real mystery," Jeannie said. "But I think we're the team to solve it." I only hoped we were the team to not make things worse for us all.

I spoke to my neighbors about the new plan, and Jeannie spoke to Matt. We agreed to meet at Jeannie and Matt's and discuss the situation. We moved cautiously to see if there was any more troubling activity, but none of us saw any more indications of anything suspicious. I operated under the assumption they may have bugged my apartment, but seeing there was never anybody there but me and my cats, all I had to do was not use my phone to call any of the other team members. Marta pointed out I had probably allayed their fears seeing they found nothing in my apartment, that most likely they were acting on suspicions they had of Sonya and Gerry.

"That may be, but I think I had better be careful trying to contact the members of previous expeditions," I said.

"True," Marta said. "Anything we do now to rekindle an interest in us could bring serious trouble."

Our first team meeting was at Jeannie and Matt's Brookline place two or three weeks after Jeannie and I had met on Comm. Ave. I told the entire story of Sonya's tapes, the electronic bugs Gerry discovered and how he even disabled one, of meeting Gerry, tracking down Dr. Farrity, and the strange tale of Harold Jennison, his coauthor Roger Reckow, and Harold's paranoid hippie girlfriend, Carolyn Truesdale. I finished with the recent discomfiting break-in of my apartment. Marta added a few more comments about the burglars, and then Matt showed us all the whale room, and explained what he was doing with the tapes. We had been talking for well over an hour when he offered to play some of them.

"Oh, good," said Marta, "Finally, some meat." We all laughed in agreement.

"Dr. Farrity made tapes of humpback pods in both the Atlantic and Pacific. I think he was trying to compare the patterns, to see if he could find similarities. And he did, listen to this." Matt played two sequences of sounds, one from each side of our planet. "You can hear both whales make a similar series of three sounds, almost like a form of Cetacean Morse code." He played the tapes once more.

"I think the similarities are more complex than that," Marta said.

"How so?" asked Matt.

Marta was fighting to find words to explain herself, then she relaxed and turned to Jeannie. "Jeannie, dear, do you have a cello I could use?"

Jeannie appeared surprised at the request at first, then her face lit up. "Of course."

While Jeannie was gone Marta explained the similarity in sounds was more nuanced than just three phrases following each other. When Jeannie came back and unpacked her instrument, Marta exclaimed, "You didn't need to bring your Scarampella!"

"Why not? You won't hurt it. This is a worthwhile occasion."

Marta set up with the cello, then asked Matt to replay the sequences, and then again. She drew her bow and replicated the intonation on Jeannie's instrument a couple of times. The last time we could all hear subtle variations in the whales' voices. After she did that with six different whale "words", three from each pod, she said, "You can hear the first sounds from both pods have the same intonation, and the third sounds nearly do. The middle sounds in the two phrases, however, are quite different, though they sound similar at first hearing. By playing the sounds on an instrument we can replicate the nuances and more easily identify distinctive sounds, and, presumably, if they are speaking a language, different meanings."

"Are you going to go through all these tapes like that and catalogue the words?" I asked her.

"I love this music they make, and will gladly do my share, but I hope you and Jeannie and my loving husband will help." It was clear Teddy had no choice, but of course Jeannie and I immediately volunteered.

Marta handed the cello back to Jeannie. "This is a wonderful instrument, but surely you have a less valuable one you could leave here so I could just drop by when I have a few moments."

"Naturally. I just wanted you to play it once."

"I thank you for that. It is lovely. Teddy, you could bring your second fiddle here for you and Joseph. That way any of us can stop by at any time to help catalogue this Cetacean tongue."

Jeannie and Marta were far better musicians than Teddy and me, but we were both more than willing to pitch in. We soon learned if we combined our efforts and passed the violin back and forth, we made more progress than either one of us alone. I had more time on my hands, so I often spent a few hours by myself either trying to imitate a phrase, or trying to find a pattern to the phrases, before Teddy showed up. Then we would spend another hour or two passing the single violin back and forth trying to capture what we were sure were words of another species.

One day I showed Teddy my attempts at parsing Cetacean on paper.

"You know, Alan Turing invented computer language and paved the way for using computers to solve problems like these, so you don't need to do that exercise again."

"But I don't have an actual computer."

"We can fix that. My lab, which is to say me, now has two Digital VAX computers I'm using to create a computer program to analyze high-speed particle collisions. I have them running twenty-four hours a day, but I could easily have one of them help you a few of those hours."

"The school bought two computers for you?"

"Well, no, they're on loan from Digital."

"Is it legal to let me use one?"

"Don't you think that's an odd question? It wasn't 'legal' for Marta and me to leave Poland, and evidently it has been decreed somewhere that what you and I are doing now is also illegal. But we could make your computer use look legal. I could hire you, you could help me with my research, and I could help you with yours."

So, unexpectedly, I had a new job. What was worse, Teddy intended to take advantage of some of the very work I had done with Clive Bernard and actually make me spend a good chunk of my time on his project. Teddy had a theory, as far as I understood it at the time, that the entire universe is vibrating, and that particles are energy packets in resonance with those vibrations. My job was to help him recognize repeating and similar patterns in his data.

Teddy's work space was considerably less than auspicious, basically consisting of a basement office with a single long L-shaped work table against two walls and two metallic shelves with his computers in the opposite corner. He had a unique method of hanging the computer cables from the ceiling with duct tape to keep them off the floor. Occasionally a piece of tape would let go, taking some paint with it, and Teddy would clamber up on his chair or desk and stick another piece of tape to the ceiling. There was nothing charming or graceful about the room, but nevertheless he was thrilled with his situation.

"These microcomputers were the wave of the future a few years ago," he said. "Now they might already be extinct. That's why Digital was willing to let me use them."

"Is there something more powerful coming along?"

"Yes and no. These aren't as powerful as mainframes, and yet they almost displaced them. A university like Northeastern might only have a few IBM 360's, for instance, on the whole campus. Even my department didn't have its own computer — all the science and engineering departments shared a single central computer. These minis spread the wealth around. I think Digital is hoping to show how useful they are, but it looks like smaller, cheaper ones are the next big deal. The point is, I can do what I want with them, and I don't have to timeshare with anyone." Teddy looked around the room with a quiet smile. "Ah, what my friends back at Polytechnika Szczeci ska would give to have these resources."

"Would they give what you gave?"

"'Aye, there's the rub', as your Shakespeare would say. They did not, and I did."

I was amused by Teddy referring to Shakespeare as mine. Though Shakespeare wrote in English, the language of the United States, Teddy and his wife, being European intellectuals, knew the old bard much better than I, and they obviously loved him.

Teddy and I worked well together, and I was able to help him enough with his research to more than offset the amount time I used his VAX. And it was nice to have a little extra income. More importantly it vastly increased my ability to correlate the Cetacean utterances with their subsequent travels. I felt I was making inroads into the meanings of their calls.

"Look at this, Teddy. Do you see what I see?" I asked him one afternoon.

Teddy examined my maps and accompanying graphs. He smiled. "I think I see what you want me to see, but yes, I see a pattern."

"It seems the power of a particular set of utterances, that is the length, volume and tone, foreshadows the length of a subsequent trip."

"Perhaps. How precise do you think they are?"

"That's a good question. I don't know how they measure anything, I see no sign of the humpbacks counting anything. And, after all, they are swimming in a pod with youngsters amid the ocean currents, so even if they were on the money with calculating a distance before they left, the actuality of a trip would introduce error. At first blush the correlation is between the effort of the call and the effort of the trip, but I think there are more nuances and subtleties involved. I would love to know what the navy has figured out."

"Let's not ask," he said. We laughed at our danger together. When I first realized I needed to include the Witkowskis in my mystery, I was fearful I was endangering them, sorry I was compelled to. It was now they who were guiding me through the danger with caution and humor.

The five of us — Teddy, Marta, Jeannie, Matt and I — made steady progress on three fronts: cataloging the Cetacean words, collating Gerry's notes with the tapes, and finding patterns in the speech and movement. But the task was immense, and frankly the data were

crude. We concentrated on the data provided by James Farrity because the work Sonya and Gerry gave us, even though of a higher quality, represented only a few months of the whales' lives — too short a period to compare the calls and subsequent movements. Also, all of their recordings had been made in the Atlantic, so we couldn't compare the differences between distinct populations. An even further complication arose when we tried to match phrases from Gerry and Sonya's tapes with those from Farrity's, even when sampling songs from the same whale populations, for there were very few matches. It was as if the whales had changed languages.

James Farrity may have been the first of the navy's civilian researchers of cetaceans, and he was largely flying in the dark. One could see an improvement in his technique, even over the course of his two-year stint. And though he began to make some beautiful recordings toward the end of his tour, he was never able to properly document their long term movements. Still, there was enough evidence to convince me not only did the whales proclaim the distance of a trip, but also the direction, and even the manner — they had an entire three dimensional geometry they could communicate to their respective pods and were able to do so accurately without numbers. An analog 3-D geometry, if you will, but without accurate documentation of the humpbacks' movements to go along with their songs, it was impossible to actually translate what they were saying into meaningful mathematics — meaningful human mathematics, that is.

One day when Jeannie and I were working together I complained to her about the paucity of data.

"It's enough to keep us busy for now," she replied.

"Yes, but something is missing. It's like only playing Chopin's left hand; intriguing, but not close to the whole story."

"How about that organic farm girl in California?"

"What about her, other than she's a paranoid hippie?"

Jeannie scowled at me, clearly offended. "First of all, you're pretty paranoid yourself these days, and for good reason. Secondly, some of my best friends are, or were, hippies, including my parents."

I felt my face heat up from embarrassment, as if the skin were going to burn off. "Sorry, you're right, I've known some exceptional people who were hippies myself, I mean I've lived in Cambridge since the early fifties. I always thought the hippies brought a breath of fresh air to this country. I'm just not sure I see Carolyn's relevance to this adventure of ours."

"The fact she's paranoid may be a clue she knows enough to know how dangerous the situation is. She might have seen or heard something that still frightens her. From what you heard she was very close to Jennison. And clearly she's no dummy, she's running a successful farm, after all."

I had a few extra dollars from working with Teddy, so I asked Jeannie if she would like to go meet this mysterious woman. "I can't drive, as you know, so I would need a chauffeur in California."

"I'm pretty wrapped up right now. The Old Town Quartet has become quite successful, it's keeping me very busy. I don't think I can break free for a couple of months."

It was early spring, so we agreed to fly to California in July. Jeannie arranged to conduct a couple of summer school seminars at the local high school and CalPoly, mostly as a cover for our trip. In the meantime I went back to playing whale conversations with Teddy on his violin. There were times I was so entranced with the sound I felt I knew what they were saying. There were other times when the whole thing seemed like a hopeless mess.

7

The Charles River was lined with blossoming cherry trees, Boston's yards were replete with daffodils, tulips and azaleas, coeds had begun to shed their winter armor, so I had a hard time spending much time in Teddy's cramped office. Besides, there were ideas swirling around in my cramped cranium, just out of reach, all of which I used to justify putting down my pen, leaving the keyboard, and spending days wandering through Back Bay and Cambridge with no particular destination. It was one such day when Sonya unexpectedly showed up. She was waiting for me on the front steps when I arrived home from a late sojourn. She didn't bring grocery bags this time.

"Sonya, it's good to see you. How are you?"

"Pretty good. I thought you might not come home tonight."

"Where would I go?"

"I don't know — where have you been?"

"We have a lot to talk about. Would you like to take a walk?"

"Sure." She hesitated, and we exchanged glances. It was evident she understood I did not want to talk in my apartment. Finally she said, "Do you mind if I freshen up a bit at your place first?"

"Of course not. Pardon me for being so rude. How long have you been here?"

"Two hours or so. We just arrived in port today."

I waited outside for her in the damp May drizzle. The rain was so light my sweatshirt didn't seem to get wet, it was more like an afternoon fog rolling in. I looked forward to talking to Sonya, not because of our project, just because I was tired and sitting around talking to her seemed like a good way to spend some time. She wasn't inside long, and when she came out she did indeed look fresher.

"You're looking good, my friend," I said. "Must be the sea air." We headed up the street without even discussing a destination.

"I do get a bit of that. And I admit, it's odd walking on solid ground."

"So, how's your adventure going?"

"I've a lot to explain. Our old biologist, Kathy Woods, evidently became ill and has left us. They replaced her with a new one, Bonnie Young. She's a little chattier, and seems to know more biology, too."

"Maybe they downgraded your importance and removed a spy."

"I doubt it. Our new captain seems to be taking security more seriously than the old one. And they replaced the electronic bug Gerry disabled. Gerry had made it look as if the original one had a manufacturing defect. We had a bet on how long it would take for it be replaced. Joanne won — it was fixed by the time we left port. There's no need for us to have many clandestine conversations anyway. How have you been? Isn't your apartment safe?"

"I don't know, probably not." I told her the story of the "Russian" burglars and everything else that had happened since we last met.

"So they're spying on you, too?"

"Maybe they figured out that Gerry monkeyed with their bugs."

Sonya was quiet for a while, then began again. "I've tried to be very careful, but I may have made a significant mistake. I once jokingly told Kathy Woods I wished you could help me. Maybe she really was a spy."

We walked in silence for a block or two. I didn't want to interfere with anything Sonya might be trying to remember. Finally she spoke up again. "You mean we are the third group that has been looking into the meaning of the whale sounds?"

"You're the third civilian voyage I've uncovered, but you said something interesting. I think, but don't know, that Dr. Farrity worked alone. I have no idea whether this Jennison guy had assistants or not."

"How could you ever find out?"

"I may not be able to. Jeannie and I are going to try to talk to his girlfriend. She's a recluse, I'm not sure she'll even see us. She might know something more."

"Where does she live? Is she from around here?"

"Hardly. She lives in San Luis Obispo. Jennison was stationed out of San Diego."

Sonya laughed. "You're going to California? When was the last time you left Massachusetts?"

"I went to see James Farrity in Maine a few months ago."

"New England, then?"

"It's been a while." We both laughed. We had reached the end of my street and we needed to make a choice. "What do you feel like for dinner? Steak? Italian? It's on me."

"Anything but seafood," she said. She looked at me with a mischievous grin. "I think I'd like a plain old pepperoni pizza and cold beer."

"Of course, the Massachusetts state meal. Welcome home." We headed up to the House of Pizza. Their pizza wasn't fancy, but it was great comfort food. Sonya and I chatted the whole way, mostly about old friends and memories. It seemed the twenty minute walk only took five. We ordered our food, grabbed a couple of mugs, sat down at one of their picnic tables, and clinked our glasses in a toast. "To us, past, present and future," I offered.

Sonya smiled in appreciation, then turned serious. "I appreciate you doing this, but I don't want you to get into any trouble. I'm just trying to keep my nose clean and my powder dry, so to speak. That's why I didn't bring you any more recordings. I'm a little worried about Gerry, though. I think the situation is getting to him."

"How so?"

"Well, there's caution, and there's paranoia. I mean, assuming the worst, the navy may not want to reveal how intelligent whales are, but they didn't hire us just to kill us off."

As she spoke my stomach tightened up. I thought about the motorcycle accident Jennison had, maybe while he was on his way to see Farrity. I didn't want to tell Sonya she might not be assuming the worst. "I suppose not," I agreed.

"I mean I'm not fooling myself. They are spying on us, and they did break into your apartment."

"We don't know the navy was behind that."

Now it was Sonya's turn to doubt me, and she didn't attempt to hide her incredulity. "You think it was professional cat burglars who speak poor Russian trying to steal your pets?"

"Point taken."

"Anyway, I'm glad I didn't attempt to bring you more tapes. I'll bet you're going to be broken into again."

"I just hope they don't lose my cats this time."

"You're cute. But your burglars know it was the open door and the cats that gave them away. They'll be more careful. Anyway, I've an idea. We're shipping out to San Diego next. I could leave you some tapes there. The navy would have no reason to suspect I would be handing you anything there."

"How far is it from San Luis Obispo to San Diego?" I asked.

"I don't know. They're both in Southern California, couldn't be too far, could it?"

"When are you going to be there?"

"In about two months," Sonya said. She smiled at me as if she had had a major revelation. "I'll let you know how to pick up my package then."

"This whole thing is crazy."

"I know."

We were rank amateurs tying to outsmart one of the deadliest institutions the world has known. Sonya said she would let me know how to retrieve her tapes. We hugged and said our goodbyes. Not five minutes after we parted I decided I didn't want her to put herself in greater danger. We had a great deal of data already, though I knew the quality of her research would be superior to what we already had. I turned back to let her know she should play it safe, but I couldn't find her and had no way to get in touch. I thought about just calling the whole thing off, but I realized I had to pick up her package in San Diego now, or potentially put her in more peril.

I came to understand the concept of the point of no return. I was putting my best friends in an unknown amount of danger, and the only thing I could do was to redouble my efforts. The day after I met with Sonya I told Marta and Teddy that if someone should break into my apartment again, they shouldn't interfere. There was nothing to find there, and there was no reason to put themselves in harm's way. I did wedge a small tuft of cat fur between the door and the jamb below the lowest hinge every time I left my apartment. It would fall without a sound when the door was opened, and was so innocuous I didn't imagine even the most experienced spy would notice it. I never found the tuft actually on the floor, but once it did seem to be higher than where I had left it. Could my intruders have noticed, and placed it back incorrectly, or had I actually placed it there? Was it one more piece of the puzzle, or just my mind creating a false image? I had to act as if I was being watched, but it would have been easier if I knew it for sure.

I began to spend most of my time entering data into Teddy's computer. I could see the cleverness in the navy's method of getting skilled researchers to gather data, but not allowing them access to the power of a VAX. Without a computer it would be extremely difficult to suss out the correlations between the whales' cries and their subsequent journeys. With Teddy's computer I began to see definite glimpses of patterns. The dominant male repeated his call several times over a period of days, sometimes with minor changes I felt might be due to the response of the others in the pod. The length of the journey appeared to be related to the length of the song. It also seemed as though a different intonation was used before the pod began traveling north or south. But even though I grew more and more confident of the patterns I was uncovering, the complexity of deciphering a language was daunting. I compared it to a new-born human learning a language solely from the behavior of the adults around her, but that infant is learning a human language and has a mother constantly nursing her along. I was alone, and of a different species.

In the meantime, my companions were working at extracting new phrases from the recordings Matt had completed, using their instruments and each other.

About two weeks before Jeannie and I were to depart for the west coast I received a package from Sonya. The package was wrapped in plain brown paper, and inside was another package about the size of a ring box, which in fact it was. Inside the box lay a keychain with a gold figure of pi attached to one end of a gold chain and a key on the key ring that was attached to the other. The key had 143B written on it with a felt pen. There was a short note that read "*I knew I had to send you this keychain as soon as I saw it. Every mathematician should carry a π around all the time. I found it on the ground with this key attached. If you ever find a lock it fits be sure to go in*". A few days later I received another package from Sonya with a real pie. It was inside a small box that was swathed in newspaper to prevent it from banging around inside the outer box. On one of the pages was an ad for a storage warehouse. On the pie box was written "*Just in case the last pie was too abstract.*"

I found an atlas in the local library and found it was a little over three hundred miles from San Diego to San Luis Obispo. Jeannie had planned for us to fly directly to San Luis Obispo because she was taking a cello with her, but because we didn't know how our meeting with Carolyn Truesdale would turn out, nor what we would be picking up in San Diego, we decided to fly to San Diego together and rent a car for the rest of the trip.

8

I had flown to Washington DC once, but Jeannie flew regularly, even to Europe, for her concerts. She was an old hand at making the arrangements, so I left them up to her. There is something fantastic about the idea of flying thousands of miles, but the reality of being cramped in a smoky airplane cabin for hours at a time is less magnificent. Jeannie let me have the window seat. I amused myself by wondering at the immense landscapes below. We stopped somewhere to change flights, I think St. Louis, but by the time we arrived in San Diego I couldn't move my neck, it had cramped so badly. The worst part of the trip for Jeannie was waiting for her instrument at the luggage claim.

"I love playing cello, but I swear I would have taken up the violin as a kid if I knew what a pain traveling would be."

"Is that your Scarampella?" I asked.

"God no, I would have paid for an extra seat for that!"

Fortunately, the instrument arrived in good condition, and my neck soon relaxed. We rented a convertible to better enjoy the California sun, but then had to devise a way of tying her cello down in the back seat, as it wouldn't fit in the trunk. The address Sonya had directed us to was in an industrial section of the city. It turned out to be several blocks of what were essentially one car storage garages. We located our garage, 143B, and inside found two grocery bags with a few groceries sticking out of the top. I explained to Jeannie this was Sonya's little joke, because that was how she had brought me the first cassettes. Instead of cassettes, this time one of the bags was half full of floppy disks. I had learned enough about computers to realize this would probably mean a lot more and higher quality data, and a much easier time organizing the travel logs. It also meant the navy was finally allowing her to use some kind of computer in her work. The day was late, so we headed out of the city, grabbed a quick bite to eat and found an unpretentious motel. I was exhausted. Jeannie, being younger and a more accomplished traveler, had fared somewhat better.

We started early the next day, but by the time we pulled onto the freeway the morning sun was already baking the land. I knew the West was drier than

New England, but this was clearly moving into desert territory. Nevertheless I enjoyed the roasting feeling, especially as it was mitigated by the fact we were driving 70 mph with the top down, so I was somewhat disgruntled to see a massive yellow cloud bank ahead.

"We're heading for rain," I said.

Jeannie laughed. "You wish. We're heading for L.A., that's smog."

Boston air is plenty polluted, but L.A. smog is downright ugly. I've been told it's improving, that there are occasional days when you can see the mountains surrounding the city, but this wasn't one of them. Nor was it a traffic-free day. It took us three hours to do what I felt should have taken one. The saving grace was that Jeannie had a much easier time managing our convertible than she had driving Matt's truck in Maine. Eventually we were past all that and heading up the rugged Pacific Coast in search of our mysterious hippie farmer.

Once we passed Ventura my mood began to change. They call California golden, but it looked mostly just dried up to me. Still, the fresh ocean air, sunshine, and dry heat helped me understand the allure of the West Coast. It seemed we had arrived in the little city of San Luis Obispo in no time, but it was already late afternoon. We rented a motel room on the south side of town, then drove over to Pismo Beach for dinner and to get our feet wet in the surf. I decided I liked California.

I had to hold Marylin, the woman I had spoken to at the chamber of commerce, to her word, so we headed there the next morning after breakfast. We were lucky and found a ten minute parking space right in front of the chamber office. Downtown San Luis Obispo was filled with upscale shops and restaurants, its sidewalks were filled with people, and the parking spaces were filled with cars. I left Jeannie outside to do her daily hand exercises and watch the car while I went inside with my map of the state.

I didn't need to ask for my informant, as she was the only person in the office and she had a nameplate on the counter in front of her.

"Marylin, I'm Joe Tenatt. We spoke several months ago about the Shanti Shanti farm. You told me I should drop in and ask for directions if I was in the area."

"I remember. You're from Boston. You came all the way here just to see a farm?" Marylin might have been a few years younger than me, but maybe she just looked that way because took some care in her appearance. She greeted me cheerfully, I assumed because she was bored.

"Well, my niece is giving a concert at the college." I pointed at Jeannie through the large windows facing the street. "I've never been to California, so I thought I'd tag along." I put my map on the counter. Marylin walked around the end and stood next to me, hip to hip, shoulder to shoulder. I gathered she wasn't just bored, more likely she was lonely.

"Here we are," she said, pointing at the map. *Indeed*, I thought, *here we are*. "You need to take Monterrey Avenue to Broad Street. Take a left, go about two miles and take another left on Tank Farm Road." As she spoke she softly pushed her arm against mine while tracing the route. "Tank Farm Road becomes Orcutt Road. After another five or six miles you'll come to a well-traveled dirt road on the left. I'm pretty sure there's no road sign, but there is a ramshackle house and a couple of sheds on the right hand side. Take that road up into the mountains. *Shanti Shanti* is in a little hidden valley, maybe a dozen miles up the road."

Marylin looked out through the window. "Is that your car?"

"It's a rental, but yeah."

"Better close the top before you start up the dirt road."

I thanked her and turned to go, then stopped and turned back again. "Like I said, my niece is giving a recital tomorrow evening. Would you like to join me?" I hadn't been on a date since my wife died, but I don't think a woman had flirted with me since then either.

Marylin blushed, but just a little. "Sure, what's she playing?"

"I have no idea." We both laughed. "I'll call you tomorrow afternoon with the details."

Jeannie and I headed out and I told her about my date. "You know what I'm playing, Joe."

"Yeah, but I'm playing the role of a doting uncle."

We found the dirt road exactly as Marylin described. I had a suspicion she had driven out here since our phone conversation to be sure she knew the way. Either that or she had a phenomenal memory. In any case, we put the convertible's top up and headed for the hills. At first the road looked like a driveway heading for one of the many grand houses perched on the coastal foothills, but it continued past the farthest one — straight for the mountains. As soon as we reached the first steep incline, the road crawled into a narrow, winding canyon. We reached a little pass and then the road dropped down into what Marylin had aptly called a hidden valley. I didn't see any other roads into the valley; it was completely surrounded by more dry hills. There was a small reservoir on the south end, but most of the rest of the basin was filled with farm buildings and verdant-looking fields and orchards.

Our road came to a T and a sign with an arrow pointing right that read "ALL PICKUPS AND DELIVERIES." There was no indication of what lay toward the left, so we went right. The first building we came to was a warehouse where a small crew was loading boxes of produce into an eighteen-wheeler with hand dollies. I approached a tall rugged man with waist-length blond hair. "Where can I find Carolyn Truesdale?" I asked.

"Who?"

"Carolyn Truesdale," I repeated.

"Hmm, I guess I heard you the first time." The man stared down at me for several seconds, then at Jeannie and our dusty car. "Wait here. Don't move," he ordered, then strode into the building.

A few minutes later another man came out. I guessed he was Mexican, and his slight accent confirmed my surmise. "You looking for Señorita Truesdale?"

"Yes."

"Why do you want to see her?"

Without getting into too long of a narrative I explained I wanted to ask her about a former boyfriend, Harold Jennison. His eyes narrowed a little when I mentioned the name.

"Mañana," he barked, and went back into his warehouse. There was nothing for us to do but leave and try again the next day. There are worse situations to be in than having to cool one's heels by the beach on a hot California day. We returned to the city in the late afternoon so Jeannie could go to her high school tutorial. When she returned and pulled out her cello to rehearse for her recital in our motel room, my only regret was I couldn't bring my own instrument, but in fact I would have no place playing with her when she was seriously preparing for a show.

The next day we returned to Shanti Shanti. We arrived at the T, where, in addition to the sign pointing to the right for trucks, there was a new sign, professionally done in the same manner as the original, which read "Convertibles" over an arrow pointing to the left. Obviously that meant us.

We drove through a small apricot orchard and then past a field of tomatoes toward a cluster of buildings that looked like residences. As we stopped at the terminal cul-de-sac a woman in a long tie-dyed dress and braids almost as long came out of the front door of one of the houses. She pressed her hands together and said, "Namaste."

Jeannie and I returned the greeting.

"I'm Carolyn Truesdale. I believe you're looking for me."

"We are. I'm Joseph Tenatt, and this is Jeannie Langlois. We want to ask you about Harold Jennison. We heard you two were close."

Carolyn stiffened a little when I mentioned Jennison. At the same time I saw her eyes grow moist, and then, as if through some amazing act of will power, dry up again. "I see," she said. "Could I interest you in some iced tea? We can sit and talk in the rear patio. It's one of the coolest places on the farm."

We followed Carolyn to the back of the house. She had met us alone, but I noticed at least two people peering at us through a window in the neighboring house as we passed between the two buildings. She led us to a patio under an arbor whose green grapes were just beginning to form in thick clusters.

After we sat down with our drinks, Carolyn spoke again. "Yes, I knew Harold. That was a long time ago, at least in my life. Why are you interested in him?"

I explained Jeannie and her quartet wanted to commission a musical piece celebrating whales' songs, and that we had obtained a few recordings from James Farrity, who had mentioned Harold Jennison as someone who might also have made recordings. I told her we had heard Jennison had died, but a former colleague, Dr. Reckow, had met her and thought she might know if the records still existed.

"You've gone to a lot of bother to get in touch with me," Carolyn said. The look on her face said she wasn't sure it was worth the trouble for the stated purpose.

"I'm a retired professor with no children, no wife, and only one niece," I said, indicating Jeannie. "She is giving a concert tonight at Cal Poly. When I heard she was coming to San Luis Obispo, I offered to come and see if we could find you. And you're right, it wasn't easy."

Carolyn still didn't look convinced. "And how did you find me?"

"We went to the chamber of commerce and the receptionist, Marylin, claimed to know you and told us how to get here. It's a beautiful location, I should add."

Carolyn's face brightened a little. "Marylin Sutliff, eh? She might be one of the only people on the entire planet you could have run into who could have directed you here."

"I guess we were lucky, but she was the obvious person to ask."

"I suppose. I think I met Reckow once, but I'm surprised he remembered me. I'm surprised he remembered Harold. I always thought he had a kind of narrow awareness of the world, pretty much only saw what he was looking for. Harold was a subordinate to him, not worthy of notice, and I less so."

"He made it clear Jennison was a junior partner," I said.

"In any case, I'm not sure I can help you. Hank, that's what I always called Harold, and I did date, but we kind of lived in separate universes." She gestured broadly as if to indicate her farm. "Are you playing some sort of whale music tonight?" she asked Jeannie.

"Oh no, tonight it's Bach only."

"Is the concert open to the public?"

"Absolutely. I can have tickets for you at the front desk. How many would you like?"

Carolyn thought about the invitation for a while as she sipped on her tea. "Three. Can I show you around the farm?"

"We'd love to see it," Jeannie said, then looked at me for confirmation.

"Certainly," I said.

"We can drive around in your convertible. It would be the perfect vehicle." As we walked back to the front of the house I noticed she gave a quick nod to the dark window where I had seen the two figures standing before. After rolling the top down, we piled into the car. Carolyn took the rear seat, but she sat in the center and leaned forward so she was practically between Jeannie and myself. She had relaxed since we arrived, and was clearly in love with her farm, so we spent nearly two hours inspecting its many fields and orchards. After we had done a complete circuit she instructed Jeannie to drive past the warehouses and we ended up at the reservoir we had seen when we first entered the valley. Jeannie parked on a small dusty beach and we climbed out of the vehicle.

"This is the one place cooler than my patio," Carolyn said as she smoothly dropped her tie-dyed dress to her feet and walked into the water completely naked. It took Jeannie and myself a little longer to shed our clothes, but we soon followed her into the lake. There may not be anything more humbling than an old overweight man skinny dipping with two beautiful women, but these two women were perfectly relaxed in their own skin, and therefore so was I. We swam around protected from the summer heat for less than half an hour, but we clambered back into our convertible far more comfortable than before, not only cooler and cleaner, but more comfortable with each other. Jeannie and Carolyn in particular developed a rapport and had quickly become friends.

When we dropped her off at her house Carolyn warned us to put the top back up for the dusty ride back.

"See you at the concert, then," I said.

"I'm looking forward to it", she said. "Shanti."

"Shanti," Jeannie and I answered in unrehearsed unison.

We were disappointed Carolyn didn't have any information for us, but not disappointed to have met her. It's not often one is able to meet someone who is doing exactly what they want to be doing.

"I don't think she believed our story at first," I said on the ride back.

"I'm not sure she believes it yet," Jeannie said. "I think the swim was a bit of a test."

"Did we pass?"

"I believe we did. At the least it showed we weren't wearing wires." Jeannie laughed at her little joke, but I thought she may have been right. I was surprised by her insight.

Jeannie dropped me off at Marylin's well before the concert was to begin. Marylin lived in an inauspicious but tidy neighborhood of mobile homes nestled in the hills on the southwest side of town, not too far from the road we had taken to reach Shanti Shanti. As I mentioned, I hadn't had a date since my wife died, and I had the feeling Marylin had as little recent experience. For some reason she liked my company, and that alone made the evening enjoyable. We sat in her back yard and had a glass or two of delicious wine while we tried to get to know each other. I had always thought the awkwardness I had felt as a youth when dating was due to inexperience, but I discovered some of it is also due to the emotionally charged nature of meeting someone you really want to make like you, no matter your age. The wine helped us settle into a more relaxed mode, though, and the time disappeared quickly. We decided to get to the recital early so we could nab front-row seats. We watched the stage hands set up the stage for half an hour or so before anyone else arrived. I explained to Marylin that Jeannie's husband was in that line of work.

"Does he ever set up her concerts?"

"I'm sure he does. He's supposed to be one of the best in Boston."

"Then I hope they get along well."

I assured her they were always affectionate when I was with them. The auditorium began to fill up about twenty minutes before Jeannie was scheduled to perform. It wasn't a large venue and it was nearly two-thirds full when Jeannie finally was introduced. She played two of Bach's solo cello suites, and I thought she played exquisitely.

During a break between the pieces Marylin said, "Your niece plays very well. You must be proud of her."

For a split second I forgot Jeannie was supposed to be my niece, but I caught myself before I said something stupid. "I am, very proud." It wasn't right having to lie on a date.

After the concert, and an encore of a short cello solo by Piatti, we went back stage to congratulate Jeannie. As we were effusing over her performance Carolyn Truesdale came over with her companions, a man and woman. I recognized the man as the foreman who had been so brusque with me the day before.

"That was wonderful," Carolyn said, "Truly wonderful."

Marylin smiled. "Well Carolyn, maybe that will get you to leave your farm more often."

Carolyn took the tease well. "Hello Marylin. I understand I have you to thank for my visitors." They hugged. "Pardon me," Carolyn continued, "This is Armando and Lorna Santillana. They are my partners at Shanti Shanti."

I extended my hand to Armando. "Good to meet you again."

He smiled and said, "*El gusto es mío*", then turned to Jeannie, "You're not only talented and beautiful, you have made wonderful use of your talent, *es exquisito. Muchas gracias.*"

We spent several minutes chatting and praising Jeannie, when Carolyn grasped my elbow and took me aside. "I have found some of Hank's records.

Can you come back to the farm tomorrow?"

I promised we would come. When we arrived the next morning the convertible sign was gone, but we headed to Carolyn's house anyway. She came out to greet us as we pulled up and led us to her veranda and iced tea again. This time I didn't feel we were being watched.

"I'm sorry I've been so coy about this, but I had to make sure you guys are on the up and up."

"And are we?" I asked.

"If my own ears were not enough, I've learned that you," she turned to Jeannie, "are quite a rising star." Turning to me she added, "And you're a professor of mathematics."

"Was."

"I also found out that you called Marylin months before your trip. It didn't just happen." Then, turning to Jeannie, she said, "And you called asking to give a recital and tutorial, you were not invited, not that you shouldn't have been."

Jeannie and I gulped and looked properly embarrassed, but neither of us replied. Carolyn continued, "I don't know if you're related, I don't know if you just want whale recordings for a possible composition, it seems like a stretch. But I'm pretty sure you're not from the navy or some other government agency."

"How did you learn all this?" I asked.

"We have friends in town, and in Boston. Let me ask you again: why do you want Hank's notes?"

"You have reliable friends," I said. "And Jeannie and I aren't related, we are merely friends."

"Very good friends," Jeannie said.

"And we have a mutual friend who is on a research voyage similar to the one Harold undertook. She feels something is amiss, that the navy is not being candid. It took us some effort to even find there were previous similar efforts, such as Harold's."

"Have there been any others since his?" Carolyn asked.

"I don't know, but there was at least one before."

"Then Hank was right."

"He was. He had even contacted the man who conducted that project, James Farrity, but he died in an accident before they met."

"He was killed in a hit and run. I'm not convinced it was an accident."

"You think he was murdered?"

"Hank was a complex man, I suppose that's one reason I loved him. He had this philosophy that we have to balance our intellectual lives between suspicion and belief. He said, 'If you don't believe, you can't learn anything; if you aren't suspicious, you can't learn anything new.'"

"He sounds like a smart man."

"He was, but I used to think he erred a little too much on the suspicious end. After he died I changed my mind."

"How so?"

"Hank was sure that the navy was lying, and that he was in danger. He learned about Farrity and talked to him once. He felt Farrity was naive, and was on his way to see him, I think in Arcata, when he was run over."

"Farrity taught at Humboldt State at the time. We've spoken to him. He was the one who told us about Harold."

"Do you think he told the navy Hank was going to see him?"

"I doubt it. He may not be as 'suspicious' in his intellectual pursuits as you say Harold, Hank, was, but he was angry with the Navy too, and wouldn't give them his research records. We have them."

"Really? And the navy asked for them first?"

"Yes, but he told them he didn't have anything."

"And all these years I just imagined him as a dupe. Why was he mad at the navy?"

"He wanted to continue his research, and to publish it. They wouldn't allow it."

"The thing is, they've been here as well, looking for Hank's papers. I denied I knew anything about them. I would love you to take them, I can't bring myself to destroy them, but I've no use for them, either. To use a mariner's phrase, they've become an albatross around my neck. I feel they have endowed me with Hank's paranoia. Come."

She loaded us on to a little farm cart and drove us into one of the large warehouses we visited on our first day. It was refrigerated and filled with pallets full of produce boxes stacked higher than I could reach. We drove down the central aisle, then dismounted from the machine and walked down an undistinguished side aisle somewhere in the middle of the building. She stopped in front of a stack that looked exactly like all the others in the building.

"I have about forty boxes of notebooks and tapes you can have. You won't be able to fit them all in your cute little car."

"It's just a rental, we'll trade it for a van." I turned to Jeannie, who hadn't spoken since we arrived. "Do you feel like driving back to Boston?"

"I think I'll need to cancel a performance or two, and some lessons, but sure. Whatever's needed."

"Can we pick them up tomorrow?"

"Today, tomorrow, the next day, those boxes will sit there until you take them."

Jeannie had a seminar she needed to give that evening, and I spent a lovely evening, and night, with Marylin. As she dropped me off at our motel the next morning on the way to her job she asked me to come back, and I invited her to Cambridge. When I was a kid my aunt hinted I should leave Draper. She always said travel broadens one's horizons — I wonder if this is what she meant.

I was beginning to wish I could drive for the first time since I left South Dakota, must have been the western air. We were able to obtain a van at the rental yard (after we washed the car) and headed back out to Shanti Shanti and drove directly to the warehouse. Armando was waiting for us and helped us load the boxes into the vehicle. "Señorita Truesdale would like to see you before you leave," he said when we were finished. He looked at our vehicle sagging on its springs. "Be careful on the road out. You might need a heavier truck."

We had iced tea once more with Carolyn. "I'm relieved to get rid of those records and delighted someone wants them," she said. "But I do hope Hank was mostly wrong about the risk and danger. If he was run over on purpose ..."

"Do you really think that's possible?" I asked.

"He was nervous towards the end, and I've been worried ever since. I just don't know. That's the hardest part, not knowing."

Armando was right about our van. Jeannie had to crawl away from the farm just to keep the springs from bottoming out. We upgraded from a passenger van to a light commercial truck in town, meaning we had to unload all our boxes in the motel parking lot, and then reload them again. We didn't want the rental agency to know we might have broken one of its springs. I felt bad for Jeannie, because the only thing they had in the yard was a stick shift truck, and we had over three thousand miles ahead of us.

The United States is huge and varied, and driving from one end to the other is an amazing, even exhausting, experience. We started relatively early the next morning and climbed over the coast range, past valleys full of farms and orchards similar to Carolyn's, then descended through a maze of evil smelling oil fields onto the flat, hot and humid farmlands of California's San Joaquin Valley. I will admit for the first several hours I kept an eye on the rear view mirror, but we were on an isolated road and I never saw anyone following us.

Our truck was meant to haul its cargo safely, but not necessarily to carry its crew in comfort. It had no air conditioning, so we left the windows down. The radio emitted more static than music, and at times it seemed like the engine was in the cab with us. Jeannie and I had to shout at each other to be understood, casual conversation was impossible. The first day we made it over the Tehachapi Pass and across the scorching Mojave Desert into Las Vegas.

"I'm done," Jeannie said. "I think nine or ten hours is my limit."

"Yeah, mine too, and I just sat here all day."

It took us nearly a week to get home, but it felt much longer. I sat mesmerized by the scenery as it zipped by my truck window. Out west, especially, I could spend hours watching a distant landmark, an unnamed peak or ridge, come into view, slowly change its shape as we passed by, but when it finally disappeared I often could hardly remember what it looked like.

As we left the Rockies behind and reached the vast expanses of eastern Colorado and then Nebraska, I recalled my trip from Draper to Boston, the first adult activity of my life. Now that I was looking at the same country from the tail end of my existence, it was hard to imagine so much time had passed. I mused that I had seen and learned so much since my callow self had launched itself onto an unknown universe, but I also realized I then had the confidence that comes from not comprehending how much I didn't know. Now I was fully aware I was undertaking a potentially difficult and dangerous mission. Furthermore, I was risking the safety of those closest to me, whereas that initial voyage was mine alone. Still, I knew what I must do, and I knew my friends felt the same way, that none of us would turn back. We were all more afraid of what would happen if we didn't act than what might occur if we did.

We left the West and the far vistas vanished. I turned my attention to sound and to how it changed with the conditions. Rain, vegetation, development all modified the incessant noise of travel, incessant because we kept the windows down to stave off the heat and boredom. It seemed softer in the evening as the light faded, harsher in the cities and as the temperature rose. I could not tell if it was synesthesia, my imagination, or some actual modification to the waves of air pounding my ears, but the idea did get me to thinking about my attempt to understand whales. I have played music and listened to music and loved music since grade school, but it occurred to me it might be folly to try to plumb the depths of whales' comprehension of sound with their massive ears and brains. But if that were so, it was all the more important to try, as our species might be killing them because of their intense aural sensitivity.

When we finally pulled into Jeannie and Matt's driveway, Matt was busy wiring some equipment in his garage. We opened the rear door of the truck to show him our treasure. I'm sure I saw his dark skin get pale. I think he knew more than we did how much work was in store for us.

9

Harold Jennison's data were more voluminous and sophisticated than James Farrity's, and Sonya's new data, while not so ample, were the best quality of any we had to work with. However it was very difficult to cross-reference any of the material because the methods each researcher used were so different.

It turned out my musings on sound during our return trip were but a prelude to the complexities Matt laid out in comparing these various collections. "Generally speaking, biologists are quite sure some whales use echolocation to find food, but we can't rule out the possibility that they use it to keep in touch with each other as well. One of the problems we face with these data is how the sound was recorded. Farrity's, for instance, had the poorest recorders, and all of his recording were from the ship. Jennison not only had better equipment, but it appears he made at least a few simultaneous recordings from different locations, as if he had an assistant, or had one of the crew help him."

"He had help?" I said.

"I think he must have, and a second boat of some sort. We find the letters "DH" scattered through his notes on the recording methods he used, but there is no explanation of who or what they mean. If he had an assistant we would like to know if he had different responsibilities and methods than Jennison, like Sonya and her teammates. If not, what else does DH mean? In addition, even local conditions change the nature the of sounds, so we need to determine whether some of the differences we see are due to differences in the environment, or to meaningful intonations."

I made a note to myself to ask Carolyn Truesdale whether she knew if Jennison had an assistant if I ever saw her again, but I wasn't planning such a trip in the near future. In any case the new evidence created many new questions for us to ponder.

One day, several months after we had returned, Matt came into the whale room while Teddy and I were imitating the cetaceans' vocalizations on our shared violin, and began to explain some of the nuances of Jennison's data. "We could see if that helps us." I paused, then continued, "You would have been a pretty good biologist, Teddy. And you, Matt, would have been a great electrical engineer."

Matt glared at me. Teddy quickly broke the icy silence. "Joe, he *is* a great electrical engineer."

I realized my error and apologized. Matt regained his composure, but remained serious. "Do you know why I do sound systems?"

"I always assumed you liked it and were good at it. Jeannie told me about your first company selling stereo systems to undergrads."

"I do and I am. But there's more. As a black man it is expected I could be good at music. I graduated at the head of my engineering class, but I knew it would never be expected I could be a good engineer. But I am, and I know I am and I didn't want to spend my life proving something that would never be accepted. Do you know how I see my work?"

I saw I had somehow missed the mark in my assessment of Matt, and admitted it. "No."

"I feel every musical event I create should sound as good as if it were being played at La Scala or Symphony Hall. Maybe better, because I set each venue up for the particular artist or artists who will use it. I enjoy what I do, but I didn't just luck my way into my line." Matt spoke quietly, forcefully.

"I understand," I said.

"I know you do. So what do we do now?"

"Get back to work."

A few weeks later Sonya showed up again. This time she took a page out of Clive's playbook and found me walking down Mass Ave. as I was heading home from Teddy's.

"Hi Joe, enjoying the end of fall?" she said, acting like we met every day. I took her cue not to act surprised, though in fact I was — it had only been six months since her last visit.

"Sonya, how are you?"

"Getting my land legs. Want to join Gerry and me for a beer and a bite?"

I knew I couldn't say no, not that I wanted to. "Sure. Where are we going? And how did you find me?"

"Actually, I was going over to your place now. You saved me the walk."

She took me to a local pub I hadn't been to before. It was mid-afternoon, the place was slow. Sitting at a booth in the rear was Gerry, looking, if anything, more wan than the first time I saw him. I mused to myself he must stay below deck all the time. I wondered how he could attach his transponders to the whales without getting a little suntan.

"Hello Gerry, good to see you again."

He gave me a forced smile that indicated it wasn't so good for him. "Hi, Joe."

"Gerry wanted to talk to you," Sonya said, which was surprising to me, given his dour countenance. "He's curious about what you're doing with his recordings."

As Sonya and I sat down a waitress came over to take our order. I was relieved to see Gerry already had a brew, so I ordered a red ale and hamburger. I think Sonya asked for the same thing, only with porter.

"We're trying to figure out what they're saying," I said.

Gerry considered this for a while. His glass was full, his sandwich sat untouched. He stared at me without replying. I decided I needed to be more voluble.

"We think ... rather we are operating under the assumption they have a mathematical language, a sort of geometry without numbers, that they use to plan, and maybe recount, their voyages. I think it's pretty much along the same lines as what you and Sonya have been thinking."

"There's more to it than that," Gerry said.

"You're probably right."

"I am right."

Gerry's certitude surprised me, maybe because, as a scientist, I feel I must test and retest any hypothesis, and I assumed Gerry had the same mind set. "What more do you think there is?" I asked.

"They don't like us."

"Who could blame them?" I said. "We haven't treated them well."

Gerry glared at me, as if I wasn't taking him seriously enough. "We have been murdering them for millennia. And they don't want us eavesdropping."

I didn't want to disagree with Gerry, I wanted to show we were on the same side. At the same time, I wanted him to explain his views. "How do you know that?" I asked.

"Isn't it obvious? Have you ever heard of empathy?"

"But, Gerry, we're trying to understand their language to help them."

Gerry laughed a very ugly laugh. "Yeah, right, that's just what the navy's trying to do too, help the whales. And the whales are so grateful."

"Maybe if we beat the navy to it, we could convince everyone they deserve to be treated as intelligent beings."

"Oh, good idea. We treat each other so well. Do you happen to know what the fundamental purpose of the navy is, by any chance?"

I couldn't think of a meaningful reply. On the one hand, Gerry wasn't off the mark, I couldn't refute him. On the other his attitude was so despairing, so hopeless, I couldn't accept it, either. Gerry and I stared at each other for a few moments. Sonya had sat there the whole time, watching both of us but not interfering. It was clear she had seen this act before. It was truly an awkward silence. Finally Gerry stood up. "I guess this meeting is over," he said. He turned and walked out the door. Sonya and I continued the awkward silence by ourselves.

"What do you think?" Sonya finally asked.

"What do *you* think?" I said.

"This has been building up. Almost from the beginning. Gerry's very talented, but I think the stress has gotten to him. And the navy has upped the ante."

"How so?"

"Well, they changed our project from sensitive to classified confidential, and they brought on a new captain, a real stickler for the rules."

"Why doesn't Gerry just quit?"

"He might. He exploded at the captain last week, accused the navy of hiding our research. He threatened to make everything public."

"What did the captain do?"

"He told him that would not be a good idea, and reminded Gerry he had signed a contract giving the navy sole authority to use the information as it saw fit. I can't see how Gerry can continue, but he's very paranoid, now he's afraid the navy will track him down and murder him."

I didn't want to tell Sonya about Harold Jennison, but the time had come that I had to. I explained what I knew, and what I feared.

"My God!" Sonya said when I was done. "What have I gotten myself into?"

"I feel I led you into it," I said.

"No, it's been my choice." Sonya took a long slow sip from her mug and I drained mine. I ordered two more and we were half way through them before Sonya spoke again. "I want to continue. To adopt Gerry's point of view is to adopt nihilism, and I can't do that. I choose not to do that. I want to know what my whales are saying, and I want to help them, if I can."

"In that case, I will continue too."

"Thank you," Sonya said. "I ship out tomorrow."

"Do you think Gerry will join you?"

"I have no idea."

10

I don't know what it would be to spend a life working at something just to earn a paycheck. I've had the happy circumstance of being good at what I'm interested in, and in having a skill in enough demand I was never without well-paid employment. I don't mean to say my work life has been completely without impossible deadlines I had to meet, or office politics with the accompanying petty backbiting, or that there were never times I wasn't up to the task or times when my assignment was so trivial, so mundane, so boring, I simply couldn't concentrate. The way I dealt with these externalities may be why I've bounced around all my life, rather than ensconce myself in some institution and percolate up through its ranks. I had assumed I would become a tenured professor when I first embarked on earning my PhD, but I've never even given that a thought once I began to earn a living doing mathematics.

Neither can I imagine what someone who's not versed in math would think watching me spend hours scratching little figures on my notepads. For myself I barely notice the pencil, the paper, the figures — I'm fixated on what they mean. I don't even notice the time passing when I'm at work because the ideas I'm working on seem eternal. In any case I hadn't approached a project with as much enthusiasm as I did deciphering Cetacean in many years.

Of course I had to learn another language — most of my work now was done on Teddy's VAX, so I had to become fluent in computer language as well. Teddy used C++, so that's what I learned. I didn't know if some other computer language might be better, but I figured if I had to choose between a great method and a great teacher, I'd go with having a great teacher.

One of our first breakthroughs came from Gerry's remark that there was more than mathematics to the whales' language. We had become so focused on discovering a mathematical meaning to their sounds we had neglected to consider that might only be part of what they were communicating. At first this possibility seemingly made our task much harder, as we had no idea which sounds might be contributing to a mathematical description, and which might be conveying other information. And even though Gerry might be right that they disliked us, and resented our intrusion into their personal world, we didn't know that for sure.

"What if we are right that only the alpha males give the directions?" Marta asked one day as our group brainstormed our dilemma.

"What if?" I said.

"Well, then we could analyze the phrases the rest of the pod makes as non-mathematical language."

"That makes sense," I said. "We could analyze those conversations separately."

"More than just that," she said. "We could remove those phrases from the large males' cries as well, which could isolate their mathematical language and make it more accessible." All our heads turned to Matt, except Matt's, of course, who was lost in his own thoughts.

"I'm sure I can manage that," he finally said. "This idea has been stalking me, but I still couldn't catch it. Nice going, Marta."

After Marta's suggestion we began to make a little more progress on the math side. We didn't have a linguist in our group, so we satisfied ourselves with merely separating the alpha male-only cries out and pursuing our attempt to understand their mathematics.

"I think we're looking at some sort of spherical trigonometry," I said to Teddy one day. We were sitting in his basement office munching on peanut-butter-and-grape-jelly sandwiches. Teddy kept a jar of peanut butter and a jar of jam in his office, as well as a loaf of white sandwich bread. If the bread became moldy he would replace it. He always bought the same peanut butter, but never the same jam or jelly. He joked one needed a little variety in life — very little.

"That makes some sense," Teddy said. "But spherical trigonometry is essentially a two-dimensional geometry over a curved space. The lives of whales are truly three dimensional. They live much fuller three-dimensional lives than humans, at least before airplanes."

"You're right, so simple vectors wouldn't be appropriate for them," I said. Vectors are a mathematical description used, among other things, to describe motion in a single direction. "Straight lines just wouldn't mean much. And I can imagine they could develop the concept of latitude, but longitude … longitude would be difficult. Humans couldn't accurately manage longitude until they had spring-operated clocks." Early mariners based their measurements of location on the positions of the sun and stars. This is easy for determining latitude, as one only has to measure the angle of a heavenly body from the north or south horizon to calculate the latitude of an observer. But because the Earth rotates, to determine longitude it is necessary to know the time differential from some reference point, now usually Greenwich, England. Sundials, pendulums, hourglasses and such did not work well on a rolling ship.

"Measuring time is hard enough," Teddy said, "but we've never discovered how they measure anything accurately. I mean, so far it seems they have some sort of analog system, a measuring system without numbers. A longer bellow may mean a longer journey, or at least a longer part of a trip, a longer length of some sort. And a rising pitch appears to be correlated with diving and a falling pitch with surfacing. But how do they determine how long, how far, how fast? And how do they account for the curvature of the Earth?"

"I've been wondering the same thing," I said. "Humans began serious math when they started laying out plots of land and keeping track of the seasons, but even before that there are some indications humans at least counted. But whales live in a liquid world. Even if they have a need to understand and communicate quantities of time and space, maybe they don't use numbers. What could they ever count? Krill? They eat millions of krill in every mouthful. Even the regular sequence of night and day may not mean anything to them. After all, they spend most of their time in ocean depths much darker than our night. The idea of number may never have occurred in their existence."

"I see what you mean." Teddy looked thoughtfully at his remaining crust, then took a bite and chewed on it for a while. "They do have the individuals in a group, that's a countable quantity."

"Yes, but they may just see each other as distinct individuals, not as countable members of a unit."

"So they wouldn't need to count them?" Teddy asked.

"Maybe not. Think of a family, an extended family. Does anyone actually count family members except when you have to set the table for a holiday get-together? We count things we think of as being identical in some way, what mathematicians call belonging to a set, having some trait in common. Maybe whales never think that way."

"Perhaps, but it's hard for us not to think that way. They must have some way of measuring, some gauge or metric."

"You know, thinking about a universe that is not filled with discrete forms, a universe where numbers wouldn't be useful, reminds me of an old mathematics saying: mathematicians can find a needle in a haystack pretty well, but they can't find the hay."

"I like that, but what does it mean, exactly?"

"Well, take the concept of the number line, a one dimensional array that increases continuously from zero to as large as we want to consider, infinity even. We can describe the natural numbers, 1, 2, 3, etc., exactly, and we can describe the rational numbers, which are defined as the result of dividing one integer by another, as well. But we have no way of exactly describing an irrational number, because they can't be described with integers. We can only approximate them as rational numbers, usually in decimal form. We use the phrase 'as precisely as you want', but it is never exact. It has been mathematically proven that rational numbers are actually countable, whereas the irrationals are not, they are innumerable. Because of this one can even prove, rigorously, that one 100% of the number line is made of irrational numbers, not even 99.999...%. In other words, we can't describe 100% of a number line exactly."

"Does that mean we know exactly 0% of what is happening?"

"Sometimes it sure seems that way."

11

When I think about it now, I realize it was over a year before I saw Clive again, but at the time I didn't think about it, I thought about whale language. Our progress was slow — we succeeded in categorizing hundreds of "phrases", and many of them had variations we also noted. We were convinced our initial surmises about their language were correct: a longer bellow presaged a longer trip, a louder one correlated to faster speed, a rising pitch indicated a dive, a falling one meant to surface. We also determined a series of clicks indicated a turn — evenly-spaced clicks meant a turn right, alternating long and short clicks meant left. At times it seemed the length of the click phrase described the angle of the turn, but that wasn't clear all the time. And all of these calls were short-term instructions. We still had no clue as to how they managed to understand where they were, but we were beginning to believe the absolute pitch played a role in what we would call counting, or more broadly, creating a metric that all the other signals referred to. It did not seem possible they just memorized their location, but we couldn't completely discount that idea. After all, most long-distance traveling animals do not appear to have a developed language. Maybe we were giving too much credit to whales.

We could find no indication the whales ever counted, so we had no idea how they determined how fast or far or deep to go. But regardless of our fits and starts, our uncertainty, our endless backtracking, the entire group felt we were making progress and that was enough to encourage us to continue. Of course, as I had less outside work than the others, I spent more time working on the whales, but even I found I needed to take major breaks to remain productive.

It was fall again. The fresh chill of a clear New England October day can rival the magnificent autumnal foliage spectrum for enjoyment. There is, to be sure, often a sense of the impending brutality of oncoming winter, but when that anticipation is obliterated by the sheer pleasure of existence, the joy and exuberance of each brilliant and refreshing breath keeping winter at bay, when all the senses join in the exhilaration, there is no better feeling, no better time nor place to be alive. One such afternoon as I was headed toward the Mass. Ave. Bridge and Teddy's office at Northeastern, I heard Clive's familiar booming voice behind me. "Wait up, Joey," he said, "Since when did you take up speed walking?"

Of course I was barely meandering down the street, my thoughts lost in watching the complex flips and flops of the leaves falling off the maples. Clive, on the other hand, ran several miles a week, and not just jogging — sprinting. He had once explained he was really lazy, and needed to find the most efficient way to stay in shape. He decided interval training was the key, which meant running flat-out sprints until he dropped.

I turned and waited for Clive to catch up to me. I knew he might have something he needed to tell me, but then realized if it was important he would leave a note in my trash. In any case, I wanted to ask him if he thought it was possible the navy had murdered Harold Jennison.

"How are you, Clive?" I asked. "Are you involved with ruining the Iron Curtain?"

Clive seldom joined in on my attempts at humor, but he surprised me today. "I consider it an improvement. The Russians should be grateful, but they never will be." Then he continued in an unusually somber tone for him, "And it looks like an especially rough ride for Ceausescu right now."

"Are you going to Romania next?"

"I can't tell you that, but no, he's small potatoes."

"Don't you ever have a chance to recuperate?"

"That's the last thing I need. Besides, there's always something going on. Ever go to Kuwait?"

"No, should I?"

"No, it's not much of a tourist attraction. Not much of a country, really. The Brits created it as part of their nineteenth century Great Game to screw Iraq, and now Hussein wants it back. Of course the Kuwaitis have tons of oil now. Everyone there is rich. There's no way they want to be under his thumb. Beer or coffee today?"

It was two in the afternoon, so I opted for beer. The Plough and Stars was a twenty minute walk, though it was in the opposite direction of Teddy's lab. I was happy to spend time with Clive, and, as he was often more at ease outside than in, a long walk might help me get answers to my questions.

We walked without speaking for several minutes, which led me to believe he had something he wanted to say to me as well. Finally he asked, "Have you heard from Sonya?"

"Not for a while, nearly a year."

"How's she doing?"

"I'm not sure. I saw Gerry too, and he was spooked. She seemed okay, but I gave her some pretty unsettling news." I could feel Clive try to look through me when I said that, so I continued. "Does the name Harold Jennison ring a bell?" Seeing it was Clive who gave me the lead that eventually led to Jennison, I thought it might.

"Maybe. Remind me."

"Dr. Harold Jennison was a biologist who had essentially the same task as Sonya several years ago. He was a bit of a hot-head and was very unhappy with the navy. He was on his way to meet with another biologist, James Farrity, who had worked on this same project even earlier, when he was run over by a truck and killed." I watched Clive's face when I mentioned Farrity. He looked concerned, but didn't flinch at the name.

"That's too bad."

I was losing my patience with Clive's nonchalance, so I took a more direct route. "There's some concern that he may have been murdered by the navy."

"Who's concerned?"

"Well, I am, if it's true." I didn't want to tell Clive about Carolyn Truesdale.

"Joey, that's circular reasoning. Very unlike you."

"And you're being coy, Clive. Very much like you."

We were walking side by side, so I felt, more than saw, Clive give me a sidelong glance. He said nothing for a while, then spoke, "You say Gerry didn't look so good?"

"He was bitter and paranoid and unhappy."

"And how are you doing?"

"I'm worried." I wasn't going to answer Clive's questions if he wasn't going to answer mine, so I changed the subject. "What are you going to do in Kuwait?"

"You know I can't tell you." He paused. "Protecting American interests."

"You travel all over the world 'protecting American interests', but who protects Americans' interests here, at home?" I asked.

Clive looked at me as if he couldn't quite grasp what I meant. We had stopped in the middle of the sidewalk, facing each other. "I've always thought it was the citizens of a country who needed to protect their own interests and rights," he said.

"Not the government?"

"Isn't it the government the citizens need protection from?" For a moment I was speechless, and Clive continued before I could think of a response. "One day when I was in Lebanon a car exploded about two hundred feet from where I was standing, I think the defense minister was assassinated. When that happens you always expect another blast, so I hid under a car with a teenage boy who also happened to be on the street. I recognized he was from an influential Christian family when he told me his name. I knew several of his cousins and uncles, so we chatted there until we felt safe. As we discussed the various factions, I asked if he ever thought the Lebanese could compromise with each other enough to allow peace to return to Lebanon. He replied, 'I doubt it. We have a saying here: money can give up money, but power can never give up power.' He was right. Asking the government to protect you from itself is a fool's errand."

I'm as sardonic as the next skeptic, but I thought Clive was preaching a level of cynicism I hadn't yet attained. "So you don't believe in freedom?" I asked.

"Indeed I do. I believe I'm free." Clive put both of his large hands on my shoulders. "And I always believed you were, too."

"Are we talking about the same thing?"

"There is only one meaningful form of freedom — removing the mind-forged manacles from oneself, to paraphrase William Blake. Living beings are always constrained, life is necessarily a precarious balance. As to politics, the act of being blissfully ignorant of the forces encompassing you, just because at that moment there is no reason for them to coerce you, is not freedom. It is ignorance."

"But, shouldn't we try to have a government that doesn't abuse its citizens, and maybe even assists them in their endeavors?"

"Of course. It's the duty of every citizen to work toward that. In fact I would say only free citizens can fulfill that duty, and it's a job that's never complete."

As we continued our walk towards the Plough and Stars I thought about the lessons Teddy and Marta had imparted to me about living under extreme totalitarianism, and realized they had learned to be free long before they left Poland.

When we sat down to drinks Clive regaled me with stories about Berlin and Tiananmen Square until we both had drunk enough that walking was difficult. I didn't make it to Teddy's office that day. Two days later in the bottom of my emptied trash can was a chunk of broken concrete with "Berlin 1989" written in chalk on one side.

12

Matt's business had taken off. He now managed several crews setting up music festivals all over the United States and Canada, as well as his original niche of creating high end one-of concerts. He had rented a warehouse in Waltham and moved most of his equipment out of his house. He would meet me or Teddy at the drop of a hat if we asked him to do something, but most of his energy went into his business, so we seldom saw him.

One miserably frigid day I ran into him at home, and he invited me to his warehouse. It was about a thirty-minute drive from Corey Hill. As we drove Matt began to talk about his business plans. "In some ways, I'd be better off working alone, or with a small crew, but it's hard to give up the opportunity to run the sound systems at the Monterey Jazz Festival, or my favorite, the Jazz and Heritage Festival in New Orleans. It's worth it just so I can meet some of my favorite musicians."

"You must spend all your time organizing your crews and setting up venues."

"That's a trap I'm trying to avoid. Ultimately, yes, it's my show, but I've hired people who are much better at organizing than I. The goal is to create a company that allows me to do what I do best — design sound systems that give the truest, most enjoyable presentation of the music. And I still enjoy the physical labor, laying out miles of cord, erecting speaker towers, meeting impossible deadlines."

As he spoke, I contemplated how much I would hate having a large organization being dependent on me, and yet how much I still appreciated his ability to see through the noise and continue to focus on his own interests.

Matt's warehouse was in an inauspicious building not far from the railroad. "It makes me wish I could use the railroad, but I just took it because the rent is cheap," he said as we walked to the building. Inside was the type of energy I expected from any company Matt might run. In the center of the main room stood three trucks, all somewhat larger than the one Jeannie and I had driven across the country, that is, that Jeannie had driven across the country while I rode. At least fifteen workers were either arranging equipment near the rears of the trucks, or loading it onto them.

"We're preparing for two concerts," Matt said.

"This time of year?" I asked.

Matt laughed. "They're both indoors. One's at the Superdome in New Orleans, and one's at the Cow Palace in San Francisco. Neither is really that big. Last year I helped set up for the Rolling Stones at the Superdome. That was an event."

"Your guys look like they know what they're doing." I was reminded of Shanti Shanti.

"They'd better. I'm not too good at micro-managing. If someone doesn't know what they're doing I don't know why they'd even be here. Ah, here's the guy really in charge of the warehouse. Richie," he said to a grizzled-looking man who must have been at least twenty years older than Matt, "Richie, I want you to meet my good friend Joseph Tenatt. Joe, Richie Jackson. If you need anything in this warehouse," he turned to me, "don't even bother with me, go directly to him."

"Corrine wants to talk to you," Richie said to Matt as he and I shook hands.

"Corrine's my accountant," Matt said to me, then turning to Richie he continued, "Do you have a few minutes to show Joe around?"

"Sure, we're pretty much just winding up here." Matt headed for what looked like an office in a mezzanine at the far end of the building.

Richie turned to me. "I've been in this game a long time, I started with Motown, but the maestro there is something else." He nodded his head toward Matt. "Are you a musician?"

"No, I'm a mathematician."

Richie looked at me quizzically, then turned back to his warehouse. "Okay, let's go look at the trucks." He spent fifteen or twenty minutes showing me around until Matt returned. After Richie walked away Matt said, "What do you think?"

"Pretty nice. I'm impressed, both with your warehouse and with Richie."

"Yeah, he's a godsend. Anyone who set up for James Brown can set up for me."

"He has a pretty high opinion of you, too."

"I guess that's why we get along. I'm done here. Want a ride home?"

There's something wonderful about watching a young adult create a new path in the world, but to see someone explode onto the scene like Matt was doing is nothing less than magical.

Similarly, Jeannie's career had blossomed, and she was spending more time abroad than in the U.S. We saw her even less than Matt. I once joked to her if I wanted to see her play again, I'd probably have to go to Paris, but she matter-of-factly agreed and offered to give me her schedule.

Marta continued to work diligently on cataloguing the humpbacks' phrases, and was of course more efficient than Teddy and I, but she left it to Teddy and me to try to find meaning in those phrases.

Teddy still taught a couple of graduate courses and spent the rest of his time in his office analyzing data from experiments conducted at Fermilab or Brookhaven, but we met several times a week at Matt and Jeannie's, and almost every day I spent a few hours in his office. I've mentioned I don't know what an observer would make of me scribbling away for hours, but in fact I have an inkling on how strange it might appear from watching Teddy at his work. One day I asked him what he was doing.

"Trying to figure out where quarks come from," he said.

"You mean looking for even smaller particles?" I asked.

"That's one possibility, and many physicists much more intelligent than I are working on that."

To listen to Teddy, one would think everyone was more intelligent than he, but strangely I have never met such a person. "What other possibility is there?" I asked.

"I'm exploring the possibility there's phenomena more fundamental than smaller particles that cause energy to coalesce into quarks and other fundamental particles."

We continued to work on our separate projects for some time. We could spend hours without acknowledging each other, or we could just chat the entire time I spent in his office. Today was one of those days when the other person could have been on Mars, but finally I turned around and said, "It's curious that I've found an unusual pattern of pitches that are constant across the different groups of humpbacks."

"What's that?" Teddy asked as he slowly pushed away from his desk and stood up. He shuffled over to my part of the long table and peered over my shoulder to see what I was doing. Though there were times when a small bomb could have gone off in our room and I'm not sure he would have noticed, he was generally as interested in my work as his own.

I showed him a series of numbers I had just calculated: 1.0, 0.6667, 0.4, 0.2857, 0.181818. "Every whale has a base pitch, not always its lowest pitch, but one that all its other tones revolve around, similar to how very piece of classical music is written in a particular key. And once you normalize for that pitch, every whale uses similar harmonics."

"That's pretty clear," said Teddy. "That's why we can isolate different whale 'words' with our violins. Each whale has the same basic vocabulary."

"Of course we already knew that," I said. "But there's something more. The absolute pitches of the vocalizations of each pod varies slightly, but if you take the base pitch of the alpha male to be fundamental, then the ratios of the pitch wavelengths of the other members of the pod are always one of these multiples of that lowest base pitch." I indicated the series on my page.

"These are the ratios of the wavelengths?" Teddy asked.

"Correct, and they are consistent to a very high precision."

"Try the ratios of the frequencies instead," he said as he ambled back to his end of the table.

The frequency of a pitch is the inverse of its wavelength, so I wrote down the ratios of the frequencies: 1, 1.5, 2.5, 3.5, 5.5. Teddy's suggestions were usually spot on, but it took me a while to see a pattern in this alternate series. Mimicking Archimedes, a man many times my better, I finally muttered, "Eureka."

"Did you find something?" Teddy asked, without looking at me.

"If I double these ratios, I get 2, 3, 5, 7, 11. Those are the first five prime numbers."

I could see Teddy was still thinking about my sequence. He appeared distracted. Instead of going back to work he sat there staring into space rapidly tapping out the rhythm of *The Trout*, a piece by Schubert we had been practicing that week. Finally he spoke up again. "In fact, I came across a similar situation in my work years ago."

"Not with whales, surely?"

"No, with sub-atomic particles. I was trying to develop a notation for the ratios of the operators of mesons when a sequence of primes popped up, and then again when I looked at quarks."

"Quarks?" Of course I knew what quarks were, but I was interested in what they could have to do with prime numbers.

"Quarks are considered to be entities that always combine in bunches of three to create elementary particles such as neutrons and protons. Conventionally, we have always looked at electric charges as based on electrons and protons and designated the charges as minus one for electrons and plus one for protons."

"Of course."

"Then quarks came along, and they could only be understood as having charges of -1/3 or +2/3, and anti-quarks having +1/3 or -2/3. When allowable combinations of three quarks are made and you add their individual charges up, the resultant charges are always -1, 0, or +1, which are the charges we find in anti-protons, neutrons and protons, respectively."

"What are the allowable combinations?"

"You can take any two identical quarks, and then the third one must be a different sign and charge. Anyway, now I feel it makes more sense to assign quarks charges of -1 or +2, and anti-quarks charges of +1 or -2, and the resultant particles have charges of -3, 0 or +3."

"Just because the bookkeeping is easier that way?"

"That's what I used to think, but you've made me wonder if there isn't some significance to the fact 1, 2 and 3 are also the first three prime numbers. Well, 1 isn't considered a prime anymore, but it used to be. I'll have to look at my notes again, I don't think I ever finished that paper." He went back to staring at the wall and tapping out Schubert's wonderful piece, humming as he did, now at a more leisurely pace.

"You know," I said, as much to myself as to Teddy, "signaling in the ratio of primes does make a certain amount of sense."

"How's that?" Teddy asked, still playing Schubert on the desk with his fingernails.

"Well, it reduces the number of consonant harmonic overtones."

Teddy stopped tapping and stared at the wall in front of him for a few seconds. Then he turned to me. "What did you say?"

"Every sound has a fundamental note that is usually accompanied by an array of overtones, and the most common overtones are harmonic overtones, which have frequencies that are integral multiples of the fundamental note. So if the ratios of the fundamentals of different whales are prime ratios of the alpha whale, then the number of overlapping overtones is greatly reduced because the primes are by definition not integral ratios of each other."

Teddy popped out his seat and practically yelled at me, "Next time you discover something I want you to scream 'Eureka'. And run naked through the streets while you're at it."

He was referring to the ancient story of Archimedes running naked through the streets of Syracuse yelling "Eureka!", which means "I've found it", after discovering a way to determine whether or not gold coins had been adulterated. I had evidently found something worthy of embarrassing myself over, but I had no idea what it was.

Teddy sat down again, then stood up, then sat down. Then he stood up again and said, "Let's go play with the whale sounds."

He was clearly excited about something. I knew I would find out why sooner rather than later.

It was mid-winter, but the temperature wasn't too bad for January. The wind was calm, the sky was clear, so we decided to walk to Jeannie and Matt's place on Corey Hill. The walk was only about fifteen minutes longer than taking the T because the walking route was much shorter, and it was far more pleasant, weather permitting. We walked side by side in silence for several blocks. I was musing on why the sky on a clear winter day seems brighter than on a clear summer day. I knew it was supposedly the lack of moisture in cold air, but I also wondered if it might be an optical illusion caused by the cold acting on one's emotions. Everything else felt sharper in winter. Finally Teddy spoke up, "Resonance."

"Resonance?" I repeated.

"That's the key to both of our problems."

"What's my problem?" I said.

"You're trying to figure out how whales establish a metric for measuring time and distance without numbers."

I wanted to think about that for a while, so I said, "And what's your problem?"

"I want to know how matter exists."

"What does that have to do with primes?"

"We know from Einstein that matter and energy are just different forms of the same thing, you know, $E=mc^2$. We also know both matter and energy only exist in discrete packages, quanta, and that's what makes it appear that particles exist."

"You don't think particles really exist?"

"It's pretty clear they don't. I mean, of course they exist, but only as packets of energy, not as actual solid objects." Neither one of us spoke for a while. I didn't say anything because nothing was clear to me. I thought Teddy might think it was all so simple there was nothing more to say, but finally he continued. "Do you think musical notes exist?"

"I've always thought they did."

"Then if I play a C twice you would say they are two different things, except we know they are just waves in the air, and from that perspective they aren't things at all, and I believe neither are any other things. It's all vibration, but because we have divided sound into discrete notes they strike us as individual items. If we only played trombones or Theremins, and music consisted only of continuous glissandi, we might not even have a concept for a note. As we've discussed before, that seems to be the kind of existence your whales have."

"And you think particles are like notes?"

"Pretty much. One of the most important and unsettling discoveries of modern physics was the realization energy only exists in discrete packets, i.e., quanta. It's kind of ironic, because we prefer to think that matter does exist in discrete units, which we call particles."

"How do you mean *prefer*?"

"Just that. We are used to thinking of matter and energy differently, even though the destruction of Nagasaki and Hiroshima offered definitive proof that matter and energy are fundamentally the same thing. One needs no understanding at all of relativity to know it must be so." Of course he was referring to atomic weapons as the most brutal proof that matter and energy are equivalent, and therefore that energy, enormously quantities of energy, can be obtained from matter. He continued, "Still, thinking of matter as waves is contrary to our common sense. I say we *prefer* to see matter as discrete packets, and energy as a continuous flux, because that's what our common sense tells us is true."

"So, if both matter and energy are quantized, they're not like music, which forms a continuum of sounds."

"You say that because you play a violin, which can create, as far as we can hear, a continuum of sound on any string. But if you played a trumpet you might have a different perspective, because trumpets use the resonances of standing waves to play discrete sounds, which we call notes.

"And you think the universe is like a trumpet?" I said.

"I do, but a very complex trumpet. It's been interesting thinking about the kind of analog mathematics we have postulated whales use, and it has me to thinking about why numbers are so important."

Teddy paused, waiting for a reply from me, but I was lost in my own ruminations, so we walked in silence for a while longer. Even though the temperature was above average for January and there was no wind, it was still well below freezing, so, as usual, we had the sidewalk to ourselves. Finally I realized I should respond to my friend. "They are a way of being precise," I said.

"They are, but that's not enough. Let's start with set theory, after all that's how the great mathematician John von Neumann proposed to generate the natural numbers, our integers, theoretically speaking: you start with nothing and create a set containing nothing, the null set, which is one item. Now you have the null set and one, which are two items. Then, obviously, you create a set containing both of these items, and now you have three items, the new set and the original two items. You can continue in this manner by creating a new number containing all the numbers in the last set, plus the last set itself, making all the natural numbers to infinity."

I was very familiar with this argument, as it is considered the basis of modern arithmetic. "So?" I said.

"Well, logically, von Neumann's argument is obviously sound, but that's not enough to make natural numbers useful or necessary. We need a reason to count, a universe with discrete items that are similar enough to each other to be worth grouping together into sets and enumerating, such as four sticks or five elephants. But, as we discussed with whales, if we lived in a truly liquid world we might never have thought of counting, integers might not arise."

"So you think resonance gets over that, creates the need?"

"Think about how our universe would be if matter wasn't created from nearly identical repetitive units such as electrons or protons, in other words if all electrons were not identical, all protons were not identical, etcetera," Teddy said.

"I think I see your point. There might very possibly be only one of any particular type of particle or combination of particles in the universe, atoms as we know them would not exist, chemistry would not be possible. If there was only one of anything in the universe there'd be no reason or ability to define groups of related things and count them. Integers wouldn't be of much use."

"Right, everything would just be an indistinguishable mishmash of energy. But that isn't the way the universe works. All electrons are the same, all protons are the same. And this leads to all atoms of oxygen being the same, or at least all the ones of a particular isotope, and so on, and therefore molecules are similar and voilà — a universe with lots of repetition in which it is worth our effort to group things together, and to count them."

"Okay," I said, "but I don't see what this has to do with resonance."

"Well, my problem is why do sub-atomic particles form into these identical patterns in the first place? How does an electron inside my eyeball know it has to be identical to one in the constellation Andromeda? I believe it is because the universe is essentially a multi-dimensional vibration, and particles are nodal resonances created by that vibration, in the same way the notes of a trumpet are made.

"Interesting way to put it. Plato thought there were such things as eternal forms, universal concepts that would always be true and beautiful in any context, and he felt the natural numbers, the positive integers, were among those forms. But if we take your position that it is the resonant nodes of our universe that create what we refer to as quanta — photons, electrons, quarks, whatever — and that we have created the concept of counting to mentally manipulate what we see, then integers themselves are a result of the nature of our universe. They aren't pure Platonic forms at all. Plato would be chagrined. It takes the purity of mathematics down a peg, but it sure shines a light on why mathematics is so useful to physicists. Do you have proof of this?"

"No," Teddy said, "I've been working on this for some time, but the thought seemed to crystallize for me when you started talking about primes. It feels right."

"How about the plus and minus?" I said.

"That's why I like your phrase 'non-consonant harmonic overtones'. Perhaps the universe needs to prevent different types of vibrations from interfering with each other — plus and minus charges fit right into that. You are probably aware that because physicists came across protons first they labeled its charge as positive. Protons probably would have been negative if they discovered electrons first instead. The concept of positive and negative works well because you can add the charges, and if you add a positive and negative charge together, you get zero, just like adding positive and negative numbers. But it is important to remember charges of plus and minus are not like the numbers one and minus one. In arithmetic $1 \times 1 = 1$, and $-1 \times -1 = 1$. Charges, however, are only additive. We don't multiply them together.

Hence, they also represent non-consonant phenomena, just like primes. And quarks have other similar properties: quarks have isospin, charm, strangeness, bottomness and, we think, topness."

"You think?"

"We're pretty sure, but we haven't seen a top quark yet.

"Why do you think all this is so important?"

"Let's take a simpler example. When we speak of notes we often think of a vibrating string without overtones, which we draw on paper as a two dimensional image that looks like a sine wave. Let's imagine particles were that simple, so we'll only talk about their electric charge. Using my previous example there are quarks with charges of -2, -1, 1 and 2, and we have electrons that are -3, neutrons that are 0 and protons that are 3. Now let us say we had another particle that had a charge of 4. But in my theory 4 is a harmonic overtone of its fundamental, 2. My theory is the fundamental tone destabilizes our potential new particle, so it can't exist."

"And you think that is true of other properties of quarks as well?"

"Exactly. If a quark possesses isospin up, it cannot possess isospin down, charm, strangeness, topness or bottomness. The same is true of each of these properties. So these properties are not even additive, but more importantly they cannot interfere with each other. That is what I'm calling non-consonant."

13

We had reached Matt and Jeannie's Corey Hill mansion. No one was home, so we let ourselves in and proceeded to the whale room to get lost trying to learn how to communicate with whales. But instead, we continued our conversation on primes and resonance. After half an hour or so Matt came into our room as were musing on Teddy's theories.

He listened for a while, then asked Teddy, "So, you think the universe is created from energy being formed into specific patterns through resonance?"

"Essentially. What do you think?" Said Teddy.

"Chladni."

"What?" I said.

"Not what, who," said Matt. "Ernst Chladni, a nineteenth century German physicist. He experimented with vibrating plates to visually show modes of resonance." Matt briefly left the room, then returned with an old book with a very ragged cover. As he carefully thumbed through the fragile volume he explained, "Chladni followed work started by the great English physicist Robert Hooke. He would fasten metal plates of different shapes to a stand at the center of the plate, cover them with fine sand and restrain the plate in various ways, then cause the plate to vibrate by drawing a bow across an edge. When the plate begins to resonate the sand settles into the areas that do not move. This book is an edition of his work that contains drawings of the patterns he was able to create."

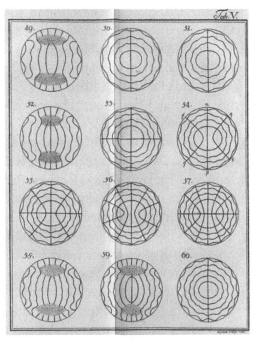

He showed us several pages of images such as this one:

"I'd forgotten about Chladni!" said Teddy. "The mathematics developed to describe his vibration modalities was used in this century to create Schrödinger's equations describing the electron orbitals of atoms."

"Exactly," said Matt. "It appears that those orbitals are just different resonance patterns of an atom's vibrations, the same as Chladni found different resonance patterns of his steel plates." A grin slid across Matt's face. "I have something else to show you. Follow me." He headed out of the door, then turned back and said, "And bring your bow."

We followed Matt to the kitchen and down a narrow set of stairs to the basement. It seemed odd how a building as magnificent as this one would have such a rickety set of stairs, but I recalled there was an equally uncomfortable set leading to the rooms above the kitchen. These were the areas meant for servants, who evidently did not warrant the grand and wide circular stairway located in the lobby of the main entrance.

Matt's basement was even more jumbled than Farrity's attic, and what's more it appeared everything there belonged to Matt, not to the history of the building. Matt turned on a long string of lights loosely hung on an electric cord strung along the center of the room, which lit a narrow passage through the clutter well enough to enable us to make our way to one of the farthest, darkest corners. Matt carefully attacked the confused stack of boxes and tools until he found an odd looking steel pipe with heavy tripod legs at one end. "Aha, found it. The plates must be close by."

He handed the tripod-like contraption to Teddy and resumed his search while Teddy and I examined the device. It was a simple steel pipe about two inches in diameter with a threaded stud welded to a cap on one end of the pipe, rather like a blunt spear point. On the stud were two nuts and two washers. Three pieces of pipe were welded to the other end to form the tripod base. The ends of these legs were flattened and bent so that the tripod sat flat on the concrete basement floor without a wobble. A small hole was drilled through the flattened portion of each leg.

We had been examining the tripod for a minute or two when Matt staggered back to us carrying a small but obviously heavy wooden crate. He set the crate down as carefully as he could, then straightened a couple of wire latches at one edge of the top, which was attached to the crate with wire hinges along the opposite side, and opened it. We could see a round steel plate resting on a piece of newspaper, and there were more plates beneath it, each separated by several layers of newspaper from the one below.

Matt unscrewed the nuts from the top of the tripod and placed the first circular plate, which had a hole in the center, over the stud and retightened the nuts with a wrench that had been in the wood box with the plates. It looked a little like a steel mushroom, or perhaps a flat cymbal. He stood there for a second looking at his device, then said, "I'll be right back."

Teddy and I immediately understood we were looking at a modern version of the instrument Chladni had used to conduct his experiments. We turned our attention to the box and began to unstack the rest of the plates. There were over a dozen of them, all of them made of a different shape, size and/or thickness. Each one weighed close to five pounds, meaning that the box when full weighed around sixty pounds. No wonder Matt had difficulty carrying the box through his clutter.

Teddy carefully drew his bow vertically along the edge of the attached plate. It made a sound, but not a particularly musical one. After we had fiddled with the device for a while, Matt returned with a bag of sugar. "Don't have any fine sand handy." He poured a thin layer of sugar over the plate, then grabbed a plate corner between two fingers and stroked the bow up and down a few times. The sugar grains danced into symmetrical rays spreading symmetrically from the center of the plate. "If you guys are interested in playing with these I'll anchor the legs to the floor. It works much better that way." He grinned as he watched us admire his handiwork.

"Why did you make this set-up?" I asked him. "Are you interested in the history of physics?"

"Not just history. Guitar- and violin-makers sometimes use this type of technique to test their instruments to this day, only now they usually use speakers to drive the vibrations. I was helping a friend of mine test his guitar faces with a speaker system, so I made this to learn more about how Chladni's original devices worked. I have a lot of literature on the subject as well, if you're interested."

We were, especially Teddy.

After we went back upstairs Marta dropped by, and as usual she accomplished in thirty minutes what Teddy and I would do in a day. It was dark by the time we left. We took the T home and I was invited to help eat some of Marta's old-country kalduny. Afterward we played our instruments in our own human musical language for a while.

One of the results of this episode for me was that Teddy started to spend a lot more time working with the Chladni plates. The next time we visited Matt and Jeannie's, Teddy was eager to see if Matt had set up his equipment. Sure enough, the tripod was bolted to the concrete floor near the basement stairs, and next to it were several more boxes of plates, different-sized bows, and an assortment of clamps, including some on stands with heavy bases. These were evidently different types of damping mechanisms Matt had built to create different resonance modalities. Also nearby was a box of very fine sand.

We experimented with Matt's apparatus the whole evening and never made it to the whale room. The next time we visited we started in the whale room, but I could tell Teddy was a little agitated, and his mind wasn't on our task.

"You want to play with the Chladni plates, don't you?" I said.

Teddy smiled a little sheepishly, but admitted I was right. "It helps me imagine the degrees of freedom as well as the constraints I need to use for my own theories."

"It's hard to imagine that these flat steel plates can help you imagine how the universe is formed."

"I'm only trying to figure out how particles are formed, Joe."

"Even so."

We clambered down to the basement and Teddy evinced a small, comfortable smile as he stared at a steel Chladni plate. "Consider the fact that this is what we call an anisotropic phenomenon. These plates are similar in two dimensions, length and width, but not in the third, thickness. Moreover, some are radially symmetrical, some not, i.e., some are round, some square or octagonal or whatever. All of these different shapes give rise to different patterns of vibrations. Similarly, as with the restraints, the manner in which we clamp or dampen the plates creates different Chladni modes."

"What you are saying appears to be the whole point of the experiment," I said.

"Yes, it is. What I need to consider is that the vibrations whose resonance I believe causes particles to form with very specific characteristics, may also be anisotropic."

"So you think they may have different properties in different directions?"

"The first assumption would be that they are symmetrical in space, and propagate through time, but I do not know that. I cannot even say they exist in three dimensional space, perhaps they create space, maybe we have time and space because of the shape of those vibrations."

"And playing with these plates helps you imagine that?" I said.

"In a way. I mean for the most part we apply a simple, steady input to every Chladni setup, and yet the patterns the vibrations form can become incredibly complex. Take a look at this." He pulled out some old photographs and handed them to me — I show some of them here:

"If one can create patterns like this on a steel plate with a bow, imagine what one could create … no, that's backwards. We can see what has been created in the universe, the quanta of particles and photons. We need to find out what kind of steel plate and bow did it. That's what I need to get my head around, as you would say in English."

"They're interesting, very interesting. And the fact that the same mathematics used to describe these vibrations is used to describe the vibrations of electrons in an atom is intriguing, but it could also be a dead end. I have a similar problem when thinking about prime numbers — I'm always led back to Riemann's hypothesis, even though I can never find a connection between it and the prime overtones of whales."

"What's Riemann's hypothesis?" asked Teddy.

"It's a bit involved, to be honest, but it concerns a series which Bernhardt Riemann called the zeta function. It can be written as an infinite series of primes, and has complex solutions, that is to say solutions with both imaginary and real components. What is interesting about it is that it appears that for every solution equal to zero, the imaginary part has no known pattern, but the real part is always equal to exactly one-half."

"Why?"

"Well, no one knows why. No one has ever even proven that it's always true, so it's called Riemann's hypothesis."

"And what has this to do with Chladni plates?"

"Mathematically, probably nothing. Psychologically, I feel I sometimes get stuck trying to find a connection which simply does not exist, like I'm going down a rabbit hole, so to speak."

"Rabbit hole?"

"It's just a saying, it more or less means going down a complex path that has no end. Not sure where it came from, probably *Alice in Wonderland*."

Teddy's face lit up when I mentioned Lewis Carroll's fantasy. "And maybe the rabbit hole will lead to a new world!"

I saw my admonition seemed to have the opposite effect of what I intended. After that I did not ask him to stay and work with me; he would have been of no use anyway. On subsequent visits sometimes I would play in the basement with him, sometimes we would work together in the whale room, passing his violin back and forth as always, and sometimes we would go our separate ways. It might have slowed my progress down a little, but in hindsight it may actually have helped, as I resolved to create a computer program to replace what we did with the violin.

14

I am sure it is needless to repeat that behind all of our actions was our concern for Sonya's safety, so in a way she was always present in our thoughts. In actuality, of course, I had seen her only a few times since she first set sail, and then but briefly. Teddy and Marta had seen her only once since she started her tour, and Jeannie and Matt hadn't set eyes on her at all. So it was a surprise to find her waiting for me at Marta's one evening when Teddy and I arrived home from his office. Though it was still February, Sonya and Marta were preparing Marta's flower garden in the front yard. I say front yard, but as our building was built about six inches from the sidewalk, it was more like a long flower box. Marta often said it was her flowers, not her food, not her music, not her apartment, which allowed her to feel closest to Poland. I'm no botanist, but I too looked forward to her early crocuses every spring. They usually arrive before winter's chill departs, sometimes even poking through a late snow, and foretell the more comfortable days of late spring and, of course, summer.

Sonya looked older than the last time I saw her, more serious, tired, maybe a little worn. She smiled when she saw me, but even her smile had a pensive edge to it. "Hi, Joe," she said. She spoke as if we saw each other every day.

"Sonya, how are you?" I said. "It's been over a year. We've been worried."

"I'm fine, exhausted, but fine. We docked at Newport News last night, I took an overnight train, just got here an hour ago."

"You look tired. Are you sure you're okay?"

Marta chimed in, "I'm making chicken soup for her. Care to come down for dinner?" The invitation was just a formality, of course.

When we finally sat down to eat I wanted to pepper Sonya with questions. "How are your companions? Has Gerry calmed down?" I started.

"I haven't seen him since our last meeting, when he stomped out of the bar." The small room grew quiet. Teddy, Marta and I quit eating and stared at Sonya.

"Is he okay?" I asked.

"I don't know. He never wrote, never said goodbye, nothing."

"Any idea where he went?"

"Not really, nothing concrete. If I had to guess I'd say West Texas. He used to talk about a place named Marfa. But I don't know for sure."

"Marfa is a real name?" Teddy asked.

"I guess so, never been there."

"Was Gerry from Marfa?" he asked.

"No, he grew up in Ohio. I think he happened to see one of those coffee table picture books on the Southwest that had a few photographs of Marfa. He told me he thought it looked about as different from Toledo as he could imagine, so maybe he'd like it. As Joe can tell you, Gerry isn't a very happy person."

"So, did you have a replacement for Gerry this last tour?" I asked.

Sonya gave me a look halfway between a grin and a grimace. "Not at first. The navy obviously didn't know Gerry wasn't going to show up. In fact they grilled us pretty thoroughly. I think he took his records with him, or destroyed them, from the questions they asked." Sonya paused and took a mouthful of soup. "Oh, Marta, you've no idea how good this tastes to me. It's been so long since I've had anything this wonderful."

"I'm glad you like it, dear," Marta said, and then turned to Teddy and me. "I think we must let her enjoy her meal before we begin another interrogation. I don't want my soup ruined by your questions." Sonya mouthed the words *thank you* to Marta, then returned to Marta's delightful soup, as did the rest of us.

After dinner, Teddy and I cleaned the kitchen while Marta and Sonya went outside. "Do you think Sonya is all right?" I said to Teddy as I scrubbed the large soup pot.

"I'm sure that's what Marta is finding out right now," Teddy said.

When they returned, Marta announced, "Sonya will tell us a little about her trip now, but she needs to get to bed early and would like to play a little Mozart with us first." Marta had taken control of the evening.

"Don't worry," Sonya said, "I have a couple of days I can stay this time, I'll try to tell you everything before I leave, including all about Gerry's replacement."

"If they didn't know Gerry wasn't returning, how did they replace him?" I asked.

Sonya raised both hands, fingers pointing upwards, as if she was going to make an important point, but Marta interrupted. "Maybe I didn't make myself clear, Joe, so I'll try again. Sonya is exhausted, she wants to tell her story, so shut up and listen." This was said without malice. We all saw both the humor and seriousness in Marta's pronouncement. I honored her demand by not replying.

Sonya continued, "Like I said, they didn't replace him at first, but they gave Joanne and me the third degree for a few days. They even moved us into separate quarters so we couldn't coordinate our replies. Neither of us knew anything though, so eventually they let us be." Sonya paused for a second, then continued as if she had just realized something. "I was kind of pissed at Gerry for leaving without saying good bye, but he did me a great favor. It was a smart move. If I had known what he was up to my interrogators would have figured that out. They were pros, and I'm not much of a liar. Anyway, we were two weeks at sea before a new sound specialist arrived, this time a navy man, Jason Noth. I'm not sure he was as clever as Gerry, but he had a lot of very sophisticated equipment."

The next day we all had a long discussion about the entire situation. Sonya began by filling us in on more details of their research. "The navy thinks it has made a breakthrough in understanding the humpbacks' songs."

"They understand the mathematical code?" I said. I was appalled that the navy may have unraveled the humpback language before me, and yet the mathematician in me couldn't help but be curious."

"Actually, no. Evidently they have decided humpbacks change their song every decade or so. Maybe you've seen that when you look at some of the earlier researchers. Anyway, they take that to indicate the whales are just having fun."

"Do you think they're right?"

"I don't have the historical data to compare, but I think the navy is seeing what it wants to see. Joanne and I both feel they want this whale problem to go away."

"Don't they listen to you?"

"They're trying to keep us out of the loop. They clearly like some of our work or they would've let us go, but they're trying their damndest to make it a one-way street, and a pretty narrow one at that."

Sonya told us she and Joanne had concluded Gerry was correct in another way — humpbacks, and likely other kinds of whales as well — were annoyed at being followed. She was clearly conflicted about whether she should return or not. "I don't entirely disagree with Gerry, but I can't accept it's in the whales' best interest for me to quit. If nothing else I can be a witness to what's going on."

"You need to think about your own safety as well, Sonya dear," Marta said.

"True, and for that reason I've concluded I should do at least one more trip. It would look too suspicious if I quit so quickly after Gerry."

We were all silent for a while. I'm sure every member of our group thought the same way I did. None of us could or would advise her to stay on that ship, and yet what she said made sense. The conversation kind of petered out awkwardly. At last Sonya broke the silence. "Joe, remember how we used to play down on Magazine Beach? Why don't we all go down there now and play a little Bach?"

"It's February, Sonya!"

"I know, but it's over fifty today. Maybe I'm just too used to sea weather."

"I think it's a great idea," said Marta, and we all knew if Marta thought something was a great idea, it was a great idea. We picked up our second-best instruments and packed into the Witkowskis' little Fiat after tying Marta's cello on top and headed down to the Charles. None of us brought up our old conversation about playing music when death was imminent, but there was no doubt in my mind we all were thinking about it, not with a feeling of foreboding or resignation, but in the spirit of defiant and joyous resolution from whence the idea was born.

Sonya left late the next day and we all tried to return to our usual routines, but I was exhausted and couldn't concentrate on my work on whale mathematics, on imitating their sounds, on particle physics, even on music.

Marylin called a few days after Sonya left. I wanted to talk to her, but as soon as I recognized her voice my paranoia raised its ugly visage. "Not interested," I blurted, and hung up. We had spoken several times since my trip with Jeannie to California, but I always called her from a pay phone, this was the first time she called me (normally a very good sign). I was afraid I might have just made a huge mistake. I immediately ran, if you can call me moving at top speed running, two blocks to a local cafe, The CambridgeSide Diner, a place where I seldom ate, but where I knew they had a pay phone in the lobby, and called her back. We had talked about getting together again, I decided to see if she was ready.

After apologizing profusely I said, "So, Marylin, would you'd like a visitor?"

"I thought you'd never ask," she said. She seemed to have taken my rudeness in stride, and to have accepted my apology. "When would you like to come?"

"Tomorrow. Today. Winter is too long here this year."

"Come whenever you want. I'll change the sheets."

15

Anyone who lives with pets knows one doesn't own cats, one cohabits with them. There's some sort of covenant wherein the human agrees to provide food, lodging and maybe even medical care in return for a modicum of hygienic behavior from the cat. Everything else is voluntary on both sides. I know from my South Dakota childhood that rural folk value cats for reducing the local rodent population, but even after that need vanishes, humans relish what we take for the emotional comfort cats provide. The mandatory part of the agreement means that cats must be fed and the litter box cleaned, so whenever the human vacates their house for more than a day they must find a surrogate. Accordingly, I arranged for Marta to take care of my cats, then left for California a few days later. The Witkowskis never owned pets, as far as I can remember, but Marta not only was willing to perform the more perfunctory chores for Cleo and Ranger, she understood she needed to spend a little social time with them, enough for them to pointedly ignore her for a while and then finally deign to sit with her.

Marylin picked me up at the airport in the evening and took me to a lovely steak and seafood restaurant in Pismo Beach that overlooked the crashing Pacific. Jeannie and I had enjoyed Pismo Beach, but of course that was during the summer when the boardwalk was in full swing. Now it was February, the beach nearly deserted. Jeannie and I mostly had eaten hot dogs and fries from street vendors near the pier, but Marylin's knowledge of eateries was more nuanced. She knew where the local nuggets were hidden. The food was nearly as wonderful as the view. After dinner, as we eyed each other over our cocktail glasses, Marylin smiled coyly. "If I'm going to share my bed with you, I think you should level with me."

"About what?" I asked. I felt I had been pretty straightforward with her.

"Not about you and me Joe, don't worry, I'm pretty comfortable about us."

"What then?"

"The thing is, where I sit in this town all the rumors and small stories go through me. For instance, I know your niece is not your niece, and it was she who asked to be able to play at CalPoly and teach at the high school, rather than be invited. And since you left we've seen more of Carolyn, a lot more. And then there's the way you answered the phone. So, what's the deal?"

I needed to know a little more about my companion before I said too much. "I thought you retired," I said, trying forestall a direct answer.

"I quit my job, not my social position, Joe, my dear. I still know just about everyone in the county."

"I guess I knew that. I've always wondered why you took a shine to me. There must be any number of eligible men around for you to choose from."

Marylin looked at me like I might look at a student in a calculus class who couldn't add or multiply. "I'm not lonely, Joe. I don't need an eligible man. I like you, very much."

"What do you think about whales?" I asked, realizing I needed to give her a straight answer.

"I love them. My girlfriends and I used to go to Moro Bay to go on whale watches."

"Used to?"

"Yeah, we really got into it, we'd often go twice a year — when they went north, then when they returned again. Don't know why we quit. Do you want to go on one while you're here? I think it's the season for gray whales."

"I have's been on a whale watch for years. I don't think we have gray whales in New England."

"You used to, they were hunted out of existence."

"Do you get humpbacks here?"

"Sure, but not now. You'll have to come during summer."

"Have you ever heard humpbacks sing?"

"Yes, but not on a whale watch. I think I still have an album of them accompanying a flute or something. Isn't that what Carolyn's old boyfriend studied?"

"Harold Jennison. Yes. Did you ever meet him?"

"Once, at Susan Truesdale's, she's Carolyn's sister. He was supposed to be very smart, but I found him high strung and nervous."

"Paranoid?"

"I wouldn't go that far, just intense. What did he have to be paranoid about?"

"He thought the navy was covering up the damage it was doing to the whales."

"How? Are they running over them? Or is it the submarines?"

"Close. It's their low-frequency sonar. It's said to drive the whales crazy." I sipped on my cocktail, then added, "What do you think? Would the navy cover up the damage it does to whales just to save face?" I wanted to understand how much I could reveal to her.

Marylin didn't say anything for a while as she digested our conversation. I finished my martini and ordered another. Finally Marylin spoke up. "A friend of mine's son went to Annapolis, Jason Sterm. Smart kid, hard worker, good athlete. Maybe not real creative, but certainly no dummy. Anyway, a couple of his classmates were caught up in one of those cheating scandals that happens once in a while at the military academies during his senior year. So that summer someone, can't remember who, some older guy who had a few too many, started badgering Jason at a neighborhood barbecue about all the cheaters at Annapolis."

"Did Jason clock him?"

"No, nothing like that. He listened until his antagonist wore out. When he finally shut up, Jason looked him in the eye and said, 'It was three cadets out of more than a thousand in one class, and none of the rest of us has any sympathy for them, but you know what I think is strange?' The man shrugged but didn't say anything, so Jason went on. 'The navy makes a big deal about honor, and they should. But you know what you want?' Jason didn't wait for an answer. 'You want a navy that doesn't give a damn about rules or regulations or honor or any of that crap. You want a navy that will protect the United States by whatever means necessary, whatever it takes. Now those guys were cheating for themselves, not their country, and they were caught so they were also incompetent, but I'd be careful about asking for a navy that just follows the rules.'"

"So you think the navy is capable of covering something up?" I said.

"Jason had it right: they feel they need to do whatever it takes to accomplish their mission."

"And what do you think?"

"It's our job to make sure they use good judgement. They're our navy."

I realized why I liked Marylin so much, and I decided to open up a little. "I have a friend who's on a research mission similar to Harold's. She also thinks the navy might be covering something up. In fact, one of her colleagues became so paranoid he just took off without a word."

"Any idea where he went?"

"We don't know for sure, but he might be in Marfa."

"Marfa? In West Texas?"

"I think so, somewhere in Texas," I said. "Ever been there?"

"No, but I've heard about it."

"Anyway, I took all of Jennison's research papers from Carolyn. Maybe knowing someone cared about his work, and didn't just think he was crazy or paranoid, helped her relax."

"How about you?" she asked.

"Do I act paranoid or crazy?"

"Just crazy."

"That's okay, I was born this way."

We finished our drinks and watched the sun quench its thirst in the immense Pacific after a long California day. We made love a little and snuggled a lot that night, between clean sheets. The next day, we hung around in Marylin's backyard drinking lemonade and lemon drop martinis. It had taken me all of twenty-four hours to understand the lure of California living. I couldn't help but wonder what my life would have been if I had applied to CalPoly or UCLA instead of BU. I wasn't wishing my life had been different or better than it had been, I was just realizing I would have become a different person.

Marylin had retired from the chamber of commerce the year before. "I enjoyed the work, I enjoyed the people, I still have the energy," she said, "I just don't enjoy having to do anything anymore." As a result we were free to do as we pleased. The next day she drove me down to Moro Bay to the fish market. The Pacific is not the Atlantic, California is not Massachusetts, much of the seafood was strange to me, but the smell of the ocean was unmistakable. Marylin was recognized by everyone, and in turn she knew all the vendors and their wares. She selected oysters, crab, halibut, squid, saying, "Seafood isn't any good unless it's fresh, you know. You have to eat it the day it's caught."

I did know that, being a bit of a connoisseur of New England seafood myself, so finally I blurted out, "But Marylin, there's no way we can eat all that today!"

She put down a large hunk of salmon she was examining and looked at me as if she had just woken up, then covered her mouth and began to laugh.

"Oh, Joe, I'm sorry, I've been having so much fun I forgot to tell you — we're going up to Shanti Shanti this evening. I told them you were coming to town. Everyone wants to see you."

"You mean Carolyn, Armando and Lorna?" I said.

"Yes, them, and the rest of the crew. They feel you freed Carolyn of a terrible burden. Everyone on the farm is grateful."

"Ah, like the song, 'Take the load off Fanny … and put the load right on me.'"

"Do you feel this whole venture is a weight on you?" Marylin asked.

I thought about her question for a while, then answered more seriously than the evening before. "The only weight I ever felt is getting my friends involved, and I've realized they jumped at the chance to help another friend, so no, it's not really a weight."

Marylin smiled at my answer and said, "And I'm sure the only weight Carolyn ever felt was not knowing what to do with Harold's papers. That's the weight you removed. You must realize she has incredible strength to do what she knows is needed to be done."

I hadn't thought of it before, but of course I could see what Marylin said was true. After we finished packing our bounty into three large ice-filled coolers we headed back through San Luis Obispo, up into the mountains and toward Shanti Shanti. To show the farm hadn't forgotten me, nor lost its sense of humor, there was a professional looking sign at the end of the road pointing right that read FRESH SEAFOOD. We drove to the residential compound, and sure enough it appeared the entire staff was there. There must have been more than thirty people, all busy preparing for the feast.

The first person to greet me was the tall rugged hippie with the waist length hair who had been the first person I met on my previous visit.

"I'm Seth," he said, extending his large, rough hand to me. "May I be the first to welcome you back to Shanti Shanti?"

"You were the first person to welcome me last time, too," I said.

He grinned down at me. "I don't think I welcomed you as much as let you live last time." He said it with good humor, almost as an apology, but it did reveal the kind of loyalty that was felt toward Carolyn on the farm. He quickly introduced me to several more workers — each one briefly left what they were doing to greet me profusely, then immediately returned to their tasks. In no time the food was ready and the festivities were on.

I will not attempt to describe all the cuisine — I've no idea of what most of the food was — but it was delicious. Armando manned the bar. There was beer, of course, and I was told there was also alcoholic and non-alcoholic fruit punch, but at the bar there were only margaritas. Armando would dutifully ask straight or with ice, and make the drink accordingly. He would also ask if you wanted salt or no salt, and if you said *no salt* he would glower menacingly until you changed your mind. Other than that he was in extremely good humor, joking in English, Spanish, and also Nahuatl, apparently fluently. He was no doubt aided in his good humor by the extraordinarily large margarita that he sipped from all evening.

"You tell me, which is better, ice or no ice," I said.

"No ice has more tequila," he replied as he crushed a lime into my glass, and that's what he handed me. I turned around to search out some food and found myself face to face with Carolyn Truesdale.

"We're so glad you came back for a visit, Joe," she said as she gave me a hug and a kiss that spilled half my drink on her dress. She laughed as she felt what she had done. "I'm sure Armando will make you another." She introduced me to several more of her — I hesitate to say employees, they truly acted like associates, but on the other hand there was no doubt who was in charge. However, the longer I sipped on Armando's second drink, the less I was able to remember any names. Finally we came upon Lorna grilling huge green peppers in some sort of cylindrical metal cage.

"Señor José," she said as she twirled her grill. "*Buenas noches,* how are you?"

"Great, and getting better. Nice party."

"*¡Sí, una fiesta grande!* And how's Jeannie? We want to hear her play again."

"You should come to Boston then, Lorna."

She stopped long enough to empty her cage and refill it. She deftly wrapped one of her peppers and some other stuffing in a tortilla and handed it to me. "*Muy bien,* I will. Can you send me her schedule?"

I promised I would and left munching on Lorna's amazing chipotle taco in one hand and Armando's otherworldly margarita in the other. It wasn't my last of either. As I was waiting in line for a seafood platter I asked the young man in front of me if they had parties like this often. He spoke English with an accent definitely not Spanish. I assumed he was Nahuatl.

"Yes, Mardi Gras, summer solstice, harvest, Christmas. And whenever we have a special guest."

"How often is that?"

He thought about my question carefully, then said, "Four times a year, and whenever we have a special guest."

"I meant how many times have you had a special guest?"

The young man grinned broadly, revealing a mouthful of incredibly straight teeth with several gold caps front and center. "You are the first. Very special."

Once I latched onto my seafood platter, I searched around for Marylin, who was sitting on a large log in front of a small bonfire with several people, including a woman who looked very much like her, though quite a bit younger.

"Joe, this is my baby sister, Jessica. Jessica, Joe."

I mumbled a greeting through a mouthful of food.

"You're quite the celebrity around here, Joe," Jessica said. "I've been calling you Mr. Sunshine."

"Mr. Sunshine?" I asked. It was one of the last things I'd ever call myself.

"Yeah. I was amazed at the effect you had on Carolyn, and now you're giving the same treatment to my sister."

The fire wasn't bright enough for me to see whether or not Marylin blushed, but I did hear it when she leaned over to her sister and hissed, "I'm going to kill you, you little witch."

It was a joyful gathering, but not a raucous one. I became pretty drunk on Armando's margaritas, but it didn't appear to me anyone else really did. And the party ended rather early for such a production. Marylin and I stayed over at Carolyn's, and by the time we woke up and had a little coffee, we noticed everyone on the farm was already deep into their respective tasks.

Carolyn showed up to say goodbye as we enjoyed our coffees and some delicious pastries that had been left in the kitchen for us. "Did you make these?" I asked, waving a half-eaten crumpet in her direction.

Marylin snorted into her coffee at my question. Carolyn poured herself a cup and simply said, "As if. If you ever see me in a kitchen, do us both a favor and remove me, please."

"By the way," I said, "do you know if Harold had an assistant or fellow scientist on his voyages?"

A pained look crept into Carolyn's eyes. It was reminiscent of the look she had when we had first spoken about Jennison during my first trip. "He did, but only for the first year. I think they had a falling out, a pretty serious one."

"Do you know what that was about?"

"Not specifically. I think the guy was a navy officer, and Hank thought that clouded his objectivity. He said some pretty harsh things about him."

"Like what?"

"You know, I really couldn't pay that much attention to his rants. It was as if he had this internal rage switch, and once it turned on, my brain kind of turned off. I believe Hank thought he was trying to bury their results. In fact, I think he caught him destroying some of their data. He was livid."

"Why would a scientist destroy his own data?"

"What I remember is Harold questioned whether he was more interested in furthering his own career than the research. Hank felt his assistant had a preconceived notion of what they should find, and to Hank that was the ultimate mortal sin for a scientist."

"Do you remember his name?"

Carolyn had finished her coffee and put the cup into the sink. She turned back to me with slightly knitted brows. "I'm not sure if I can't remember, or if I never even knew it. Anyway, it was great to see you, Joe, and of course you too, Marylin. Please come back soon." She bowed toward us and said "Namaste." With that simple goodbye she turned to leave the room, then turned back with a slight smile. "I think Hank usually referred to this guy as 'Lieutenant Dickhead,' when talking about him. But I don't think that was his real name." With that she was off.

We drove to the warehouse and said our goodbyes to Armando, Lorna and Seth, as well as a few other associates, then headed back to San Luis Obispo, or SLO as the locals call it. We were both quiet for most of the ride, but as we approached the outskirts of town Marylin spoke up.

"I've been wondering about that technician."

"Gerry?"

"Want to go find him?"

"Where?"

"I guess we should start with Marfa."

I turned toward Marylin, as if watching her speak would help me understand her words. "Why?"

"Maybe he knows something. Isn't that what you're looking for? More knowledge?"

It was interesting to hear Marylin put it that way. Of course, it was true that more knowledge was what I was looking for, what I had always looked for. It occurred to me I had always assumed that was what life was for, that that is what everyone did. But when I heard Marylin enunciate the idea so clearly, I realized even though looking for more knowledge was what I did, it wasn't for everyone.

I didn't answer for a while. I was trying to unravel a tangled skein of thoughts twisting through my consciousness. I felt if I pulled on the wrong thread, I would tie myself up in mental knots I might never unravel. "Gerry is an interesting person," I began. "He is very smart, and I don't mean in a small way." I paused for a moment, trying to determine whether the string of thoughts I was pulling on would unravel or tangle my mental skein more. "He is appalled at what the navy is doing, but I would say he sees it as a natural extension of what the human race is doing."

"He may be right, you know," Marylin said.

"I'm sure he is, but a person can't survive thinking only that. The way he sees it, everything humans do is ultimately destructive, and not just to whales or animals or the planet. To ourselves as well."

"What does he suggest we do, then?"

"He has no suggestions as far as I can tell, no solutions, only anguish and despair."

"So, you don't think he'll help us?"

"If he sees me, he'll know I was following him. Who knows how he will react? Maybe he'll think we're from the navy."

"Didn't he trust Sonya?"

"I think he may have trusted her not to betray him intentionally. I'm not sure he trusts her to see reality as clearly as he does. If we're not in cahoots with the navy, he might still think we could lead them to him. Or he might conclude if we could find him, so can they." Marylin reached her house. She pulled into the driveway and switched off her car engine and sat there for a second, then turned to me.

"So, you admit Gerry might be right, but you just don't want to accept it?"

"Not quite. I can't prove Gerry is wrong. Perhaps the human race is hurtling headlong into certain destruction. Perhaps. But anyone who has such a despairing outlook is certainly heading towards personal destruction. One has to have hope."

"And therefore, by your own logic, we need to search for him." Marylin had proven to be a worthy debater. I had no further grounds for objection. We began planning for a trek to West Texas that afternoon.

16

As I've mentioned, I'm not much of a traveler, and had been grateful that Jeannie, who travels extensively, took care of the details of our earlier trip. However, Jeannie was primarily a professional musician who traveled as a necessary adjunct to her profession. Marylin, who had run the SLO Chamber of Commerce for several decades, was a professional trip planner. She organized the details of our trip so thoroughly and efficiently that everything seemed to materialize from thin air. Every step she took was obvious and simple, and yet without her I wouldn't have been able to get her car out of her driveway.

She wasn't hurried, but because she knew what she was doing there were no delays either. The most difficult tasks turned out to be convincing her sister to take care of her cat and to find a neighborhood kid to water her flowers. We headed out two days after the Shanti Shanti party.

Marylin drove a Chrysler New Yorker. She had explained to me that Brian Winthrop, who had been president of the chamber of commerce off and on over the years and was one of the largest land developers in the central coast area, bought a new one every year and sold his old ones at very large discounts to local acquaintances. "He could never just give one away, for temperamental and philosophical reasons, but he finds it prudent to curry favors from people like me who can be useful to him."

"How often do you get one from him?"

"It used to be every three or four years, but unless he changes models, this may be the last."

"It's a great car, especially for this trip. You don't like it anymore?"

"I love this car, but Chrysler's changed everything about the New Yorker but the name. The new New Yorker is just a cheap Dodge with a fancy hood ornament."

"Do you ever feel used?"

"I'm no more used than he is. All life forms need to make a living somehow. I'm not in the least bit envious of him, if that's what you mean."

"I'm not sure what I meant, Marylin, but I take your point. I've developed many ideas that have made millions for others, but I can't imagine living their lives. I would be an unhappy failure if I tried, and even more miserable if I succeeded."

And as we headed over the same route Jeannie and I had traversed two years previous, I settled into a comfortable reverie in a nearly silent vehicle that smoothed the pavement under its wheels. If this was being used, I could get used to it too. Marylin clearly enjoyed driving in general, but I think even Jeannie would have enjoyed driving this gentle beast.

I'm sure if I drove the same route as often as Marylin (this was her beaten path to Las Vegas) the trip would lose some of its magic, but there was something both perplexing and exhilarating about traveling a route the second time after the memory of the first has begun to merge into the rest of my past. Some parts were entirely familiar, some vaguely familiar, some entirely new. I was traveling as much through my own mind as through the actual environment.

The trip from SLO to Vegas in March is not the same as in July. For one thing, instead of the dry, golden grasses of summer, the slopes were covered with California poppies. If God has a flower garden, it might well be a field of these golden poppies. When we reached the Central Valley, instead of taking the highway through Bakersfield as Jeannie did, Marylin drove on backroads through farmlands and farm towns. To be honest a couple of the places we went through made me feel I had been transported to Mexico. Everything but the traffic signs was in Spanish.

"Welcome to the San Joaquin Valley," Marylin said. "This is the most intense agricultural land in the country, maybe in the world. But I'm afraid it comes at a cost."

"What cost?" I said.

"Two, actually: salinization of the soil and running out of water. See those pumps?" She pointed to an industrial-looking arrangement of pipes and shacks inside a chain-link fence enclosure. "Every year they need to drill deeper and install bigger pumps. And every time they do that, they force their neighbors to drill even deeper, and so on. And the deeper the water, the saltier it's likely to be. Pure water is either absorbed by the plants or evaporates, leaving the salt behind."

Of course I was familiar with the concept — I had worked on a USDS-Syrian project that tried to reclaim soil similarly spoiled in the Middle East. I had promised myself to see how it turned out, but I never did.

We sailed over the Tehachapi Pass and through the Mojave in comfort, then pulled into Las Vegas an hour or two before dinner. When I made this same trip with Jeannie, we had arrived exhausted. She and I had stayed at a motel on the southern edge of town and left early the next day without even making it into the city. Marylin drove straight to the front of Caesars Palace. Valets opened the car doors for both of us. I remembered being scorched by the hot desert air before, but this time it was a mild evening with only the slightest hint of a breeze. I recalled a physicist explaining parallel universes to me. At the moment, I felt as though I was living through a second version of my original Nevada sojourn.

"Gustav, it's good to see you again. How's Carol?" Marylin addressed the valet.

"She's doing well. Are you staying in town long? She'd love to see you." Gustav had a slight accent, formal, definitely European, maybe German or Austrian.

We left the car and Marylin ushered me into the large hotel. "Do you know everyone in this place?" I asked.

"No, but I know plenty. I've organized the trips for a lot of small business groups from the central coast to Las Vegas, and I always sent them here. It's as good as any place in town, and once a destination realizes I'm a repeat client, they are more generous with the discounts, spruce up the packages a little, you know."

Our first stop was the front desk. "Ah, Ms. Sutliff," the young clerk said. He looked like he was barely out of high school. "Business or pleasure this time?"

"Neither, Frank, we're just passing through."

He looked down at a large ledger on his stand. "A single night? It's pretty busy, but I could offer you a courtesy room on the third floor. It only has one queen bed, though." He looked up to read Marylin's face, to see if that was acceptable.

"That would be nice. Thank you." He gave her a key. She didn't sign anything, we just walked away.

"Do you get a free room every time you come?" I said.

"Not necessarily. He had a room for one night he knew he wasn't going to fill anyway." She looked at me with an amused smile. "It's not such a big deal. The hospitality business is run by mid-level operatives like Gustav, who's the head valet, Frank and me. We're the ones who deal with the public, field the complaints and demands, smooth over the logistics with each other so everyone enjoys themselves. If we all do our jobs well, we learn to appreciate each other." She paused for a second, and then continued, "And of course, they see I have a special friend, so they're going to be especially felicitous." Marylin hooked my left arm with her right. "Let me show you around. As a mathematician, you'll love this place."

"As a mathematician, I would love this place if I had years to spend here. I think I'd better just enjoy it as a tourist tonight."

"Fair enough." She led me through several of the gaming rooms. We gawked at the posters advertising the show rooms and perused the various restaurants before deciding on Cajun.

"Why don't we relax at the slot machines before dinner?" Marylin said. I had never played slot machines or even been in a casino before. I felt I had gone through my entire life without winning anything, and my expectation wasn't that I would enjoy losing money to a machine, but there was no choice.

An hour and a half later and forty dollars lighter, we strolled to the far end of the hotel for a bowl of jambalaya.

The next day we continued into the desert — endless light-brown sand punctuated by small discontinuous mountain ranges. About three hours into our trip Marylin asked me, "Do you want to see the Grand Canyon?"

"Is it around here?" I said.

Without answering she turned onto a side road and headed north. The road headed through some pretty barren and even innocuous territory, although I had noticed a few groves of evergreen trees scattered around. It looked like there was nothing ahead, so I began to wonder how many hours out of the way this trip would take us. I wasn't in much of a hurry to get to Marfa, as I had no idea what I would do or say if we ran into Gerry, but I was learning Marylin could bring serendipity to new heights. The trees thinned out, then in half an hour or so began to repopulate again. After we passed through a touristy-looking town I had to ask, "How far is it, anyway?"

"Are you in a hurry, dear?" she said. Just then, a sign proclaimed we were in Grand Canyon Village. She pulled into a large but nearly empty parking lot and said, "Well, we're here in any case."

When I opened the door, I was surprised by a blast of winter. I knew we had been climbing in elevation, but the comfort of Marylin's limousine had protected me from the change in temperature. We scrambled through our suitcases for any sweaters or sweatshirts we could find, bundled up, and headed toward the canyon. Until I got to within ten feet or so of the rim, I had no idea what to expect, or even how close we were to the spectacle, but once we reached the edge and peered down into the gaping chasm, I was flabbergasted. I was looking into a geometrical puzzle I knew was too complex for me to solve but that I wanted to understand anyway. My mind simply couldn't comprehend what I was seeing.

"This is one of my favorite times to visit," said Marylin. "Any earlier and it's likely too cold, there may even be a lot of snow. We're lucky there's none now. Any later and it gets too crowded." She turned to examine me, to see if I was adequately appreciative.

I said, "This makes me realize the word *mind-boggling* is overused. This is mind-boggling. Do you come here often?"

"I try to make it every few years. My husband and I used to come every spring. We'd hike down there," she pointed to the canyon floor far below "and camp out for a few days." We didn't speak about our departed spouses to each other much, but I could see from the way her eyes watered up that the memories were powerful.

I put my arm around her. "I can't take you down there, but I think I could take you over to the restaurant for a drink and a meal."

"Good enough, Joe, that'll be good enough."

As we walked shoulder to shoulder toward the restaurant I was amazed at how well we got along, but I also wondered if either one of us would have even taken a second look at each other when we were younger. My wife had been an art historian. Like me, she lived in a world of ideas and abstractions. I knew Marylin's husband had been in construction, and, like her, he was a doer. And I was sure their marriage was every bit as powerful and complex and nurturing as mine had been. But having weathered our lives, Marylin and I now had a different, yet still very strong connection based on experience, on overcoming sorrow, on respecting sorrow. We were not afraid of the past, but I felt we both knew we had to move on, and we both relished finding a friend and lover who had no regrets about the pain they had been through.

After eating we spent more time gazing into the incomprehensible abyss again, watching it disappear as the sun set, then headed back on the road. Somehow viewing the Grand Canyon snapped me out of the mindless reverie

I had been in since leaving SLO. The vastness of the West had hypnotized me. You can see so much and so far, the mind simply can't hold it all, so you see nothing at all. Although I knew we were going up and down hills all day long, I hadn't paid attention to the details. Las Vegas is two thousand feet above sea level, the Grand Canyon Village and Flagstaff, where we ended up for the night, are nearly seven thousand feet. There is a difference.

The area around Flagstaff was gorgeous in its own right, although the city center looked a little run down, if still quaint and lovely in many ways. The next morning we got off to a fairly early start and resumed our trek. A couple of hours into the trip I decided we needed to try to formulate a plan. "How do you think we're going to find Gerry?" I said.

"Not we. You. I don't even know what he looks like."

This simple fact hadn't occurred to me. How was I going to find him? I had no idea, so I went on to the next question. "What do we do when we find him?"

The question hung in the air while we hurtled toward Texas. By the time we pulled into El Paso, we were both tired of the road. A couple of beers, a big Texas steak, a clean motel room, and a long, hot shower together helped us regroup. The next morning we slept in a little, then found a pancake house not far from our motel.

I was chewing on my last piece of bacon when Marylin said, "I think the main thing is to stay relaxed."

I knew immediately she was talking about Gerry. "Should we pretend it's a coincidence?"

"We can try. But if he sees through it, stay cool."

I wasn't sure how her advice would play out, but I accepted she was right. The last three hours of our journey as we approached Marfa seemed longer than all of the first three days. I was worried I would upset Gerry more than anything. Not just because he might retaliate against me, or our mission would fail, but simply because it seemed he had enough agony in his life, and I didn't want to add to it. We passed through a few very small towns that morning. They weren't ghost towns, but they weren't alive either. I labeled them zombie towns, suspended between existing and not existing. It was hard for me to imagine how one could make a living in some of those places.

Finally, we came to Marfa, and I had a feeling it too might be a zombie town, but in fact it was alive, if not quite robust. There was a dusty little diner named Jack's Burger Bar on the east end of town, so we pulled in for lunch. Our waitress had spiked pink hair, multiple earrings in one ear, and wore a tight black dress that barely covered her butt. I couldn't tell if she wore underwear. She stood over our table and glared at us. She just stood there, didn't ask what we wanted, didn't say hi, just glared.

"How's the hamburger?" Marylin said.

"This is Texas. It's great."

"And the coffee? I said.

"It sucks. Get a Coke."

"Two hamburgers with everything and two large Cokes," Marylin said.

Our waitress smiled to herself and turned away to place the order. She came back a few minutes later with our drinks.

"What's your name, dear?" Marylin asked.

"Gloria. What's yours?"

"I'm Marylin and this is Joe. What do you do for fun around here?"

"Me? I fuck and I smoke." She had gone back to glaring at us. Marylin was going to say something, but our waitress cut her off. "But I ain't telling you who I fuck or what I smoke."

"That's all right, I'm not interested, honey," Marylin said. "Is there a place around here we can get a cold beer?" I was glad she was taking over the conversation, I felt a little intimidated by our young friend.

"Sure, there's two. Mitch's and El Chapo. I recommend Mitch's"

"Why?"

"They speak English."

"*No es importa, hablo español.*"

"*Entonces vayan a El Chapo. Su cerveza es mejor, es de México.*"

"*Gracias.*"

"*No hay de que,*" Gloria said and left to get our burgers.

I can't speak Spanish, but had listened to my wife's family enough to know what better beer was. "What do you make of our waitress? Is she mad at the world or just us?" I asked Marylin.

"Neither, especially not us. In fact, I'm sure she likes us. She's just young and beautiful and sexual and sexy and she loves it and hates it."

"What does she hate?"

Marylin stared at me for a while as if she couldn't believe what I had asked her. Finally she said, "Young, beautiful women don't always get treated well, you know." As she said this, I looked at her wonderful face. I had perceived her as a lovely and wonderful companion, yet also as just another old fogey like me, but I saw she was speaking from experience, and I understood she had had her years of being gorgeous too. She continued, "Frankly, a lot of men are real pigs, and there's always the possibility of an unwanted pregnancy. Surely, you've noticed people more or less leave young guys alone, but everyone has strong expectations of young women and they aren't shy about voicing those expectations."

"What kind of expectations?"

"Oh, Joseph, really? Be pretty, be chaste, put out, keep quiet, talk to me, behave, lighten up."

"You make being a young woman sound tough."

"It is tough, and young women are the only ones tough enough to handle it. I couldn't do it anymore." The hamburgers arrived and were delicious, as promised.

We headed toward El Chapo, passing a dingy motel where we figured we'd spend the night. As Marylin drove down a couple of half-abandoned streets to the bar, she said, "We have no idea where we might find Gerry, but I'll bet he's as likely to be at El Chapo as Mitch's if he likes to drink."

"He might. The last time I saw him was in a bar, but he left a full glass on the table when he walked out on us."

El Chapo was a low-ceilinged adobe building about two blocks south of the highway. It was early afternoon, the place was pretty quiet. We ordered our beers, then sat out on the rear patio and looked out over the West Texas desert. We were on the south edge of town, so there were no buildings obscuring our view. It was broad, rocky country, the horizon was littered with numerous small mountains of random shapes. To a New Englander it might seem the dry scrub couldn't support much life, but the loud incessant buzz of insects, which reminded me of my childhood in South Dakota, proclaimed otherwise. Marylin had ordered our beers in Spanish, but there was no one else on the patio, so it didn't matter what language anyone spoke.

After forty-five minutes or so we left for Mitch's. We tried to see if Gerry had shown up as we trudged back through the bar, but our eyes didn't accustom themselves to the darkness very quickly and we weren't sure we saw everyone.

Mitch's was in a newly renovated building, higher ceilings, not adobe, but it was also dark inside. It was near the center of town and didn't have a patio, so we grabbed a corner table. We watched the ranchers come and go for an hour or two, then decided to go find a motel room and get some dinner. Still no sign of Gerry.

After renting a room, we returned to Jack's and were handed menus by an older woman. "Is Gloria's shift over?" Marylin asked.

"Who?"

"Gloria, the pink-haired waitress we had this afternoon."

"Gloria? Did she tell you her name was Gloria? She's no Gloria. Her name is Kathleen. What else did she tell you?"

"She told us the beer at El Chapo is better than the beer at Mitch's."

"Well, she might have a point there, though all beer pretty much tastes the same to me. Do you know what you want?"

"I'll have the chef's salad," said Marylin.

"A Coke and hamburger," I said. The lunch had been pretty good, so I decided to do it again.

"Why did that girl tell us her name was Gloria?" I asked Marylin after our waitress had left.

"I told you, she's testing the limits of her reality."

After dinner, we went back to our motel room. Neither one of us wanted to watch either of the channels on the crummy motel TV. Marylin wrapped herself in a long novel. I lay on the broken bed and mused on some of the ideas about primes Teddy had planted in my brain.

The next morning we decided to drive to Alpine, a town about thirty miles east of Marfa. The restaurant there wasn't any better than Jack's, but at least it was different. We drove back to Marfa and wandered around town for a while. There was a small grocery store and a couple of gas stations, a very small laundromat, several empty storefronts, and a beautiful, stately town hall that was beginning to fall apart. Clearly Marfa had seen more prosperous times.

We returned to Jack's for lunch, mostly to ask our waitress what her name was that day.

"Good afternoon, Gloria," I said.

"Wait, I thought your name was Kathleen," said Marylin.

"You two should make up your minds," said our waitress, unperturbed.

"Maybe you should too," said Marylin.

"I don't need to, I'm not confused. I know who I am. Do you at least know what you want for lunch?"

She had checkmated us, so we laughed and ordered. We were about half way through our meal when Gerry walked in. As he walked past our booth, he stopped short and stared at me. "Gerry?" I asked, trying to act surprised.

"What are you doing here?" he said, ignoring my question but answering it anyway.

"Vacation," I said.

"Right," he said. He turned on his heels and walked to the farthest booth. Our waitress, Gloria or Kathleen or whoever, sat down next to him and gave him a substantial kiss. They could see us, so Marylin and I just continued eating as if nothing special had just happened. The two of them, however, put their heads together and were obviously discussing us. Finally our waitress went back to work. Gerry stood up, walked over to our booth, and said, "Can I join you?"

"Of course. Gerry, this is Marylin. Marylin, Gerry." I gave a perfunctory introduction. I didn't want to explain anything. I felt the more I said, the more likely I was to screw up. "How are you, Gerry?" I asked.

Gerry sat down across from us. "Katie says you've been here since yesterday," he said as he sat. "What are you doing here? Are you following me?"

Marylin saved me from an awkward, unbelievable story. "I wanted to see if Donald Judd had opened his museum yet and try to understand why he settled here." I had no idea what she was talking about, but clearly Gerry did.

"You know Judd?" Gerry said.

"I met him once in Los Angeles. It was years ago. I'm sure he doesn't remember, but I was struck by his work and recently found out he moved here."

Gerry turned and stared at me, clearly unnerved by the idea our presence might be a coincidence. "You still trying save the whales?"

"You mean with Sonya? That's too big a job for me. Just trying to help a friend."

"Yeah, she told me you used to play music together down by the river. She's a sweet kid. Say hi when you see her again. You will see her, won't you?"

"I'd love to, but I think she's still on that secret cruise. I'm a little afraid for her."

"You should be."

"Why do you say that?"

"That whole thing is phony. That's why I left."

"You sure didn't do her any favors when you did."

"She'll do fine without me. We were tight for a while, but that cooled off."

"I don't mean that way. They interrogated her for days. They thought you had stolen some classified intelligence and that she was in on it."

"They did, did they?" Gerry said. He turned to Marylin. "Sorry to disappoint you, but Judd's foundation isn't open, and he's out of town. He's gone a lot."

"You know him?" Marylin said.

"Not really, but Katie claims he's her father, or rather her mom did." He gestured with his head toward our waitress.

"Didn't think he'd ever marry again," Marylin said, mostly to herself.

"You don't have to be married to produce kids, you know. Anyway, he denies it." Gerry stood up and walked toward the door, opened it, then came back and sat down again. "I'm not sure I believe you," he said to me.

"I'm not asking you to."

"So, are you still working on whale languages?"

"Sure. Your idea that it wasn't all math helped a lot. But we have a long way to go."

"Follow me then. I have something for you." He strode toward the door, then turned again. "You sure no one tracked you here?"

"No one knows where I'm at. I was visiting Marylin in California, and she asked me if I wanted to go on a trip. No one followed us."

"Okay. Follow me."

Gerry was riding an off-road motorcycle, which he mounted and kicked into life. Marylin and I climbed into her car and followed him down the highway out of town. We headed west for a mile or two, then he turned on to a dusty, unpaved road heading south. We crossed a cattle guard onto some sort of ranch, at least we noticed one or two head of cattle munching on the sparse desert fare. Less than a mile from the highway he stopped at a wretched looking house trailer with litter from years of occupation scattered over the grounds. Along the side of the structure there was a sort of home-made awning constructed out of a tattered green tarpaulin.

Gerry motioned for us to sit at the picnic table under the tarp and disappeared inside. He came back with a hard, flat container of some sort in one hand and a semi-automatic pistol in the other. He sat down at the table facing us, laying the gun on the table, not pointing directly at us, but it was threatening nevertheless.

"Are you going to shoot us?" I said.

"Are you going to tell me the truth?" he said.

"Does that mean telling you something you'll believe?" I said.

Gerry smiled, a small but significant smile. "Maybe it does." He took the gun and put it on the seat next to him, out of sight. "So, you claim you're not trying to save the whales?" he asked.

I thought about his question a while. "Gerry, I'm a mathematician, it's what I love and all I've ever done. If the whales do math, I want to know how. And, like I told you, I'm trying to help a friend. She may be in danger."

Gerry's eyes widened little when I said this, then he looked down, drawing his eyes away from my scrutiny. "I always thought we were in danger."

"From what I've learned, it depends on your attitude."

"What do you mean by that?"

I thought I knew Gerry well enough to figure he was better off knowing exactly what his situation was. I explained I knew of two researchers before him. One had gone on to have a long and satisfying career as a biologist, the other may have been murdered by the navy.

"So why do you say it's the attitude?"

"The one who is living was pretty blasé about the whole thing. The navy irked him, but he let it go and never looked back. The one who is not wouldn't let up and became a trouble-maker. We're not sure what happened, but a semi ran over his motorcycle while he was on his way to see researcher number one. If they think you're a trouble maker, they'll likely brew up some trouble for you. If not, probably not."

"And you, are you a trouble-maker, Joe?"

"See, there you go asking questions. Sure sign of a trouble-maker."

Gerry grinned and picked up his pistol from his seat. With a sharp snap he pulled the magazine from the handle, aimed at the sky and fired the remaining bullet. "Guess I won't need this." He put the empty gun back down on the table.

Even though we weren't quite touching, I could feel Marylin relax.

"Sonya gave you copies of my notebooks and tapes," he said.

"Some of them."

"I took everything with me and burned it all."

I tried not to show any concern.

He continued, after scanning my face for a reaction. "But not before I copied them onto these." He opened his plastic case and dumped a pile of five-and-a-half inch paper floppies onto the table. "Not sure why. I didn't want the navy to have them, but it was too hard to just destroy all that work." We stared at each other for a few moments. It was still his turn, I didn't dare interfere. "Do you want them?"

"Do you want to give them to me?"

Gerry pursed his lips, looked at the sky, then said, "Yes, yes I do."

"What are you going to do next, Gerry?" I said.

He looked back at me sharply. "I'm not going to ask you what you're going to do with those floppies, so don't you ask me what I'm going to do with my life."

"Fair enough, Gerry, but you do know what I'm going to do."

For once, Gerry relaxed. It was the first time I had seen any sign of his tension abating. "Touché. To tell you the truth, I'm gonna take Katie out of this place. I like it well enough, but I didn't grow up here."

"Katie did?" Marylin asked. "I thought she might have grown up in New York."

Gerry's eyebrows drew together, as if he didn't understand the question, then relaxed again. "You mean because she might be Judd's daughter? It was a one-night thing. Katie and Don don't have much to do with each other because he wouldn't have much to do with her mom."

"Is she gone?"

"She died last year. Overdose. Hit Katie pretty hard, but she's getting over it." Gerry stared out over the endless Texas landscapes, then continued, "I told her we're just like the whales. We just gotta keep on swimmin'."

It was kind of incongruous thinking about the whales in that arid expanse, but I decided we'd better start swimming ourselves, before Gerry changed his mind. I gathered the floppies together and put them back into the plastic case. "You don't mind if I take this case too?" I said.

Gerry watched me fumble with his floppies but ignored my question. "You know, I still can't figure out whether you're really here by coincidence, or whether you planned this visit."

I stood up, keeping Gerry's floppies firmly in my hand. I wasn't going to try to answer his question. "Well, Judd isn't in town, his museum isn't open, so I guess we'll head back home. I don't know where this whale thing is going, but I do thank you for this." I lifted the package up as a gesture.

"You know, I hope it helps you. Just don't run into me again, okay? I've had my fill of the navy."

"Not likely to happen, Gerry. If you don't raise a ruckus, they would just as soon forget about you."

With that, Marylin and I left Gerry and Marfa, Texas. I think we held our breath for at least thirty minutes as we headed toward El Paso. Finally, after passing through a couple of my zombie towns I turned to Marylin and said, "You sure know how to show a guy a good time."

"I'm a pro," she said. "But I prefer not to have guns involved."

"Yeah," I said, "I wish Gerry and Katie the very best, but I'll be damned if I have any idea how that will turn out."

"I get the idea he hopes you never will. But all in all, he treated you pretty well. Why do you think he hauled out that cannon, anyway?"

"I'm not sure he had a clear idea, just wanted to be in charge."

"Well it was pretty stupid. I'm sure he didn't know what he was doing."

"How do you mean?"

"Joe, can you hand me my purse? It's in the back seat."

I turned around and grabbed her purse and handed it to her, but she motioned for me to keep it. "Open it up."

It didn't have a zipper, so I snapped it wide and peered inside, wondering what she wanted me to get. For men, the interior of a woman's purse is a foreign land with a different language and unintelligible culture, but in this case something very obvious stood out — a revolver.

"I almost shot him, Joe. The fool." Marylin didn't take her eyes off the road as she spoke. "My husband taught me how to use a gun, and he warned me never to let anyone see it unless I was already firing. I had my hand in my bag, I was aiming right at his gut. When he picked it up to put it on the seat, I nearly let him have it."

I didn't say anything for a moment, then I began to laugh.

"What's so funny? Don't you think I could do it?"

"No, I'm sure you could, I was just laughing at the kind of women I hang out with." I told her the story of Marta and the cat burglars. "I think you two would get each other."

"I'd love to meet her. I guess I'm going to have to visit you in Boston."

We drove in silence for a while, revisiting the vast territories we had passed through just days before. I began to think about my work back home. I said, "It'll be interesting to see what's on those floppies. By the way, who is this Judd guy? Did you really meet him?"

"Barely. It was at a gallery showing his work in LA. I had forgotten all about him, but he popped into my mind when Gerry started questioning us, I just remembered he gave a little talk about doing something new and exciting in Marfa. That's why I had heard about Marfa in the first place, I guess. Anyway, it worked for us."

"Probably saved our trip."

17

Marylin made the trip back to SLO more interesting than the trip out to Marfa. From El Paso we headed due north instead of northwest. We drove for a couple of hours watching the horizon, discussing anything that came up. We understood each other in an odd, implicit way, and that led to relaxed and wide-ranging conversations, made all the more interesting because our pasts seemed so different. At one point Marylin said, "There's some very interesting history out here, you know."

"Really? It looks pretty desolate."

"That's why some of it happened here. Do you remember Trinity?"

"The Father, the Son and the Holy Ghost?"

"Wrong Trinity. The first atomic bomb."

"Oh, yeah. Not sure which brings up worse memories."

"Were you Catholic?"

"No, my first girlfriend's family was. The whole church thing was pretty strict, and she was becoming an atheist. Her parents definitely were not. Pretty sure they blamed me."

Marylin had turned off the highway onto another of her backroads. "Trinity took place out here. Like I said, desolation was the whole point." We crossed a dark lava field, then passed through a gap in a long mountain range onto a flat unoccupied expanse. In short order, we were at the site of the first nuclear explosion, which was marked by a stone obelisk about fifteen feet tall. There wasn't much to do or say there but shudder at the significance of the place, so we left quickly.

Marylin eventually pulled back onto a real highway and we headed west. Another hour, another mountain pass, another wide plain. Marylin broke the silence. "Hey, I forgot about this, but here's a more uplifting point of interest." She pulled off the highway again and headed for a cluster of small buildings barely visible from the highway. I had been half dozing until she spoke.

"What's this?" I said.

"The Very Large Array, or the VLA. The largest telescope in the world."

Now it was my time to brighten up. "I know about the VLA. I helped design it. Well, a very small part of it." The VLA is actually an array of twenty-seven movable radio telescopes which sit on nearly forty miles of railroad tracks spread out over a large flat high desert plain.

"Damn, what a coincidence. My husband helped build it."

"What did he do?"

"Something to do with the rail tracks. Prepared the site, I think. He was a heavy-equipment contractor."

"I helped develop the algorithms on how to space the dishes on those tracks. Amazing project." We spent an hour or so examining the exhibits, then headed out on the road again. The fact that Marylin's husband and I had both worked on the same project seemed to have made us feel even more comfortable with each other, as if our past as well as our present was beginning to merge. I nearly forgot about Gerry, the navy, the whales, the whole mess, for a while.

We wound our away through deserts, mountains and forests for a few hours, when Marylin decided to stop for gas, water, and to use the facilities in a town called Alpine. This Alpine, located in Arizona, was very different from the one we visited in Texas. For one thing, it was in a little valley surrounded by immense forested mountains, not in the middle of an endless scrubland. As I filled the car Marylin disappeared into the ladies' room. When I finished I browsed around the store. The place had a little of everything, but not much of any one thing. It had some fishing and hunting equipment — fishing line, bait, some ammo, a few poles and reels, even a couple of rifles, serious-looking weapons with scopes, but they had the look of having been there a long time. The store had the standard convenience store food — soda, candy bars, potato chips and beer — and what looked like a lunch bar, but it was closed by the time we arrived. It had a few gewgaws for tourists, including some very old looking post cards with humor from another era ("How to get to Texas: go east until you smell it, then south until you step in it"). It had some nice-looking woven rugs with indigenous motifs, and turquoise jewelry, some of it very nice. In a far corner under glass there was a more serious looking display — what appeared to be authentic arrowheads and other ancient stone implements. These had no price tags, but were by far the most interesting items in the store. As I was looking at them a man a few years my senior called out to me from one of the booths, "What are you looking for?"

"Nothing really, just looking."

He ambled over to a cooler and pulled out a couple of beers. "Want one?"

I say he ambled, but really it was more like he floated across the aisle and back, then sat down lightly, silently. His voice was almost quiet, but easily carried across the room. He had dark-brown eyes, dark-brown skin, and long white hair. I'm not one to turn down a free beer, so I shuffled over to his booth and squeezed in between the bench and the table.

"Those arrowheads are from these hills. I collected most of them myself," he said as he handed me a bottle.

"They're lovely. It's hard for me to imagine the skill it must take to shape those small flakes from a stone."

"Yes, but first you need to know which stone to use, and where to get it."

"Are they for sale?"

"Never," he answered, as I expected. Then, as I did not expect, he walked with his easy gait over to the case I was looking at and came back with one of the smallest and most exquisite pieces and laid it on the table in front of me. Its tiny gray facets glittered in the dark light of the store. "I only give them away."

I fingered the arrowhead while we sipped on our beers. When Marylin showed up, he fetched a beer for her and a large bowl of peanuts in their shells for all of us.

"I'm Joe, by the way," I said as he sat down, "and this is Marylin."

"Jack."

"Do you own this place?" Marylin said.

"Yes," he said.

"Well, thanks for the beer, Jack".

"You're welcome." We all sipped on our bottles a bit and munched on the peanuts.

"I'm a curious person," our host said to me at last, breaking a comfortable silence. "I feel your lovely companion is like me, she's not searching for anything. But you are, and I'm sure it's not in this store." His eyes, which had looked so somber when I first met him, twinkled a little as he said this.

"Maybe not, but I found this," I said, sliding the arrowhead over to Marylin and avoiding his question. "He just gave this to me."

Marylin examined the little stone for a while. "Wonderful, amazing. The least you can do is give Jack a straight answer." Turning to my interlocutor, she said, "You're right, he's always looking for something. He's a mathematician."

"A mathematician, that makes sense. You have to look for answers."

"More difficult is finding good questions," I said.

"Same as hunting. Finding the track is harder than following it. So what question are you trying to form?"

"I am trying to decide whether whales speak a language, and even more, if they have a mathematical language."

Jack took this in quietly, then said, "Have you tried to speak with them?"

I had not expected this question, so I thought about it for a while. "No. In fact, that is probably a different track. I am looking for a language they speak among themselves." My new friend didn't reply, so I continued. "I have heard that the Inuit claim to be able to speak with whales, to be allowed to hunt them. Do you think that's possible?"

"I don't know. I don't know any Inuit." He paused. "I don't know any whales either."

"Neither do I. Does it seem absurd to you for humans to try to understand what another species is saying among themselves by just watching what they do?"

Jack took his time to answer. "No. That's how my people learned English. Are you making progress?"

"I don't know. Sometimes yes, sometimes no. It's very difficult."

Jack fetched three more beers, and also served us each a bowl of cold potato salad from the lunch counter cooler. "Time for dinner." The cold potatoes soothed my throat in a way even the cold beer did not. As we ate I thought of stories about the legendary hospitality of the desert peoples of North Africa and of Japanese tea ceremonies. Jack's simplicity and directness made me understand what it meant for a weary traveler to get a little sustenance and companionship on a long voyage. Not that we were so tired, but there is a fatigue that arises from being a stranger when traveling. He had taken that away.

We talked a little more as we ate. Marylin's easy grace helped me overcome my normal reticence around strangers, so I too joined in the conversation.

"You bring up an interesting point," I said to Jack. I think the beer had gone to my head. "How do you begin searching for something if you don't know what it is? You can ruin the entire venture from the start."

"Would you like to hear a story?" said Jack.

It was getting dark. Marylin and I looked at each other, then nodded at each other briefly. We had begun to communicate without words like an old couple. "Sure, we'd love to," said Marylin before I could speak.

"This is a story about three brothers. Their father hunted and fished, their mother grew corn, and they lived well. But the boys grew up and the parents grew old and one day they gathered their three sons, and the father said, 'It is time for you boys to decide what you want to do and spread your wings. Your mother and I can no longer take care of you.'"

"The eldest son, Takashim, spoke first. 'I know what I want. I want to feed people. I want to have stores where people can buy the best food to feed their families, and if they can't afford it, I want to be able to give it to them.'"

"The parents were impressed with their oldest son and they asked how he was going to start."

"'I'm going to Santa Fe and open up a stand from my pickup, selling tacos and hotdogs to construction workers.'"

"Then they asked their second son, Tarik, what he was going to do. "I want to find Sasquatch,' he said, as seriously as the first."

"They asked him how he was going to start. 'It's been seen in the Cascades, so I'll hitchhike to Seattle and start searching from there.'"

"The next day both boys left home. Over the next few years the first son opened up several food trucks, then bought a small grocery store, and then a few more. Soon he merged with a larger company and was made president because he was so good at what he did. He moved to LA and bought several chains and became one of the largest grocers in the Southwest. True to his initial promise, he also gave generously to charities and supported food banks anywhere he owned stores. He became admired and wealthy, and succeeded well beyond his even parents' expectations."

"The second son spent years searching for Sasquatch in the Cascades, both in the States and in Canada. He became an expert on the local fauna and earned a PhD and several honorary doctorates as well. He expanded his travels, searching the Himalayas, Siberia, and Indonesia, and was soon one of the most respected biologists in the world."

"When his elder brother's health took a turn for the worse, Tarik moved to LA to help him. 'Tarik', Takashim said, 'I admire your success, but I too did well, and yet here I am with diabetes and only one leg to stand on. Perhaps you chose the wiser path."'

"'I don't think my path was wiser, but it is true I was not so relentless. You had a firm idea of what you wanted and what you needed to do. I had a goal, but no idea of how to pursue it. Maybe that gave me time to heal along the way.'"

Jack quit talking and looked at us as if we should have learned something from his tale. "But, Jack," I said, "You said there were three brothers."

"Well, as I told you," he said, "I didn't feel the need to search for anything, so I just stayed here. And here are my brothers now."

We turned around and saw two men about Jack's build, though the one in the wheelchair appeared to be a bit heavier. They were talking and laughing energetically. As they came into earshot, we heard the one being pushed say, "Hey, Tarik, where the hell did you get your wheelchair driver's license?"

"I don't have a license, never saw the need."

"Well, I see the need," said the passenger. With that, they arrived at our booth.

Takashim pushed himself to the end of the booth and Tarik sat down lightly next to Jack. He looked at us, and at the table, and stood up again to get some potato salad and beer for his brother and himself. Meanwhile Takashim introduced himself. "I'm Takashim, Jack's oldest brother. What kind of horse shit has he been feeding you?"

"He's been telling us a tale about three brothers from this area. One of them even had your name," said Marylin, easily joining into the irreverent conversation.

"Hmm. Did he mention that I used to own half the grocery stores in California while he tried to make a living selling fish bait from this shack?"

"Something to that effect."

As Tarik sat down Takashim continued, "And that our great explorer here became famous for not finding anything?"

"He mentioned that too."

"Well then, I guess you're caught up on our family history. What brings you here?"

"We're just passing through," said Marylin. "We're returning to California from a short trip to Marfa."

"Marfa? Our ancestors fought the Comanche near Marfa. Why did you go there?" said Takashim.

I did not want to tell too much, but I gave the brothers a brief recounting of my travails learning about whales and their communications.

"We know about the U.S. military," said Tarik, with a wry but not unkind smile.

"You also know about looking for some which can't be found, Tarik," said Takashim.

"Maybe, but perhaps I also know about finding more than one is looking for," Tarik said.

"What have you found?" said Marylin.

"It's not easy to describe. Nowadays everyone knows about many things they have never seen, and still we think know them. But how can we be sure of what we know? What do we know of the sources of our information? Have you both been to LA" he asked, looking at Marylin and me.

"Well, I spent two hours driving through it, but didn't stop," I said.

"Good enough, in fact all the better for you," Tarik said. "And how about you, Marylin?"

"I lived there many years ago and visit often enough. And I have done a lot of business with places in LA"

"Takashim has spent most of his life there, any neighborhood he goes to he knows people, and they know him. So we all know it differently. Could we agree on what we know? If we were there years ago, is it the same now as what we know? How about someone who has never been there? What can she know about the city?"

Tarik took a sip from his bottle, and Takashim interjected, "I know you made a living being long-winded, little brother. Get on with it."

"When I started looking for Sasquatch, I thought I knew what I was looking for, namely an animal that no one else had ever seen up close. There were only stories of glimpses from afar as it disappeared into the trees. I did not find that animal. What I found was a cultural icon that everyone knows, that they know, even if slightly differently, all over the world. It is an essential element of the universe for some, if only as an acknowledgment that there are things in the universe we do not know, perhaps cannot know, maybe even should not know, and a foolish chimera for others. And I have found and documented many of its forms, probably in more detail than anyone else ever has. So, I'll let you answer your own question, Marylin." Tarik then turned to me. "You think the whales do mathematics?"

"I am beginning to be more and more sure, although it's quite different from human mathematics."

"Maybe that's a good thing."

I had become a little defensive about my trade, so many non-mathematicians see no point to it. "Mathematics is a very powerful tool, you know. It's responsible for the success of modern science."

"I'm well aware of that. From your point of view, I'm sure it is a tool of discovery and creation, but from another perspective it may be nothing more than the trigger of a slowly exploding bomb that we're all inside of."

Tarik's comments sounded much like Gerry's, but Tarik did not appear to share Gerry's despair. "I understand what you are saying, but do you think it's that bad?" I said.

"Don't forget, we" Tarik said, pointing to himself and his brothers, "are the survivors of such a bomb. Of course I think it's possible."

The serious faces of our hosts made it clear what Tarik was referring to. But Takashim quickly interjected. "I wanted to send Jack to school to learn mathematics. He was always the smartest brother. I wanted him to be my accountant, but I guess he is even smarter than I knew."

Jack laughed, "And a good thing for you. Where would you be if I hadn't hung on to this place?"

"Agreed, little bro."

We had spent hours talking, it was too late to continue to Show Low, the town we, or at least Marylin, had planned to reach that night. "Is there a motel in town?" she said to the brothers.

"You will stay with us, tonight," Jack said. "My wife would love to meet you."

We politely protested, but not too vigorously. Takashim and Tarik went one direction in a pickup, Jack climbed into Marylin's car with us and directed us to his place, about a mile and a half from his store. Jack's wife did not appear surprised or put out when we all barged into her kitchen. "Ricci, this is Marylin and Joe. I invited them over for the night."

Ricci was a petite woman, as brown and as spry as her husband. She had a smile as sweet as the evening desert air. "Welcome to Alpine," she said. "Jack and I always have tea before we go to bed. Would you like some too?"

Of course we did, and she served them with some delicate pastries full of poppy seeds. "These remind me of croissants my mother used to make," said Marylin.

"I'm sure there not as good as your mother's" said Ricci.

"Oh, yes, they're every bit as good. They're delicious."

After tea, Ricci showed us to a small room in the back which was already made up. We slept soundly, so soundly that by the time we were awake the house was full of the noise of laughter and cooking. When we got to the kitchen, we found it crowded with people. Ricci and Jack were there, of course, as well as Takashim and Tarik. There also three other women, one of them much younger than the rest of us.

Takashim was walking today, it appeared he was wearing a prosthetic leg that had been absent the night before. He was the first to see us. "I hope we didn't wake you," he said, handing us a cup of coffee each. "The whole family had to meet you. This is Cynthia, my daughter." He brought the younger woman over. "Cynthia, meet Marylin and Joe."

Cynthia welcomed us with a hug and a laugh. "I hope we didn't wake you. Tarik brought some fresh venison sausage. You're not vegetarians, are you?"

We assured her we were not. Another woman came over. "Hello, I'm Laura. I'm the lone sister in this family."

"She was the little princess of the family," said Takashim, who had just returned with the third woman. "And this is my guiding light, my wife, Doreen."

"You probably weren't expecting a party for breakfast, were you?" she said.

"Jack," I said, "why didn't you include your sister in your story?"

"Daughters are too valuable to send away."

We gathered around the table in short order. There was a lot of food, and the pace was leisurely, so it was noon before we finally said our goodbyes and headed for the road. The visit with Jack and his family had broken a kind of hypnotic rush we had fallen in to, so we spent a relaxed day with many stops marveling at the beauty of Arizona. We finally ended up in Show Low that night, a sleepy town for sleepy travelers.

The next morning after sharing a burrito for breakfast, we headed west again, but into more heavily forested land and more rugged mountains. By this time, we had both shaken the angst of Gerry and Marfa and spent the time telling each other more about our own histories. Our trip had loosened up our tongues, had made us both realize we could occasionally visit the past without stirring up misery.

At one point we began a long descent through the evergreen-covered mountains. "This is the other side of the Grand Canyon," Marylin said.

"I thought we were way south of it, not north." I was confused, as we had visited the south rim a few days earlier.

"I should have said 'another side,' I suppose. Maybe you know that the Grand Canyon was created when the land surrounding the Colorado River was uplifted by continents crashing into each other."

"Yeah, tectonic forces. I do remember something about that."

"This is the southern edge of the slab that was lifted. It's called the Mogollon Escarpment." We continued down the mountain for at least fifty miles. It struck me that I had spent almost five decades in Cambridge without leaving the Boston area more than three or four times, and now I was getting used to traveling hundreds of miles every day. It was a wonderful show.

We skipped the Grand Canyon on the way back but stayed a couple of extra nights in Las Vegas, courtesy of Frank the concierge and Caesars Palace. I had never had much desire to hang out at a casino. I understood the odds behind most of the games, and was even familiar with attempts, some quite successful, of mathematicians to find ways to beat the house. It just never was interesting to me. I think I underestimated the power of glitz, and not just at Caesars Palace. Marylin took me to see Frank — the singer, not the concierge — Wayne, Sammy — the whole gang. I don't think she actually knew any of the stars, but she had become so familiar with Las Vegas that first names just came naturally to her.

We arrived back at Marylin's double wide in San Luis Obispo late one afternoon. It was T-shirt weather, something one would seldom find in Cambridge in March, so we hung out on Marylin's patio the rest of the day recuperating with more lemonade and martinis.

The next morning over breakfast I told Marylin how much I enjoyed her company.

"Likewise, Joe. You can stay as long as you want. I mean that, move in with me."

I thought about what she said as I munched on an English muffin. "It's lovely here, but I wouldn't have the resources to work on my whales. Why don't you come back with me?"

I think Marylin's eyes became a little misty for a second, but only for a second. "Do you remember that day down at the fish market?" she said.

"Yes, I was impressed. You knew everyone, and they all liked you. Not that that's surprising."

"See, that's the thing. Here I have a place, a place I relish. If I moved to Boston, I'd just be another old lady to be ignored."

We stared at each other for a while, then I said, "I understand. It would be the same for me if I moved here. There isn't enough time left in my life to rebuild what I have at home."

We sipped on our coffees in silence, then Marylin said, "Long visits, then."

"Long visits."

We went to the Morro Bay fish markets again, but only for a small meal's worth of clams, and to Shanti, Shanti to say goodbye. Marylin drove me to Monterey along the coast highway one day, she didn't want me to miss "the most beautiful road in the world". The drive was exhilarating — hundreds of sinewy miles of breathtaking cliffs hung between impenetrable mountains and ceaseless waves. It was certainly the most beautiful road I've ever seen. In Carmel-by-the-Sea we had a tuna dinner which was not just exquisite, it made dining an entirely different experience. Of course the entire staff there knew Marylin, and those at the hotel where we spent the night as well.

The next day over coddled eggs and hash browns Marylin asked me if I was up for the return trip. As she put it, "Some folks get ecstatic, some get car sick on Highway One."

I assured her I was the ecstatic type, and the road was no less wonderful on the return trip. A couple of days after we got back to SLO Marylin brought up the idea of going on a whale watch again. Of course she knew all the agencies, so I have no doubt she received free tickets.

The tour didn't start until 9 am, so we were able to enjoy a leisurely breakfast. The tour boat was quite a bit smaller than the ones I had been on in Boston, which suited me just fine until we got to sea and I became a little nauseous. The discomfort passed before we reached the prime viewing area. A young woman named Dora was the guide. She was a biology major at CalPoly, and led the tours twice a week. She knew her biology, and explained the habits of grey whales as best one could through the squawking megaphone she used.

Dora punctuated her lecture with admonitions to us to keep a close eye on the ocean for any signs of the behemoths. She emphasized the astounding nature of their existence, but slowly her excitement seemed to turn into rather plaintive pleading for us to enjoy the trip as time went on and we saw no evidence of whales. Finally we did see a solitary whale in the distance, it disappeared, then may have reappeared again briefly before disappearing permanently. She tried her best to convince us of how lucky we were to have seen such a beautiful creature, but one could tell from her voice she knew she could not alleviate the disappointment of her audience.

I reminisced that I felt similarly frustrated when I agreed to teach a class of remedial algebra to freshman at BU one year. I realized several weeks into the course I was not going to impart my wonder at mathematics to my charges, but I had to labor on with my fruitless efforts until the end of the semester.

Though I would have loved to have seen a grey whale, the tour importantly reminded me of the type of experience Sonya and her companions were going through, with long, uncertain periods of searching between brief actual encounters with their quarry.

On that day I did not mind anyway, as Marylin and I kept our arms around each other to stave off the chill and were both happy just to observe the swelling sea pulsate beneath our craft.

Time passed at a different speed on the West Coast, but my mind turned more and more to wondering what was on Gerry's floppies. Did whales have a complete language? How did they measure distance? Or time? What did prime numbers have to do with all of it? In a couple of weeks, I elicited a promise from Marylin to visit me soon and flew back to Massachusetts. That plane ride made up the loneliest six hours of my life.

18

My loneliness disappeared as soon as I entered my front foyer and smelled Marta's cabbage rolls. The next day I handed Gerry's floppy disks to Matt to put into the same format as Farrity's and Jennison's records. We looked forward to getting more data, but we also knew that we would have to translate a new whale language, because, as Sonya had warned us, the whales apparently change their songs every ten years or so. Fortunately we had already begun to do that from Sonya's data, and we had already discovered, despite the fact that each separate whale population, in fact each decade of each population, had its own dialect, there was still a lot of overlap, and the logic of all humpback languages appeared to be very similar.

In the weeks following my return from California Teddy and I made strong progress on understanding the instructions encoded in the humpbacks' singing, at least insofar as it pertained to an ongoing journey. We felt we had narrowed the precision of a destination to several hundred miles and a few days. Our task was made easier by the fact that their travels, in either the Pacific or Atlantic, were pretty regular.

Our feeling of success was tempered by the fact there was an anomalous set of voyage instructions in all language sets that seemed to be discussions of a journey to the Indian Ocean, at least if our understanding of their geometry was correct. We couldn't make out the context, but if our surmises about their geometrical language were correct, humpback whales from around the world described a destination in the Arabian Sea. Currently a population of humpbacks resides there year-round — in fact it is the only population that does not migrate. Furthermore, humpbacks from other parts of the world don't currently travel there, at least not frequently. None has ever been documented. We couldn't ignore these accounts, however, because though the actual songs they sang were quite different from each other, as the whales were living on opposite corners of the Earth and using different dialects, all the destinations were undoubtedly the same location — the Arabian Sea.

We had learned the earliest fossil records of whales came from this area as well, but that didn't explain why humpback whales in particular would all refer to this area. Our confusion was heightened by the fact that these descriptions were enmeshed in a lot of what we hypothesized was their non-mathematical language.

However, Teddy and I were confident we were on the right track. We had taken our first discovery of how they favored the prime-numbered overtones in identifying individuals in a pod, to further understanding how they used resonance in general to tune their songs when they first met, much like a guitar player uses it to tune her strings. Further, it appeared that just as we usually use base ten (or in computer language, base two) for our number system, the whales, in fact, used what I call "base prime" for their form of mathematics.

One day as we hunkered down for our daily peanut butter sandwiches I brought up the subject of numbers again. "You know, Teddy, I've spent my life manipulating numbers, but I realize I had never thought about why we need them before your explanation of how resonance may create the conditions which make them useful."

"I'm glad to have broadened your perspective," said Teddy.

"For one, it has made me see Euler's identity, $e^{i\pi} + 1 = 0$, in an entirely new light."

"How so?"

"To a mathematician, the Euler identity is like a poem. It rivals any sonnet Shakespeare ever wrote. We have marveled at it for a couple of centuries now. It is one of the best-known equations in mathematics, but it still seems to hold a secret meaning away from view."

"I know it comes from a very important equation, $e^i = \cos + i \sin$," Teddy said, "that showed the power of using imaginary numbers. I also understand that when the angle is set equal to π, then $\cos \pi = -1$ and $\sin \pi = 0$, and the formula becomes $e^{i\pi} = -1$, or $e^{i\pi} + 1 = 0$, the way you put it. But the full formula, which is essential in physics and electronics, is a more important and powerful statement, don't you think?"

"Of course, but it's like comparing a dissertation to a poem. $e^{i\pi} + 1 = 0$ contains what are considered the five most important quantities in mathematics and combines them in such a neat and tidy way that we can't help imagining it has some deep underlying meaning, but no one has ever come up with anything more than a confirmation of its validity. Obviously 'π' and 'e' are two of the most important numbers. 'π' is the ratio between the circumference of a circle and its diameter, but that does not begin to do justice to its importance. For instance it's found in Einstein's formula of general relativity, as well as Heisenberg's uncertainty principle, it is essential to describe anything to do with space, the key to describing any kind of shape. And if π is essential to talk about space, then 'e', the base for natural logarithms, is necessary to talk about anything that changes with time, which is everything, from electricity to compound interest. They are both irrational numbers, which constitute the haystack I told you about earlier. 'i', the square root of -1, on the other hand, is not even a real number but the basis of the imaginary numbers. It was the concept which allowed mathematics to explore multiple dimensions, to leave the number line, so to speak. These three numbers are truly the basis of mathematics."

"You consider them more important than integers, the numbers we actually count with?" said Teddy.

"You have admitted that numbers only become useful in a world of discrete objects with shared properties. π, e, and i would be useful in any universe. Of course, 0 and 1 are the most important numerals, which is why Euler's equation holds so much fascination, but I think we are overlooking the obvious."

"I hope you'll be so kind as to point out the obvious to me," said Teddy. A wry grin had crept onto his face.

"First, I think the equation should be written in a slightly different form. It's a convention to write an equation equal to zero to make it easier to analyze and solve, but every equation can be written that way, so the presence of '0' is superfluous. Let's write: $e^{i\pi} = -1$, as you just pointed out."

"Is that an improvement?" Teddy asked.

"You believe the phenomena we understand as particles are created by resonance with some underlying vibration of the universe, no?"

"I do."

"But in order for particles to be stable, those vibrations need to be constant."

"True. The universe we know would vaporize as soon as that vibration changed at all, because all of the particles in the universe would disappear."

"The equation $e^i = \cos + i \sin$ is really a description of how a vibration repeats itself. In mathematical terms, it maps a sine wave onto a circle. And the Euler identity, $e^{i\pi} = -1$, represents the first cycle, a single beat of a vibration. In that sense, given the universe you postulate, this equation defines the number one."

"Actually, it defines negative one," said Teddy.

"That's just a historical accident."

"Accident? A mathematical accident?"

"Sure. The Greeks defined π as the ratio between the diameter of a circle and its circumference. As a result the angle represented by π is half of a circle, and so $e^{i\pi}$ points left on the number line and represents negative one. I guess it's more accurate to say the equation represents a half beat. If they had chosen instead to use the ratio between the radius and the circumference, the number would be twice as large. We designate this number as , and radians would be a full circle and the equation would be $e^{i} = 1$. In fact, today many mathematicians think that would be a better choice for mathematics in general."

Teddy's wry smile had changed into a broad grin. "People often ask me 'what's the difference between a physicist and a mathematician?' I think you just demonstrated it admirably."

"Guilty as charged. But haven't you ever wondered that one cannot write π down exactly with numerals? It just keeps going on and on. And the same with e. Yet this simple equation gives an exact and concise relationship between all of these quantities. And it illuminates the basis of how digits arise out of vibration."

"You may be right, but frankly I still can't visualize what it means."

"But that makes it even more important!" I said.

"Why is not understanding something important?"

"Because it shows us our brains have been evolved to understand the environment we perceive, but in physics we are trying to describe a universe totally unlike anything we normally perceive. For instance, the equation 2+2=4 is easy for us. We can imagine having two cookies, and then being given two more, voila, we have four cookies. But the reality of our universe is, as your own studies show, the discrete items we use numbers to keep track of are a result of an opaque process of the universe resonating to an evidently complex multimodal system of vibrations, and that is not the type of reality our brains have been evolved to visualize."

Ever the physicist, Teddy said, "I see your point, but I'd better stick to trying to discover how matter is formed."

Teddy returned to his seat, but instead of resuming his work, he turned to me. "You know, it's funny how our fields are so rigorous, so dependent on facts, on research, on proper protocols, that it's easy to lose sight of the fact that there is so much chance in actually making a new discovery."

"How do you mean?" I asked.

"Well, it took me studying full time until I was thirty just to be able to earn my PhD and actually start working. And ever since then I've had to study every day to keep up with the field, but my important work actually consists of trying to discover which ideas among what I've learned aren't true."

"That's pretty much what Carolyn said was Harold Jennison's mantra."

"Really?"

"Yeah. He'd say, 'If you don't believe, you can't learn anything; if you aren't suspicious, you can't learn anything new.'"

"Beautiful. I think I've just gained new respect for the man." Teddy paused for a while, and I assumed he was returning to work, but then he spoke up again. "Do you know how the Big Bang got its name?"

"If I recall, the mathematics of the expansion of the universe, if carried back in time, leads to a singularity, that is, it seems to collapse to an infinitely small point. So, it appears that the universe just came into existence out of nothing, like an explosion."

"Well, that was the theory more or less, but the actual phrase was coined by Fred Hoyle, who adamantly disagreed with the whole idea. It's kind of ironic to me, because Hoyle's opposition to the idea of the Big Bang crippled his own career. More than once he has been called the greatest physicist who never won the Nobel Prize, and it's said to be largely for that reason."

"And the irony is that his name stuck?"

"I've come to believe it's much more than that. Of course it's a wonderful, evocative phrase, but I think it's unfortunate in that it did exactly what Hoyle wanted it to do."

"I don't understand. He lost the argument. Do you think he was right?"

"Not at all. Remember, I am trying to create a theory of how matter is created by resonance to some primordial vibration."

"Of course, we just went over that."

"So, as I started to work it out, I realized time, space, and force may also be created by the same phenomenon. In fact, the more I think about, the surer I am."

"I can see how that would make sense."

"Well, as you know, every explanation of cosmic expansion points out that the expansion of the universe is not an expansion into pre-existing space, but an expansion of space itself."

"True. So how does that relate to Hoyle's phrase?"

"Well, I started by postulating that this vibration must at least have four degrees of freedom."

"Is that because we have a four-dimensional universe?"

"That, and because there are also four forces. Of course there may be more. There is a convenient math for eight dimensions, but let's assume it's four for now."

"Okay, but what does that have to do with calling the origin of the universe the Big Bang?"

"I haven't proven my theorem yet, but I believe I'm right, and I wonder if more progress could have been made if someone who viewed the idea more favorably had provided the accepted moniker."

"Like what?"

"Right now my own favorite name is The Primordial Chord".

"Primordial Chord, very nice."

"I imagine the chord as being like a tuning fork one uses to get an orchestra in tune."

"And then the universe, existence in fact, is the symphony?"

"Something like that, although, as you pointed out, the original chord has to keeping vibrating, like a drone string on a sitar. Of course, one would need to presume someone in the fifties already had my approach in mind for them to give it such a name, but the thing about calling the beginning the Big Bang is that it just jumbles everything together. I think it has affected everyone working in the field since then. It makes everything inexplicable."

"Interesting. That's certainly how I've seen it, but I'm not really a physicist. The Primordial Chord gives one a lot more to think about."

"Exactly. At the least it indicates the beginning of the universe might have a complex structure. And, of course, it plays into my own theory that particles are formed from the resonant modalities of that Primordial Chord."

"I think you've trumped me, Teddy."

"How do you mean?"

"As much as I'd like to explain Euler's identity or prove Riemann's conjecture, they pale in comparison to explaining the Big Bang ... that is, the Primordial Chord."

Teddy's normally placid face almost beamed with appreciation at my self-correction. "Of course, neither one of us has succeeded yet."

"I'm sure it's just a matter of time, Teddy." With that, we both returned to our respective tasks, though if I recall correctly we left his office earlier than usual that afternoon so we could continue our discussions on chords and primes.

19

One day as I was wandering around Cambridge thinking about primes and Riemann's hypothesis I almost tripped over my old friend Flora.

"Joe? You are Joe, aren't you?" she said as I apologized.

"Flora! Yes, I'm Joe Tenatt. You remembered me."

"Of course I did, it's not often one finds someone with such natural spiritual strength as yourself."

I didn't want to get into a discussion of chakras or whatever, so I tried to think of a way to politely extricate myself from her company, when she asked me if I still thought whales were mathematicians.

"As a matter of fact, I do. My colleague and I think we have deciphered their code enough to predict where they are going to go." I let that sink in for a moment, trying to subtly rub in the fact I was right all along. Flora didn't respond, so I continued, "Right now we are wrestling with the interesting fact that humpback whales from all oceans describe an event in the Arabian Sea, a place where there is an isolated local population, but where no other humpbacks currently travel to." I thought that would stump Flora, and I would be able to take my leave, but for the first time she showed an interest in what I said.

"That's amazing. Maybe they all used to meditate with yogis from the Indus River Valley." The first time I had met Flora had been under streetlights and I hadn't been able to make out her features or coloring well. As I looked at her now, I saw her eyes were an intense dark green, a color I don't believe I had ever seen in eyes, in human eyes at least. Maybe in cats. Her skin was olive, smooth, nearly wrinkle-free, but I was sure she was at least in her forties. She had long, straight, very black hair. I realized she could have been from India herself, although there was no trace of an accent in her speech.

"Meditating?"

"Of course. That's where yoga started for humans. There are talismans from then that show yogis meditating with animals. Why not whales? Maybe the original yogis learned to meditate from whales. That would certainly be consistent with my knowledge of whales."

"But surely there are no talismans of people and whales meditating together?"

Flora took a long time to answer me. "I still don't know if you're putting me on or not, Joe. By the way, your Anahata and Vishuddha chakras have developed since our last visit. Anyway, there is a very strange legend about the Indus civilization. It was very developed, the most advanced and largest of all the ancient civilizations, but it completely disappeared. There are remains of ancient cities, such as Harappa and Mohenjo-Daro, but there's a lack of cohesiveness to the whole of the civilization. It's believed there is a sunken city off the coast of the current state of Gujarat that was the capital of the entire civilization."

"Has it ever been found?"

"Unfortunately, no. It's hard to do archeological studies in that area now due to the extreme religious intolerance of the current population."

The next time I was at Teddy and Marta's apartment I mentioned I needed to brush up on the Indus River Valley civilization. I related my conversation with Flora.

"You should just talk to Jaime Huddersfield instead of going the library," Marta said. "You remember Jaime, don't you?" she asked Teddy.

"Sure, and his crazy wife."

"Crazy?" Marta asked.

"At least flamboyant." Teddy turned to me. "She's a professor of drama, and has to be at least twenty years younger than Jaime."

Marta scowled at Teddy briefly, then continued, "Anyway, you want to talk to Jaime, not Ginny. He's in the anthropology department at Northeastern. Once he gets going, though, you may not be able to stop him."

I was able to schedule a lunch date with Jaime later that week. "Any friend of Marta is a friend of mine. I think my wife has a crush on her," he said over the phone. I didn't relay Teddy's comments or Marta's scowl to him.

We met in the cafeteria at Boston's Museum of Fine Arts. "I spend more time here than on campus," he said. "Did you say you wanted to talk about the Harappan Civilization?"

I recounted my conversation with Flora. Jaime grinned when I was finished. "It's interesting seeing a set of facts one is familiar with in an entirely new, even alien, context. It's true the treatment of sewage was more advanced in the cities of the Indus River Valley than in any of the contemporary great civilizations. It is also true there are seals from that era that depict human figures in what could be a yogic sitting position, and that animals are also shown on the same seals. Whether or not they are all meditating together I can't say."

"Isn't that where yoga started?"

"The Harappan civilization completely died out as far as we know. We didn't even know it existed until a century ago. Yoga must have started somewhere in India, perhaps there."

"Flora claims there's a sunken city off the coast that was the capital of the area."

"I've heard that story, but there's no concrete evidence to that effect." Jaime looked at me as though he was trying to decide how to phrase what he wanted to say next. "It would make sense though. We know there was significant trade between this area and Sumeria, and it seems Egypt as well. In fact, there is evidence there was even some trade with southern Africa. It appears gold-mining techniques used in what is now South Africa came from India, and some gold in ancient Indian jewelry is of African origin. And yet we have not found any major Harappan seaports. A sunken city would explain a lot." He looked at me as if to discover if I made too much of his uncertainty.

"What I want to know is whether there is any mention of whales in their records."

"I don't know of any pictures, but of course all of the seals and talismans we have are from inland cities. And we haven't deciphered their writing. So, we just don't know. We don't know much about them at all, just that they had a phenomenal sewage system."

Jaime Huddersfield and I spoke for another half hour, until his class showed up. "We're going to look at the Egyptian exhibit. Would you care to join us?"

I declined and left not knowing much more than when I had arrived. When I returned home a young woman was sitting on my front steps. "Dr. Tenatt?" she said. It was a question, but there was no doubt in her tone.

"Yes. And you are?"

"My name is Joanne DiLeonardo." She stood up to shake my hand. Joanne was a few years older than Sonya, and somewhat more austere in countenance. She had a serious look and the kind of eyes we call hazel, which is to say they were multi-colored, and, like a chameleon, they changed color with their surroundings. She surveyed me as if to discover hidden meanings in my actions, and she followed my words as if they too contained hidden meanings. Her hair was short and brown, her skin was also brown, which wasn't surprising, considering she had been living on a ship for two years. "Can we go inside?"

"If you've anything important to say, that's probably not a good idea." We stared at each other for a moment. "Meet me at Huxley's Coffee, don't get there before three," I said, and gave her directions. I figured that would give me enough time to hang out at the cafe for a while before she arrived. I knew Huxley's well enough to know if someone new or unusual was around. I felt I had actually learned something from my old buddy Clive.

As I watched her walk away I noted her deliberative movements. She had something she considered important on her mind.

I made it to Huxley's by 2:30. Clive's table in the empty hall was taken, so I sat at another in the farthest corner of one of the rooms, with my back to the wall, a la Wild Bill. There were a few students scattered among the tables, but no one else entered the room until Joanne walked in at 3:10.

She sat down and said, "I've just left the *Grinsby.*"

"You mean you've quit?"

"Yes." Joanne was very deliberate in her speech.

"Do they know?"

"Yes, I didn't pull a Gerry. That would be a good way to attract attention, which I don't want."

"Have you done anything to be afraid?"

"Just by getting involved. I didn't abscond with my official notes like Gerry, either."

"So, what's going on?"

"It's a long story. May I call you Joe?"

"Please do. And take your time."

"That whole outfit is creepy. Sonya must have told you something about the project."

"She did, and she felt the same way."

"I know. She's a bright kid."

I found it kind of funny the way Joanne called Sonya a kid when there couldn't have been more than five years difference between them, and they were both less than half my age, but I didn't say anything on that subject. "She told me about the electronic eavesdropping," I said.

"Sure, start with that, and the fact they wanted our input but didn't want us to learn anything. Sonya told me you said there were previous expeditions."

"At least two." I was willing to tell Joanne everything I knew, but I didn't want to distract her from her story.

"But what made me leave was I was afraid of the whales."

"The whales?"

"Yeah, they're angry at the *Grinsby.* Very angry. And I can't blame them."

"What's going on?"

"You know I'm a linguist, right?"

"Yes."

"And I've made some headway in understanding them. Sonya says you've made some progress deciphering their instructions."

"We're treating it like mathematics. We think we understand some of their code."

"The operative word being *some*?"

"True."

"Anyway, I think they're basically the same as us. Most of the time they're occupied with living, mostly eating and breeding and raising their young. But sometimes, especially in their winter home, I think they're telling stories."

"Would you like to come to my computer lab? I could play some of their songs for you, we could compare notes."

Joanne didn't hesitate. "No, I'm going to tell you what I know here, and you will never hear from me again."

"Okay."

"Thank you for accepting my terms. Anyway, I've come to believe they are recounting both the near and far past. And one passage in particular I think is like a retelling of a horrific episode in their history, I think it was a bloodbath."

"You're kidding."

"If you knew me, you would know I am not kidding. Here." She handed me two floppy disks. "I didn't keep my official notes, but these are my personal ones. In some ways, they have more information than the official ones. I used these to record all my speculations."

"So how did this bloodbath occur? Who would have attacked the whales like that before the last three centuries?"

"I think the whales did the attacking. But it may have been some kind of suicide attack. They say they used their voices."

"You mean in their story?"

"Yes. I'm not sure what they mean."

"Could it be using resonance?"

"How would that work? You mean like an opera singer breaking glass with a powerful high note?"

"Exactly. It's not just the strength of the note that's important. It has to be at just the right pitch to cause the glass to vibrate until it shatters."

Joanne looked a little surprised at this thought, then said, "I hadn't thought of that specifically, but it probably means I'm right. I tried to get Sonya to leave as well, but she didn't think we should quit together." Joanne stared past me at the blank wall behind me for a while. I could see she was gathering her thoughts, so I just sipped on my coffee until she was ready. "As I said, the navy knows more than they let us in on. Recently they have been talking to the humpbacks."

"Sonya told me the navy had decided they didn't have a real language."

"I think they have their doubts. Anyway, I gave them a few phrases I thought might make sense, and then they just made up other stuff, some which sounded similar to what whales actually sing, some was just garbled whale sounds. I should say they were talking *at* the whales, and at first the whales seemed to think it was other whales, and responded accordingly. But at some point they figured us out. I think it pissed them off."

"Gerry also said he thought they were angry at us."

"He did, but this is new, more intense. They started making very loud sounds, and often there were many more whales in the pod than usual."

"Do you think they were yelling at you?"

"I did, until just now. They were actually capable of making our ship shudder. Maybe they want to pull your opera singer's stunt. It was very unnerving."

"Shudder?"

"I have a very good ear for sound."

"Are you a musician?"

"Yes, in fact, I used to play piano. And sing."

"Used to? Did you quit?"

"It wasn't intentional, I just have moved around too much. Maybe when

162

I settle down, I'll start up again. I'm no virtuoso, I play mostly standards, a little jazzy, but like I said, I have a good ear for sound, as I think you'll find when you listen to my cassettes. Anyway, now that you brought up resonance, it did seem they were tuning up, trying to make the ship shudder, then they'd back off."

"Maybe they're trying to scare you?"

"Possibly. I just didn't want to be part of hassling the whales, and my superior officer didn't take it very well when I voiced my objections. I kind of felt it was best I just leave. It wasn't much of a job anyway, not what I expected."

"How was Sonya doing?"

"I think she feels the same way I do. She told me to give you my notes, that's why I'm here. Now I just want to forget the whole thing."

"I think that's a good idea."

"I expected you to try to convince me to help you."

"I'd love that, under normal circumstances, but these aren't normal circumstances. Frankly, you should assume you're being watched. I'm assuming they already know we have met."

"What if they catch you with those tapes? What are you going to do with them?"

"I don't want to be rude, but you don't need to know, so it's best you don't know."

"Is it that bad?"

"Maybe."

Joanne left before I did, and although she seemed to be, as Sonya had told me, a thoughtful and sincere person, I hoped I would never see or hear of her again. Before I left, though, I had to consider whether or not I wanted to carry her floppies around and decided not to chance it. I had tried to be careful since my first clandestine meeting with Sonya and had come to the conclusion I was no longer being closely surveilled. Of course, out of caution I still assumed my apartment was bugged. But I did assume Joanne might be watched for at least a while after leaving her ship, and for now, so might I.

I considered leaving the disks with the barista but concluded that would be too obvious. Instead, I wandered over to the bathroom. The ceiling was a little low and consisted of a grid of the dreary fiber panels all offices and public buildings seem to have. By standing on the toilet seat, I was able to touch the ceiling. There was something holding down the first tile I tried, so I moved to the next stall. This time I could lift a tile up just enough to slip the cassettes into the plenum above the ceiling. That done, I decided to head for home, but no more than a block from Huxley's I was stopped by a couple of city cops, or at least they were dressed as police.

"Hey, buddy, what's up?" one of them said to me. They were both broad men with red faces and serious eyes.

"Nothing, just enjoying the evening."

"Maybe doing a little business?"

"No, I'm a retired mathematician, there's not much need of that in a coffee shop."

I knew what was coming, but I wanted to remain non-confrontational.

"Maybe doing a little something on the side, a little dealing?"

"No."

"Then you won't mind if we look in your pockets?"

Of course I minded greatly, and under normal circumstances I would make that clear, but in this situation I felt if I let them search me now I might avoid a future home invasion. "Sure, go ahead," I said, as I raised my arms over my head and let them thoroughly paw me. When they were done I lowered my arms, but didn't move. The two cops glared at me for a while, then one of them said, "Okay, you can go for now."

"Thank you. I appreciate what you guys do for us." They glared at me some more as I left.

I hoped that would be the last I saw of Navy Intelligence, but the next morning, as I was drinking my coffee, I heard a knock on my door. I opened it to see two navy officers in uniform. They were going from surreptitious to direct.

"Mr. Tenatt?" one of them asked. These men were taller and thinner than the cops from the previous evening. They looked more dangerous.

"*Dr.* Tenatt," I said.

"Dr. Joseph Tenatt. May we call you Joseph?"

"I prefer Dr. Tenatt. What do you want?"

"We're here to talk to you about the woman you were with last night."

"You mean Ms. DiLeonardo?"

"Yes, Joanne DiLeonardo. May we come in?"

I didn't mind being rude today, I didn't want to let them think I was intimidated or had any reason to be worried. "No, I'm just leaving. What do you want?"

"What was the nature of your visit?"

"She was visiting me. It was personal."

"May we ask what you talked about?"

"You can ask, but I'll tell you it's none of your business."

As my interlocutors were deciding what to do next, I stepped into the hall, locked the door behind me, and began to descend the stairs as fast I as I could. I wasn't trying to outrun them, just surprise them. "Pardon me, there's something I need to ask my neighbor before she leaves for work," I said.

The navy officers skipped down the stairs, much quicker than I, when they realized what I was going to do. They exited the front door as I knocked on Marta's. I didn't care if she were home, but as luck would have it she hadn't yet left for work.

"Good morning, Joe. What's up?"

"There's something I want to show you outside. But pretend we're going to look at your flowers."

She immediately understood she should just follow my instructions. As we passed through the front door, a US Navy car that had been parked directly in front of our house sped away with a quick screech of its wheels. The passenger, who was on the near side, was leaning forward, his face out of sight. I began to laugh.

"What was that about?" Marta said.

"Two Navy Intelligence officers were quizzing me about Joanne DiLeonardo, and it occurred to me they wouldn't want you to see them."

"Why not? Why were they quizzing you about Joanne DiLeonardo?"

As I turned toward Marta, Teddy also came outside. "What's going on?"

"You must remember Joanne DiLeonardo was the name of the linguist on Sonya's project. She has left the *Grinsby* and came to see me last night. While those two clowns were interrogating me, I realized they wouldn't want you to see them. I think they're the two you almost shot."

"I didn't almost shoot them, Joe."

"Close enough. Anyway, I told them I had to see you and they took off, like bats out of hell."

"Do bats leave hell that quickly?" Teddy asked. "I always thought they might enjoy it there."

"It's a saying, Teddy. And maybe they're leaving to do more damage more quickly elsewhere," I said.

"Is Sonya okay? What did this Joanne have to say?" Marta asked.

"I think she's fine. Invite me in for coffee and I'll tell you."

We went inside and I recounted Joanne's conversation and what happened after. "I haven't been back to retrieve the disks."

"I could do that," Teddy said.

"I almost fell off the toilet stuffing them overhead, Teddy, and you're shorter than me. Besides, we don't want them around here anyway. Maybe I should ask Matt."

"I think that's a good idea," Marta said. As usual, her vote was the one that counted.

Teddy and I walked to his office that morning. It was a miserable day, spring often leaves with a vengeance in Massachusetts. The walk normally took just over an hour, but I think it took us twice as long that morning. I remember thinking we might get blown off the Mass Ave Bridge, the gusts were so powerful. None of this mattered to us — we were fascinated and perplexed by the possibilities before us. We talked ourselves hoarse trying to shout over the wind, but in the end we knew we needed to analyze Joanne's notes if we hoped to make any headway.

Once we were off the bridge and among the buildings, the wind was more constrained and we could easily converse again. In order to pass the time I decided to question Teddy about what more he had learned about primes.

Teddy had an electric tea kettle in his office, and a stash of exquisite English tea for the right occasion. This appeared to be one such time. As he prepared us both a cup, I said, "Do you remember how we wondered what kind of metric humpbacks could use if they had developed a mathematics?"

"I do, and I'm not sure you've fully explained that to me."

"You're right, and I still haven't fully explained it to myself, but I believe it is related to another question just as important."

"And that is…?" he said as he handed me a pleasantly hot cup.

"How do they remember things with precision, their location, past trips, anything?"

"Good question."

"Our mathematical symbols are visual mnemonic devices we use to keep track of the relationship developed while doing math."

"True. Oliver Heaviside had a great quote about that, but I can't quite remember how it went."

"I'm sure it was accurate and to the point, he was a unique and profound mathematician. But whales cannot produce permanent records — they need to do everything from memory."

"Like Homer. He was blind, of course, and recited both the *Iliad* and *Odyssey* from memory. Scholars believe the repetitive form of his epics comes from the need to remember them."

"I hadn't thought about Homer, but he is a case in point. Another example is the manner in which South Pacific Islanders keep track of time and distance with their chants."

"We heard a group of them sing in Warsaw," Teddy said. "They were spellbinding."

I didn't want to get off track discussing beautiful music. "I've only heard a few recordings myself, and they were beautiful, but my point is that they are crafted to keep track of time over long voyages, to allow the sailors, or rather rowers, to navigate by the stars. They change the octave of their chants in a regular pattern to mark long periods of time. Remember, without a good clock, the heavens can only reveal your longitude. That is what I think the whales do."

"You think they navigate by the stars?"

"No, I think their songs help them measure how far they travel. Only instead of all of the octaves, they use the prime-numbered overtones."

"I would say ingenious, but of course I believe that's what the universe does as well. By the way, I've been thinking about Riemann's hypothesis."

I'm sure I stared at Teddy when he said this. "You haven't proven it, have you?"

"No, nothing like that. But didn't you say that in every non-trivial solution equal to zero, the real part always equals one half?"

"Exactly one half."

"I was just thinking that in the scheme of things, one half is a very interesting quantity."

"How so?"

"As you remember, both energy and matter are always quantized."

"Of course."

"That means all of the information in or about the universe can be written in digital format, specifically zeroes and ones. And if you average all those digits I'm sure you'd get one half."

"Do you think that's important?" I asked.

"I have no idea. I don't even know if Riemann's hypothesis is important."

Some other time I might have been interested in pursuing Teddy's line of thought, but at the time I had whale mnemonics on my mind. "Anyway, I believe I have come up with a scheme the humpbacks use, based on primes."

"What's that?"

"It appears that they have several songs they sing. I'm not even sure which song they sing at any particular moment matters. They're all about the same length, and that does matter."

Teddy looked at me as if I were speaking a language he did not understand, and which he knew I did not understand either. "So?"

"The trick is they modulate them by a prime number sequence."

"How does that work?"

"Well, they start by singing one of their songs, each of which lasts about a day and a half, thirty-six hours. When they finish one they start over in the 'key' of the next prime number. They seem to know that when they reach a certain pitch, say seventeen, they might have to change direction."

"And they can sing high enough for their entire trip?"

"Easily. Humpback whales have a vocal range of around eight octaves, from thirty hertz to eight thousand hertz. The eighth octave is 256 whole overtones above the fundamental, and there are fifty-six prime numbers in that interval, so theoretically they could go over eighty days. I think their longest journey is about eight and a half weeks, or sixty days."

"Interesting. I wonder how they find the prime overtones."

"I think I've figured that out as well. It's kind of like singing in rounds."

"Rounds?"

"Like Frère Jacques, or Row, Row, Row Your Boat."

"I don't know what those are."

"Like the Canon 7 of Bach's Musical Offering."

"Oh, of course! How does that work in this case?"

"So, one of the males blows the fundamental, and then other whales join in harmony, singing the next whole overtones until one whale sings an overtone that only belongs to the first whale's voice. It's like the Sieve of Eratosthenes. Actually, I haven't figured out how they get past the second octave. The overtones of the fundamental become pretty weak. They appear to have the ability to memorize the difference between the original whole tones, which obviously can change, as every male has a different fundamental pitch."

"There is much to learn."

"I guess that's why we like doing what we do."

20

That evening I took the MBTA to Matt and Jeannie's. I always felt welcome at their place, but they both had begun to travel extensively, so I was never sure if I would see either one. I could have called from a pay-phone, but I was so preoccupied with Joanne's visit, I decided to just go to their place and hope for the best. As it turned out both of my friends were home. They were involved in a serious conversation in front of the house when I arrived, but they welcomed me and invited me in.

"We just got home ourselves. I've been in Paris and Matt flew in from New Orleans this afternoon," Jeannie said.

"The weather's a hell of a lot nicer in Louisiana right now," Matt said. "Spring is not my favorite season here."

"I should try somewhere else sometime," I said, "but it's nicer now than it was this morning."

"Ah, but we understand you've been in California again recently," Jeannie said. "And you made it without me." If she was trying embarrass me, she succeeded.

I updated them on my trip to Marfa, meeting Gerry, and then explained a little about Joanne's visit, as well as the navy's obvious concern she might be spreading information they want kept secret. I included my encounters with the cops and navy officers. "I think she really irritated them when she protested over their treatment of the whales."

"Why do you think they even use civilians?" Matt asked.

"Not sure. Sonya says they want to show they're taking the welfare of whales seriously, even though for military reasons in the end they feel they need to continue using low-frequency sonar no matter what damage it does to the environment, and to cetaceans in particular. After all, the military is a professional risk-taking institution, and this is just one more gambit."

Matt opened a bottle of wine and Jeannie whipped up a delicious stew she had previously frozen. "To homecoming," he toasted.

"Amen," said Jeannie. And we sat down to a small feast.

"What were you doing in Paris, Jeannie?" I said.

"A lot. Too much. I'm in a new string quartet, but this one has a European base. Two French violinists, Guy Blaise and Marie Giroux, and a renowned Spanish violist, Sophie Abele. I loved my old group, but everyone had other duties, and it just became too hard. And frankly, this is a step up. It's funny — on the one hand, the more famous you become the more in demand you are, so you're busier. On the other hand, you can choose what you do, so in a way it's more relaxed. And together we offered a master class at the École Normale de Musique de Paris. It was a lot of fun. Oh, and before I forget, Armando and Lorna came to one of my concerts in Paris, and then had dinner with my group. They're such a lovely couple."

"They are indeed."

"Did you know Lorna's great-grandfather was a famous Mexican classical musician and composer, Manuel Ponce? I promised her we would play one of his pieces if she came to Paris again."

"I'm jealous. I guess I'll have to make it over there too, if I want to hear you. How about you, Matt?"

"I had to make an emergency trip to the Jazz and Heritage Festival. I'm supposed to be in Charlottesville right now, but my crew has that under control, so I flew home to see Jeannie. But it's good to see you too."

"Before I forget, I have a favor to ask. I hope you're not leaving again tonight."

"He'd better not be," said Jeannie. She was smiling but not joking.

"No, nothing like that," said Matt. "What's up?"

"Joanne gave me a couple of floppy disks of her notes. I thought I might be followed, so I stuffed them in the ceiling of Huxley's bathroom. It turns out I was followed, and I don't want to go get them myself, I don't want to have them at my place, so I thought you might retrieve them in a day or two."

"I can do that. Do you think the navy tracked you here?"

"No, I think they're going for the obvious. They will probably try to keep close track of Joanne for a while. If they're watching Huxley's to see if she returns there, and I show up, they might stop me again." I explained where the floppies were, we had a couple more glasses of wine, then I left early so they could spend some obviously much needed time together.

One of the breakthroughs Teddy and I had accomplished was to develop a computer program that parsed and compared the Cetacean words and phrases from our whale tapes. This greatly reduced the amount of time Jeannie, Marta, Teddy and I had to spend trying to ferret them out with our instruments. We were excited by our work but were faced with the fact we still didn't know what most of the singing meant. We hoped Joanne's tapes would help us advance on that front.

It took several days for Matt to get back in touch with us. Everyone knew no one should use my phone for important calls, but we had no reason not to trust Marta and Teddy's phone. One day Matt called in the evening while we were struggling through a piece by Bartók. Marta spoke a few words and handed the handset to me.

"Hi Joe, I've got a gift for you." It was Matt's voice.

"That's nice, what is it?

"It's a surprise."

"When do I get it?"

"It's ready now. Why don't you drop by tomorrow evening?"

"Great. I'll bring Marta and Teddy. I'll supply the pizza."

"We have plenty of beer. See you then."

I had made the date without consulting my friends, but they were willing and able, as I had presumed. The next evening I ordered pizzas from a place near Jeannie and Matt's, then called them so they could pick it up hot. The Witkowskis and I trundled onto the subway from Teddy's office, as Marta had walked over the few blocks from the New England Conservatory. We hadn't all been together for several months. We were excited to see our friends and find out what information Joanne had left us.

Jeannie greeted us at the door, and Matt arrived a few minutes later with several large pizzas. Before we started eating Matt went over to his stereo and turned it on. "You have got to hear this," he said.

Over the speakers we heard Joanne's voice. For several minutes she explained her methodology: she would attempt to mimic a whale phrase, then explain how she believed the phrase was used. As we listened to her narration we sat down to our meal. Finally, her introductory explanations were done, and she began her demonstrations. At the first sound of her singing we all stopped and put our food down. Obviously her pitch was much higher than a whale's, but other than that she sounded very much like one of them. We had been justifiably proud of our ability to mimic the whale's phrases with our instruments and to differentiate minuscule nuances in their voices, but our work was crude compared to Joanne's. I don't think any of us listened to her explanations the first time we heard the cassettes, or the second time either, as Matt played them for us twice that evening. I do know our pizzas were cold when he finally turned his system off. We looked at each other, dumbfounded, for several minutes.

"We have just heard genius," Marta finally said.

"I just wonder how we're going to integrate this with our work," said Matt.

"I may have an answer," I said. "One of the things Teddy and I have managed to do is computerize the work we have done on our instruments. I don't think it will be difficult to expand our program to be able to include Joanne's voice. If her commentaries are as brilliant as her mimicry, this should help us a great deal. By the way, Matt, how do Gerry's disks look?"

"Also brilliant. It's a shame the navy didn't want to sincerely include these people into their research. They chose some fine minds. I think the tapes are ready for you now."

"The only bad news," I said, "is we won't have an excuse to meet here so often. I will miss that."

Jeannie and Matt exchanged glances. "That will make what we have to say a little easier though," Jeannie said. "Matt and I are going to sell this place."

"Where are you going to live?" asked Marta. "Not moving far, I hope."

"Well, yes, I'm afraid so," Jeannie said. "I'm spending much more time in Europe, and as I told Joe the other day, I've joined a European quartet, and also have a position at the École Normale de Musique de Paris. So, it makes sense for me to have an apartment in Paris."

"Are you separating?" Marta said.

"No, of course not," said Matt. "This place is much too small for my company. We've been working out of two warehouses recently, one in Waltham, as you know, and one in Denver. I fly around so much anyway, getting to Paris is almost as easy as coming here." No one said anything for a while. We knew we were basically saying goodbye to Jeannie and Matt, at least for a while. Before the Witkowskis or I could respond, Matt continued. "Of course the Waltham warehouse will still be available anytime you need to listen to high-quality recordings. I don't mind continuing to keep all of the records, and Joe has already met Richie, the warehouse manager. I have a large climate-controlled safe there, I'm sure we can work out the details of how you can use them when needed."

"The VAX does a good job of picking out the phrases now, so I guess we won't have to do that very often," I said.

"But I'm sure I speak for all three of us when I say we're sorry we're going to be seeing a lot less of you," Teddy said. Marta and I agreed.

For all the wonder and advancement of the evening, we left with a little sadness. We were delighted for the career successes of our friends, of course, but we still felt our own loss.

21

Before I continue, I will quote a few lines from Joanne's introduction to her notes:

> *All linguists, whether they agree with Noam Chomsky or not, are familiar with, and need to take heed of, his concept that a universal grammar underlies all human languages. There may even be a few stalwart followers of Dr. Chomsky who would try to extend this same universal grammar beyond human language, but from what I have learned of whales, I think we should set aside any such notion. Linguistic structures such as person (I, you, it), singularity and plurality, subject and object, possessiveness, or even shortcuts such as pronouns and contractions, do not exist in humpback communication.*
>
> *Instead, I think we need to consider their language to be a cross between painting and musical composition. Paintings, of course, have long been used to tell stories, but they lack the dynamic aspect of whale communication. The closest idea in music that I am aware of comes from composers such as Mussorgsky (Pictures at an Exhibition, for instance), or Debussy. However, that is only to a point, for it would be a mistake to not realize how specific their language can be in conveying ideas.*
>
> *Before getting into the actual sounds, I will try to give an example of this with the concept to go, to travel, or to swim, which are all more or less denoted by the same sound in Cetacean. For simplicity's sake, let us say this idea is denoted by the human sound "swim". Now, each whale has its own base pitch, and so a simple utterance of this sound at its base pitch would more or less mean "I am swimming," except the whales listening to this would know which whale was singing, so we must not imagine there is a real pronoun involved. If it uttered the same sound with some gurgling overtones, it would mean "we are swimming," and the more gurgling, the larger the indicated group. If it sang louder,*

it means "I (or we) are swimming fast." And if it stretched it out (III aaammmssssswwwiiimmmiiinnnnnggg), it would indicate "I am swimming for a long time." This begins to bring tense into the picture, but more of that later.

Note that these sounds, like music, can meld together. I will attempt to show a sample of a young whale expressing a concept we might translate as "I enjoy frolicking with other whales," as well as adults exclaiming, "We're getting tired of this trip," all using this single sound and its transformations. [At this point she sang a couple of beautiful, lilting phrases, quite distinct from each other, but with unmistakable similarities.] Before going on with this type of explanation, though, it is necessary to understand at least a small catalogue of such sounds, a basic vocabulary, as it were.

After this brief introduction, Joanne proceeded to mimic many of the whales' intonations. Her ability to do this is what left my colleagues and me so amazed at our dinner meeting. She was able to do with her voice what we had attempted to do with our instruments. She was greatly aided by the fact that she appeared to understand what the whales were saying. I will relegate to an appendix the technical details of her discoveries and speak now of what she learned about the mysterious epic whales all over the world sang about.

Biologists already know the lives of humpback whales are centered on the yearly migration from breeding ground to feeding ground. Each population, with the exception of the Indian Ocean humpbacks, goes to the Arctic or Antarctic region in the summer to feed, and then migrates back toward the equator to breed. Before a migration Joanne picked up the same idea we had — a male would sing out instructions for the trip. Naturally these songs were very similar from year to year. During the migrations they would edit the song a little, perhaps to account for changing conditions, perhaps to gauge their progress. Her ideas were very much in alignment with my own concept of how they sing in what I call base prime. She pointed out, as I had also discovered, that though it is the male voices we have been familiar with, the females and young sing as well, albeit more softly.

Joanne noticed, as we already had ourselves, that during the breeding season, when they are not actually traveling, the whales also appeared to sing a song about a different journey. These were the songs we felt referred to traveling to the Arabian Sea, a fact Joanne hadn't discovered. What she did postulate through her knowledge of the Cetacean concepts of time was these journeys were placed in the deep past, and they recounted a horrific scene where a huge number of whales were destroyed.

Joanne likened these tales to ancient human epics, such as *The Iliad* or the Bhagavad Gita. But according to her, the overriding emotion was sorrow, not victory or pride, for there was immense destruction on all sides.

As Joanne had told me, she hadn't thought of the concept of resonance, but she had noticed a similarity in some of the phrasing in the ancient tales with the ominous phrases accompanying the situations when they began to circle the *Grinsby* and cause the ship to shudder. In an aside at one point, she recalled a discussion she once had with Gerry, in which he came close to predicting a strong reaction from the whales before he left the ship.

Gerry, as I knew, felt the whales were angry at the ship, and likely at all humans, but I had more or less discounted Gerry's ideas as resulting from his generally bleak attitude. In fact, he was evidently not only accurate in his assessment of the whales, he pretty much nailed the human arrogance embodied by the navy.

According to Joanne's account, she had been able to isolate some of the language that accompanied this perceived anger. Her notes indicated she felt this language had greatly intensified after the whales discovered the navy was broadcasting fake whale messages to them. It was at this time she protested to her supervisor and was told more or less she could take a hike home on the water if she wished.

We continued to enter data into one of Teddy's VAX computers and work on the software we had invented to break down the songs into their constituent phrases, and now, with the help of Joanne's work, even decipher their meanings. Teddy, Marta and I would also discuss the possibilities of the ancient tale we only had glimpses of. These discussions were so involved that some evenings we wouldn't even break out our instruments. We were interested in two main issues: first, who or what had the humpbacks been fighting? We considered it might have been two populations of humpbacks, or even two different whale species, having a battle. In that case the supposed lost city off the Gujarat shore might just have been collateral damage. Or maybe there was no connection — the area is known to be prone to major earthquakes. Or maybe the city never existed. Or if it did, perhaps we were looking at two separate, unrelated events. After all, we had no idea when the events of the whale epic took place.

But what if there was a connection? There were indications in the whale account humans were involved. Joanne had discovered enough about the whales' language to know when they referred to humans and therefore was able to recognize when they did so in their epic as well. What did that mean?

We had familiarized ourselves with the so called "yogic" talismans. They did indeed appear to show men sitting in a meditative position surrounded by various animals. Perhaps whales and human civilization had interacted, but in the throes of a dying civilization, something had gone wrong. Perhaps the whales had been attacked or betrayed. Perhaps one segment of the human society had betrayed the goodwill of another, and the whales blamed everyone. Perhaps they had destroyed the civilization after a battle, or destroyed its capital, which led to the demise of the rest. If so, how? Perhaps there had been no great initial interaction, and the whales wanted to keep it that way, but the people of the Indus River Valley had presumed to interfere in whale affairs. Maybe the sailors of the lost city just took to whaling, and there was simply an all-out pitched battle. We realized we could speculate forever, but unless some record emerged from the ancient human civilization, either from the desert or perhaps a lost city beneath the waves, it seemed unlikely we would ever know.

We also wanted to know what methods and strategies the whales used. We tried to imagine what would happen if the whales did manage to create a resonant vibration so powerful it would topple a city. If the resonant frequency that destroyed the city was the same as that which would destroy the whales, it would be a suicide mission. The whales would die as the city did. Even if the frequency the whales used wasn't fatal to the whales themselves, if the whales needed to be extremely close to the port city to launch their sound attack, then the resulting debris and tsunami might still kill many of the attacking whales. We could never learn this part of the story from human records, but if we learned enough about what the whales were singing, we might be able to understand what they did and what happened next. And what they were trying to do, or about to do, now.

Although we spent much of our time trying to improve the way our computer operated, there were times the computer just chugged away, and there was nothing for me to do. Teddy, of course, kept busy on his own resonance problem. He was sure the universe was in its most basic form a multi-dimensional, multi-modal vibration.

"Have you ever seen Chinese two-tone bells?" he once asked me.

"Never even heard of them," I answered.

"My friend, you need to get out more. The Chinese government allowed a huge exhibit, including the famous terra-cotta warriors and two-tone bells, to be shown in several cities in the States. It was a huge concession. Every piece in the show was beyond priceless. It was wonderful. Anyway, each of these bells is capable of producing two different tones, depending upon where it is struck."

"How do the bells work?"

"Well, the bells are rectangular, not round, in their cross section. They also have what look like rows of knobs all over them. If you hit them on the larger, flatter section they produce one tone; if you hit them on the sharper edge they produce a sound off by a major or minor third from first."

"Have you heard them?"

"They were very closely protected in the exhibit. The guard said the government would take the whole thing back if anything was touched."

I took his non-answer for a yes. "How did you do it?"

"We didn't — a guard did. We explained the bells to the guard, a young man with no apparent reverence for authority. At the end of the day, he told us, there would be a few minutes when they had cleared everyone out. We were to come back to the bell room just then. When we arrived, he stationed me at one door and Marta at the other to warn him if his boss and the museum director were coming, and he snuck under the ropes, took off a shoe, then tapped one of the bells with it. He managed to create both tones just before the bigwigs showed up to throw me and Marta out."

"So, are you going to take up a new instrument?"

"Joe, I'm too old to try anything new. But as I've explained to you, I think the universe we are aware of is created by a harmonic structure underlying even time and space, and that it is the universe resonating to some primordial vibration which creates the energy packets we call particles. And as you pointed out, primes provide one form of non-consonantal systems, but so do positive/negative relationships, and these two together constitute the way quarks can coalesce to form electrons, neutrons and protons. My task is to find an entire system of vibrations that has the relationships we see in all different forms of matter."

"Which you call the Primordial Chord," I said.

Teddy looked at me blankly at first, then laughed. "Of course. I've explained this to you before. I hope you're not bored with my ramblings."

"Never, Teddy. Are you getting anywhere?"

"To tell you the truth, I have been sidetracked the last few months by studying these Chinese bells. I know it's only an analogy, like the Chladni plates, but it has helped me think about multi-modal vibrations. Now I have to go back to the data."

"It's interesting, don't you think, that you are trying to discover a way in which resonance has created our universe and I'm working on how resonance may have destroyed the greatest of the ancient cities."

"In a way, though, it makes complete sense," Ted said. "The destructive power of resonance goes right to the point of why I think particles with wavelengths that are harmonic overtones of other particles cannot exist."

We looked at each other with ironic amusement, an amusement we knew few other humans would understand.

One day in particular, I was weirdly out of sorts, restless and bored at the same time. I didn't feel I could help Teddy, though I did make a few suggestions about how to approach group theory. Instead of hanging out in the dingy office, I spent the afternoon and evening walking around, and finally hanging out on one of Boston's many bridges, I think it was the BU Bridge, watching the Charles River and its crew teams. The water grew darker and darker, the crew teams disappeared, the traffic grew quiet. Finally I headed for home, my head full of the possibilities of an ancient war and even a current danger.

I turned up my street and noticed the lights were on in the Witkowskis' apartment. I determined we wouldn't discuss the whales or Sonya or anything related. I was sure I could convince my friends to revisit a Vivaldi concerto we hadn't touched in months. As I replayed the tune in my head I was suddenly grabbed from behind, an arm thrown around my neck and a very hard rod like object rammed into one of my kidneys.

"You motherfucker, I should just shoot you now, but I want you to know why first," a harsh voice hissed in my ear. It was Gerry Watkins, and I guessed the rod was the barrel of his .45.

"What do you want, Gerry?" I tried to act as calm as possible, and I didn't resist as he pushed me into the narrow yard between our building and our neighbor's.

"You led the navy cops to me, you asshole. There's no way you just happened on me. You ruined my life, and I'm going to ruin yours." He maintained his hissed whisper as he spoke.

"What happened, Gerry? The navy didn't follow me. They had no idea where I was. Did they find you in Marfa?"

"Not in Marfa, in Toledo."

"At your parents'?"

He jammed his gun harder into my kidney. "How the fuck did you know that?"

I realized I needed to be very careful in what I said — Sonya had told me where he grew up in the same conversation she mentioned Marfa. "Pretty much a guess on my part, but certainly not on the navy's. I think you now know how they found you."

My last sentence caused Gerry to pause. He relaxed his grip on my neck and pulled his .45 out of my back a little. "What do you mean by that?"

"Think about it. They should have just taken us all in Marfa — they wanted your notes."

"Maybe you gave them to the navy yourself."

"Not a chance. I still have them."

"Okay, let's just go to your place and you show me."

"Come on, Gerry. I'm not going to keep them at my place."

"Where are they then?"

"In a safe in Waltham."

"Right. And you can't get to them now, is that what you're going to say next?"

"It's a long, long story, and it's a little late, past business hours." I paused, but before he could respond I said, "How did you find me?"

"I looked your name up in the phone book. Not too hard. And then I waited here. Been here since morning, but I'd have stayed days if I had to."

"Well that's how they found you too. I didn't have to know where you lived to know that. And they didn't have to wait outside behind the bushes either. They probably had hidden cameras aimed at your folks' house 24/7. If they needed to, the navy could have even bought a house on the street. Tell me what happened."

Gerry pulled his gun out of my back again. "Katie and I left Marfa a couple of weeks after you did. We drove around awhile and lived in her pickup, but we got tired of being poor. I called an old high school buddy and he offered me a job in St. Paul, so I decided to go see my folks on the way."

"Is Katie with you now?"

"No, I'm getting to that. So the very first day we spent at my folks' place some navy MPs bust in, tear the place apart, tear my pickup apart, fuckin' tear everyone apart. They were there all night. My parents started screaming at me, Katie freaked out and started crying, said she wanted to go home. My whole life was ripped apart in a matter of seconds."

"So, they were still looking for your records. That should show you I didn't give them anything and that they knew nothing about me visiting Marfa. Did Katie go back to Marfa?"

"Not sure. My brother was supposed to take her to the bus stop, she was going to go to Dallas. It was her truck, but she can't drive."

"Neither can I. Are you going to see her again?"

"I don't know. This whole thing freaked her out."

"So, Gerry, the thing is I didn't lead the navy to you, but you might have led them to me."

"No way. I gave my brother Katie's truck to take her to the airport. As soon as he took off a car did follow him, it was parked just down the street, probably followed him to the bus station, I'll bet they picked up Katie before she even got on the bus."

At this point Gerry was talking to himself as much as me, trying to disentangle his thoughts.

"What does she know about all this?"

"Nothing, never told her a thing. Maybe that's why she became so upset."

"She saw me, though. I saw you two talking about me."

Gerry laughed. "I asked her if she thought you guys would like some weed. She wasn't sure about you, but she thought your girlfriend might. She thought we went to make a deal."

"Then how did you get here?"

"Took my brother's car, left as soon as he and his shadow were out of sight. My folks wanted me gone anyway. Not sure they'll ever forgive me. What a shitty mess."

I decided I needed to tell Gerry about Harold Jennison and how dangerous the navy could be, but I wasn't sure he hadn't been trailed. As far as I knew they had heard every word we had just said. And I didn't want to take him to my place. "Gerry, we need to talk. Can I interest you in a pizza and beer?"

"What a riot. I was going to shoot you, now you're offering to buy me a meal. And who knows, I might shoot you yet. This whole thing still doesn't add up."

"You can walk behind me if you want." I headed across the street to go to the Spring Hill House of Pizza.

22

I was vaguely aware I was in a hospital. There was no one else in the room. I was attached to a plethora of tubes, and I recognized the steady beep of a heart monitor. I may have lain there for minutes or hours. I'm sure I nodded off and woke several times before I was aware that a nurse walked in.

"Ah, we're awake. My name is Alisa. How are we feeling?"

I could never understand the medical use of the first-person plural. "I suspect I'm feeling different from you," I said. "Where the hell am I?"

"You're at the Naval Medical Hospital."

"Where's that?"

"Portsmouth, Virginia."

"What am I doing in Virginia?"

"It's the best hospital the navy has."

"What's wrong with me?"

"You were in an automobile accident. You had a severe concussion. We're not sure what else. It's hard to tell when someone's in a coma."

"How long have I been here?"

"About five days, but you were at Mass General for a few days before that." As we had this conversation my nurse was busily watching my monitors, arranging my tubes, replacing my drip, draining my urine bag. When she was through she said, "I'm going to send a doctor in. We need to find out if there's anything else wrong."

She left and I was alone again for an interminable amount of time. I tried moving, and noticed my arms and legs were strapped to the bed. Not a good sign.

Soon after two men strode in purposefully. The man in front had a slightly stooped frame, white hair, pale freckled skin weathered by the years and the sun, and light-blue eyes that were simultaneously friendly and serious. There was nothing stooped about the second man. He did not have the robust build of someone like Clive; rather he appeared rigid, even brittle, as if something would break if he relaxed too much. He was missing an eyebrow. In fact it appeared there was scar tissue in its place above his right eye.

"Mr. Tenatt?" asked the older man. He was taller than the second man and appeared less severe. "I'm Dr. Jones." He did not introduce the other man, nor did the second man offer me even a gesture of a greeting. He had a military bearing, which did not surprise me considering where I was, and studied me intently, as if we had met before and he was trying to remember where.

"*Dr.* Tenatt," I corrected him. I was still foggy, but also upset I was in a navy facility, a prisoner in a navy facility.

The second man scribbled on his clipboard while the first one continued to speak. "Are you a medical doctor?"

"No, I'm a mathematician." The second man took a step forward and whispered something into Dr. Jones's ear, then stepped back.

Dr. Jones continued, "A professor?"

"Retired. Or at least semi-retired. I'm a consultant."

"I see. What field do you consult in?"

"Right now? Particle physics." I realized this was probably as much an intelligence interrogation as a medical examination. I struggled a little to get my story straight, but I felt I was in danger and the resultant adrenalin helped sharpen my wits. "What happened to me?"

"You were in an automobile accident. Hit and run, apparently."

"What happened to Gerry?"

The two men looked at each other for the first time but didn't answer.

I persisted. "Why am I in a naval hospital?"

This time they didn't bother to look at each other. Dr. Jones removed the blankets, then my confining straps, and began manipulating my torso and limbs. "We'll answer everything in due time. Right now I just want to see if you're injured, besides the concussion, that is. Can you feel this?" He slid his hand down my right arm, then my left. The examination went on for several minutes, maybe half an hour, when he said, "Why don't you take a rest now. We'll talk more tomorrow."

As he said this, he injected something into one of the tubes leading into my body. I was asleep before they closed the door behind them.

The next time I woke up I noticed my hands and legs were still free, and there was a different nurse standing next to my bed. When she saw I was awake she said, "Good, you're awake. My name is Betty. How are we feeling today?" I wanted to repeat my lame joke about feeling different than her, but I decided the nurses might be the only friends I had in the hospital, so I decided to be on my best behavior. "Pretty groggy. I have a headache."

"Not surprising. You sustained a pretty bad blow to your head. Now we need to find out how the rest of you is. Let's see if you can sit up." As she spoke she operated the bed so it gradually raised to a half sitting position.

I realized the tubes had been removed, and the heart monitor was no longer beeping. I took that as a good sign, for my health at least. My head began to throb violently. "Can you put me down again? I feel like I was run over by a truck."

"Not surprising. We'll try that again later. Here, take two of these." She handed me a small glass of water and two pills.

"What are they?"

"Percodan. They'll help your headache."

I swallowed the pills, she slowly lowered my bed, and I went back to sleep.

I awoke to the nurse named Alisa. "Good afternoon," she said as she hooked up a blood pressure cuff to my arm. I was glad she mentioned the time of day. I had no idea what time it was, what day of the week, what week, or even what month. I had the odd feeling I existed outside of space and time. Nurse Alisa's routine was much the same as the earlier one, except I was able to half-sit a little longer, and my headache was more diffuse.

"We'll have you running laps in no time," she said.

She was young and very fit looking, she looked like she could run laps herself.

I remained under her care for another day or two.

Dr. Jones came by once or twice, alone. "You appear to be okay, Dr. Tenatt," he finally said, "but we'll keep you here a while courtesy of the navy. And frankly, you should spend as little time in bed as possible. Walk as much as you can."

"Can I walk anywhere?"

Dr. Jones looked at me over his reading glasses. "Of course not. You'll need to stay in this ward." That limited me to round-trip walks of about two hundred feet, but I figured it only took about twenty-six round trips to make a mile. I got to know the nurses pretty well.

"I told you we'd have you doing laps," Alisa said one day as she took my blood pressure and other vitals. As soon as she left the room, she was replaced by two men I immediately recognized as the navy men who had come to my door the morning after I had met with Joanne DiLeonardo.

My first thought was that I wish I had left. My second was that the ward was locked, I wasn't able to go anywhere.

"We meet again," I said.

"Good morning, Dr. Tenatt, how are you feeling?"

"Confused and irritated. What am I doing here?"

"Recuperating from a serious accident."

"But why here, in a naval hospital in Virginia?"

"It's a good place to finish our conversation, perhaps without interruption this time. And we have a few new questions as well."

At that point I felt I might not leave the hospital alive, but I was going to give it my best shot. "What questions?"

"To start with, what were you and Gerald Watkins discussing just before your accident?"

It took me a second to translate Gerald to Gerry. I realized I had better think about what I said and answer carefully. The fact that I was recuperating from a coma allowed me speak slowly. "He wanted to know where Sonya Perez was."

"Did you tell him?"

"I don't know where she is."

"Haven't you seen her?"

"She used to drop by every once in a while. It's been a couple of years, I think, at least one."

"You didn't see her a few months ago?"

I figured it wouldn't sound so good to say she had just stopped by after taking a hurried overnight train from Virginia. "No, it's been at least a year, I think a little more." This was a fateful answer. If they knew I was lying I would be in big trouble. If not, I would know they didn't know that much.

"Why did Gerald want to see Sonya?"

"Not sure. She's very pretty. If I was his age I'd like to see her a lot too."

"Why was he armed?"

"I wasn't aware he was. Maybe he thought I live in a rough neighborhood."

"How do you know Sonya?"

"She and I are fellow mathematicians. I was her professor at one point. Afterwards we collaborated on some projects."

"Do you know what she's doing now?"

"No, I think I answered that."

187

"Are you friends with her?"

"I'd like to think so, yes."

"And with Gerald Watkins?"

"No, I hardly know the man. Only talked to him a few minutes, but I could tell he's not my type."

"Why not?"

"He seemed pretty nervous, cynical even. Kind of set me on edge. How is he, anyway?"

They ignored my question. "Don't you think it's strange Sonya should suddenly just disappear?"

"Not really. It's not like we were inseparable, we didn't see each other that often after my seminar was over, unless we were working on a project together."

"And you never asked her what she did?"

"Take a look at my record. I've worked on a lot of defense projects, I had some pretty high-security clearances, in fact I still have one, and I know Sonya did too, because we collaborated on a project for the army. And neither of us would consider asking the other what they were doing if they didn't offer to talk about it first. We take our work seriously."

The guy who had been questioning me stopped to write something down, but the other guy, the blond, chimed in, "Was Joanne DiLeonardo asking about Sonya too?"

"No, she did convey greetings from Sonya, though she didn't tell me what they were doing, or where. She mostly wanted to ask me about the Boston area universities. She wants to be a professor. Sonya must have told her I had quit working for almost all of them at one time or another."

"Can't keep a job?"

"More like can't stave off boredom. I suppose it amounts to the same thing, except I'm happy and they'd all take me back."

"How about your downstairs neighbors? What kind of people are they?"

"Good people, an amazing couple." I told them the story about escaping from Poland.

"Are they dangerous?"

"Only if you try to bully them. Do you think you could navigate a broken motor boat across the Baltic? I doubt I could."

This interrogation went on for quite a while, but the longer it took the more I was sure they hadn't learned anything important. Teddy and Marta were right again — the navy was dangerous, but not always that smart. However, the fact that they couldn't get anything out of me did seem to irritate them.

I was transferred from the intensive-care room soon after my first bout with what I presumed to be intelligence officers, into a room with an old sailor who appeared to have suffered a major stroke. He did nothing but stare at the ceiling — at least his eyes were open and his face was pointed upward. He never moved and received no visitors while I was there. My interrogators, always the same two men, would drop by at seemingly random intervals — sometimes two or three times in a single day, sometimes a day would go by without an appearance. They never threatened or even cajoled me, but they asked me the same questions endlessly, with only slightly different phrasing, and they always made it clear they did not believe a word I said.

The TV in my room was never on — the nurse said it seemed to disturb my roommate. For my part, I couldn't have cared less; I never have watched TV regularly, not even for the evening news, and I was glad to help the poor soul in that bed gain whatever peace he could. I continued to spend my time walking in circles around the ward. I assumed all the doors were locked, but I never bothered to try, it was all part of the cat-and-mouse game, and being the mouse I wanted to be on my best behavior.

I knew I was under this pair's control, and I knew how ruthless they could be, but it seemed while I was in the hospital there were limits to their power. My job was to make sure I gave them no reason to go beyond that.

Then one day, about half an hour after another interrogation, my nurse, Alisa, hunted me down on my walk carrying a clipboard. "I guess the navy is tired of you. You're being discharged." We went to my room where she filled out several pages of paperwork, then stopped as she reviewed the pages. "I can't find your navy I.D. number," she said.

"I've never been in the navy."

She looked at me, or maybe through me, as if I wasn't there, for a few moments. "Why are you in a navy hospital?"

"I wish you could tell me. I have no clue."

She took the handful of papers and left. I think I dozed off before she returned and handed a bunch of papers to me. She also gave me a plastic ID to hang around my neck. "This will get you through the front gate. You can leave it with the guard." I looked at her quizzically and she saw I didn't understand what she meant. "This *is* a naval base," she said. "Follow me, I'll have to open the ward door for you."

I followed her to the nursing station but decided I didn't want to be released to the street in hospital pajamas. I was sure my friends from Intelligence were determined to make my life miserable, but I was determined to survive.

"Can I have my clothes back?" I asked Alisa before I went any further. She said she'd look into it. She sat at the desk and made a couple of phone calls that didn't last very long. She looked up at me. "I guess your clothes must have been ruined in the accident. Mass General didn't send anything along."

"How did they get ruined if all I did was bump my head? And how about Gerry?"

"I don't know anything about him. I heard there was a man who died. Was that Gerry?"

"And my wallet? Was that destroyed too?"

"I'm sorry, Dr. Tenatt, I'm just a nurse here, I don't know what happened. Maybe someone stole it."

"So I'm just going to walk out of here in hospital skivvies with no money or ID?"

"Don't you have family?"

"No, I don't. I don't even know anyone within a thousand miles of here."

My nurse finally looked concerned. "I'll see what I can do." She left me standing in the hallway. I waited while the hospital bustle continued around, ignoring me.

Half an hour later another woman, a little older and not nearly as fit looking as my nurse, walked up to me. "Dr. Tenatt?"

I had the feeling they used the honorific 'Doctor' as a sly insult more than as a term of respect. "Yes."

"I'm Adrianne Weston, director of outpatient services. I understand you need some clothes."

"A little cash and my ID would be nice too."

"She handed me a bundle of clothes. "I'm Sorry, I can't help with the money or ID." She spoke without apparent malice, or concern.

"Do you have a phone where I could call some friends?"

"Is it a local call?"

"No, I don't know anyone around here. It's to Massachusetts."

"I'm sorry, we can't allow long-distance calls from the hospital lines without approval." I didn't bother to ask how I could get approval, because I was sure I couldn't.

The clothes almost fit, though certainly not my style. They looked like they would be appropriate for an overweight sailor in his twenties. After I dressed, an orderly led me through interminable halls in silence to the front door. At the door an MP was waiting. He accompanied me to the base guardhouse, where a guard brusquely looked at my papers, took my plastic ID, and wished me a good day. My MP had already retreated into the base behind me. I started walking without any idea where I was going, but with an overwhelming desire to get away from anything navy.

I found myself on a busy thoroughfare. The air was hot and sticky, the heat made me a little dizzy. The sidewalk I was on looked like an afterthought, as if someone knew a road should have a sidewalk even though no one would ever use it. I kept going straight because I thought I saw some stores in that direction, although I didn't know what good they would do me as I was flat broke.

I was soon joined by a small black woman with a nonchalant air, an attitude that said she was completely comfortable with the situation. She began a little small talk, about the weather, her parents, her boyfriend, whatever. I wasn't used to strangers being so friendly. I wondered if Virginia was that different from Massachusetts or if she was just crazy.

After I told her my story, she said, "You look like you could use a few bucks. Take this." She pulled a few folded bills from her purse and handed them to me.

"I don't know you, I can't accept that," I said, then realized how stupid I sounded. Maybe I wasn't over my concussion.

The woman smiled at me, a very sweet smile. "Of course you can." As she spoke she surreptitiously unfolded a corner of the small wad with her thumb and showed me a note tucked inside. "There's a convenience store about four blocks from here. You look like you could use a soda." She pointed down the street, then abruptly took off across the highway and disappeared down a side sheet. I was left to myself again.

I stuffed the bills in my pocket and continued down the street following my erstwhile companion's directions. Her odd appearance, disappearance and quixotic manners made me realize I might still be followed. When I arrived at the store, I went in, bought a sandwich and asked for the key to the bathroom. Once inside I sat on the toilet and opened up the note:

> *Hopefully you are in a private place when you read this. If not, find one. Go to the 7-Eleven bathroom. You will see a small valise on the floor. It has your new clothes. Remove all your clothes, including socks and underwear, and put the new ones on. Leave your old clothes and this note in the valise where you found it. There will be a taxi parked around the corner. Ask the driver if he can take you to the bus station. If he says yes, tell him you left your money in the store, go back in and try another cab later. If he says no, get in.*

I changed into the new clothes, which looked like they could have been taken out of my own trash, walked out and saw two taxis. The one in front was piloted by a Sikh, or at least I took him for a Sikh because of his turban. The one in the back by a large, rough-looking man who looked like he had just stepped off of a Viking ship; he had a massive blond beard and pilot-style sunglasses that completely hid his eyes, and wore a tight T-shirt that looked like it was going to be torn apart by his pecs and biceps. He looked dangerous, but when I approached the first taxi the Viking guy in the second taxi gave me a quick nod, so I walked up to his open window instead and asked if he could take me to the bus station.

"No," he said, or rather growled. I crawled into the back seat. As he pulled away without speaking, I saw a man wearing the clothes I had just discarded leave the store and slowly walk away. After a block or two my driver looked at me through his rear-view mirror and said, "How the hell are you, Joey? You look like shit."

It was Clive. "I'm great, it's just my rags," I said, tugging at my sleeve.

"You should be grateful, Joey."

"I am, Clive. What's going on?"

"Can't quite say, but things have gotten out of hand. What have you been up to?"

I realized I had never told Clive exactly what I'd been doing, but I assumed he knew enough. "I think I've been hanging out with the wrong people."

"Present company excluded, I hope."

"No, I was specifically referring to the present company, Clive."

"You're probably right." We pulled into the bus station.

"We had to have you change clothes. They may have wired the ones they gave you. Someone in the navy has started to play hardball."

"What are you going to do with them, my old clothes, I mean?"

"We'll deliver them to your house. Just don't wear them again, throw them out. If they are bugged, it will look like you managed to hitch a ride home, but we thought the bus would be safer for you." He paused, then continued. "There was never a question of not helping you. This ruse is to protect our identity."

Of course I wanted to ask him who he was working with, but I knew better. "How did you know I was being released?"

"The harder part was finding where you were. The ambulance took you to Mass General, which is where you should have stayed. But when the navy offered to take you, I guess they saw a way to cut their losses. You must be on Medicare. Once we figured out where you were, it was pretty easy to keep track of you. Hospitals aren't all that secure, even a naval one."

"Do you think they killed Gerry on purpose? This was no accident, was it?"

"One of the fallacies one falls into when dealing with an institution like the navy is to identify every action that emanates from it as being a conscious effort of the entire outfit. I've spent the last fifteen years engaging with the most nefarious governments on earth, and I've learned even the most autocratic of them are rife with factions, rivalries and dissensions."

"Are you saying there's a rogue element in the navy?"

"I don't know if it's rogue, but it's not mainstream either, I don't know if there is more than one agitator. I do think there is a faction that is trying to protect itself."

"Do you know who it is, who's behind this?"

"No, do you?"

"No," I said, then remembered something I had meant to ask Clive before. "Do the initials WD mean anything to you?"

"No, should they?"

"I'm not sure, but they might be the initials of another researcher, he may have worked with Harold Jennison. I already asked you about him once."

Clive adjusted his head. Even though his eyes were hidden behind the dark lenses of his glasses, I could tell he was scrutinizing me through the rear view mirror. It appeared he was going to say something but then stopped again and stared some more. Finally he started the cab. He said, "I'll look into it."

"But it wasn't an accident, was it?"

"Of course not. From what I do know, they want Gerry's records."

"He destroyed them."

"How do you know that?" This time, Clive turned around to face me. He was remarkably limber for a man of his size.

"I saw him in Marfa."

"Marfa? Marfa, Texas? What was he doing in Marfa?"

"It wasn't Toledo."

"And what were you doing in Marfa?"

"Looking for Gerry."

"But he had already destroyed his records?"

"Yes." I decided I didn't need to tell Clive everything. Like he said, things were getting out of hand.

Clive took his glasses off and stared at me. "What are you getting out of this?"

"I'm learning a lot about whales."

"You're a very clever man, Joey, but even clever people can do stupid things. Watch your step. You're fooling around with very dangerous people. Here's a bus ticket to Boston."

I took the ticket and climbed out of Clive's taxi. There would be no coffee, no beer, this visit. We said goodbye, and as I walked away, he said, "Don't forget your trash."

The trip home was uneventful. Rather, it was tedious. Sleeping on a bus is uncomfortable, being awake is uncomfortable and boring. Boston never looked so good as when we finally pulled into North Station. It was about three in the afternoon when I arrived, the weather not as hot as Virginia, and the air was fresher. I had to buy a newspaper to find out the date. June 12, one day short of a month since I had been run over. I had been unconscious for a little over two weeks.

I took the Red Line to Central Square. Though it was a beautiful day, I was too tired to walk the whole way. When I finally arrived home, just walking down the street I had lived on for more than three decades felt like a new experience. I heard some noise in the Witkowskis' apartment, so I knocked on their door before I went up to my own place. Marta answered the door and just stared at me. She turned white, as if she was looking at some horror.

"My God, you're alive," she said. "Teddy, Joseph's here," she called into the apartment. Then she threw her arms around me and began to cry.

Teddy walked up behind her. I could see his expression over his wife's shoulder. He was grinning from ear to ear. That these two, who had been through so much pain, seen so much misery, were so moved by my return reduced me to tears as well. It was as if I dropped a coat of armor I had been forced to wear to survive at the Naval Medical Center. We must have all cried for half an hour. Finally Marta wiped her tears on her apron and said, "Have you been up to see your cats yet? Teddy and I have been feeding them, but I think they are very angry at you."

I turned to climb my stairs, but Marta called after me, "Then come back down for *galumpkis* or I'll be mad at you too."

I entered my apartment and Cleo came to rub against me as usual, and soon afterward Ranger followed her out, also as usual. I sat down in my big chair, expecting them to resume their usual places, but instead they both sat on the floor at the far end of the room and stared at me. After a while they both got up, but instead of climbing up on my chair they both just left the room. They were pissed. I was exhausted and fell asleep in my chair. I was awakened by the phone — it was Marta asking me if I wanted dinner.

Teddy, Marta, and I didn't play any music that evening, we just talked and sat in silence and talked. I told them I couldn't remember anything that had happened.

Teddy spoke up. "You know Rico, who lives across the street? He says he saw everything. He's the one who called the ambulance. You should go talk to him."

Rico was a retired cop, he always saw everything. He had lived on our street longer than I had. It was only seven in the evening, so I decided to find out what he knew. Teddy went with me, I think he was afraid to leave me alone. As we crossed the street, it struck me the last time I had done that, I had nearly been killed. I knocked on the door and Rico answered.

"Great God, you made it, Joe! I swear if I were a betting man I would have just lost a fortune. Are you all right?" Then he called back to his wife, "Annemarie, they couldn't kill Joseph. He's come back from the dead to haunt us."

Annemarie came running out and grabbed one of my hands with both of hers. "Oh Joe, we weren't sure you made it. We couldn't find you in any of the hospitals. We thought you were dead, didn't we Rico? He saw the whole thing, you know."

"I can't remember anything, Rico. Would you mind retelling the story?"

"I'm about to burn the kitchen down," Annemarie said. "I have to go."

After she left, Rico said, "Sit down," as he motioned to a long wooden bench on his front porch. "I'll be right back."

He returned quickly with half of a cigar, which he lit. "You don't mind if I smoke, do you? My sweetie won't let me smoke indoors. In fact, that's why I saw your accident."

"What happened?" I asked again.

"Well, it happened very fast. You and that other guy were crossing the street, it was like you guys came out of nowhere. Anyway, you were in front, he was half a step behind when this truck came roaring down the street. Don't know where it came from either, but it was screaming." Rico took a puff or two on his cigar, then continued, "How a truck is even able to go that fast on this street, I don't know. Weird. Anyway, all of a sudden your friend cries 'Watch out!' and pushes you, I mean he really shoves you from behind and you both go sprawling, kind of sideways. I don't know if the driver panicked or what, but it looked like he swerved into guys."

Rico stopped and chewed on his cigar a while, as if that was the end of his story. "What happened then?" I asked.

"Teddy can tell you as well as me. The whole neighborhood came out, I mean it made a lot of noise. The fuckin' truck didn't even slow down, it squealed around the corner and was gone." Rico looked at his cigar, then put it back in his mouth. "Tell you the truth, I'm losing my touch. The truck was a Dodge, black, pretty new, but I didn't get the license plate. Back in the day, I mean when I was still working, you'd better believe I would have seen it and remembered it. After that, all that was left was to pick up the pieces, your pieces. Teddy was there, we were all there."

"I didn't see the truck, but I saw you and that Gerry guy lying on the street," said Teddy. "He was a mess. Poor guy, I guess he saved your life."

I didn't want to speculate in front of Rico, but several scenarios were going through my head. I didn't believe it was an accident, but I wasn't sure who was being targeted. But there was no denying Gerry went from almost shooting me to trying to save me. And it may have cost him his life.

Rico picked up where Teddy left off. "Damn right. Anyway, it didn't take long for the ambulances to arrive, and off you went. Where did they take you, anyway?"

"Mass General for a while, then the Naval Medical Center in Virginia. Gerry had something to do with the navy, I guess they thought I did too."

"Did you know him?"

"I knew who he was. He was just looking for an old girlfriend, a former student of mine. I guess he thought I might know where she was."

"Did you?"

"No, but you know, even if I did, I wouldn't tell him."

We sat on Rico's porch while he finished his old stogie and talked about the times we had seen. It was good to be home again.

23

I didn't resume my work on Cetacean for many weeks, months in fact. I had a constant headache — something as easy as walking around the block could be excruciating. I didn't play music with Marta and Teddy for quite a while either, but I often sat in their apartment and listened. It may have been my imagination, but their music seemed sadder than before.

Eventually my life resumed some normalcy. My cats quickly forgave me and sat with me on my chair. I think the fact I just sat there for hours in the dark pleased them. Perhaps they thought I was finally coming to my senses and living life as it should be lived.

Next, I picked up my violin and joined my neighbors once in a while, a very good sign, though I still felt the pieces we played and the way we played them were more somber than previously. Soon I was wandering around Cambridge, enjoying the heat of late summer along with more than a few cold red ales. It occurred to me I should call Marylin, I had promised to invite her to Boston, but I put it off — think I was embarrassed, even ashamed, not that I was still weak, but that I had let my guard down — until I just let the idea fade.

After a while I began to drop in on Teddy at work, but I didn't resume my own efforts. We did have some interesting conversations about the relationship between mathematics and physics.

Gradually our conversations led me to begin thinking about whale communications again, but I still couldn't look at the immense amount of data I had.

I did make sure I examined my empty trash can every week. My visit with Clive in the taxi had been very unsatisfying, even though I was grateful for the fact he extracted me from Portsmouth. I've no idea if my clothes really were bugged, as Clive had indicated. They had appeared in a bundle at my upstairs door the morning after I returned, and I promptly threw them in the trash as directed. I took this as a sign they were wired, and we needed to keep up the ruse that I wore them home, but Clive did not communicate anything directly to me about them. I did know the navy, or at least someone in the navy, didn't have any affection for me. I hoped Clive would provide clear answers someday.

One day as I looked into my empty trash barrel I noticed some wet paper sticking to the side, wet newspaper. I wasn't sure if it was a message from Clive or just some of my own trash that had become soaked. I tried to peel it off, but it began to tear. I decided to borrow Marta's hair dryer but had to wait until she got home. When I finally dried the paper enough to peel it off my trash can, I could see it was part of an obituary:

Admiral Charles "Chuck" Hentoff died today of injuries sustained while riding his bike to work on Bayside Rd. in Chesapeake Beach, MD. No further details are available at this time.

Admiral Hentoff was born in Wichita, Kansas. He is succeeded by a son, Dennis, of Chattanooga Tennessee.

Admiral Hentoff earned a PhD in electrical engineering from the University of Missouri and was director of the Institute of Naval Studies on Marine Animals at the time of his death.

According to colleagues, he was an avid deep-water fisherman and exercise enthusiast.

The notice was torn out of a newspaper, there was no date or the paper's name. There wasn't a lot of information in the notice, but the fact Clive had seen fit to leave it for me said a lot, or at least gave me a lot to speculate about. I immediately assumed this was the person in charge of the persecution of my group. Was he also responsible for Dr. Jennison's and Gerry's deaths? And what was I to make of the fact he was evidently run over? Would Clive send me more information when it was available? How long ago had this happened?

The same day in the mail I received an unsigned get well card, but I recognized the handwriting as Clive's. It was a plain white card. On the front it said, "Get Well / Stay Free". Inside was the following poem:

In every cry of every Man,
In every Infants cry of fear,
In every voice: in every ban,
The mind-forg'd manacles I hear

Wm. Blake

The poem was more ominous than the death notice. I recalled Clive's admonition that it was the duty of every citizen to oppose his own government's malfeasance, as well as his quoting the phrase *mind-forged manacles* from this poem when telling me we each had to create our own freedom. Was Clive indicating he was responsible for Admiral Hentoff's demise? I had to face the reality it was this type of activity that was Clive's profession. He had spent decades traveling around the world advancing US interests through clandestine methods, and I always knew those activities could include assassinations and other violent mayhem. Had he turned against his own government now? Or did he see it as fighting an element within that government that had itself turned against the country? I had no answers to any of my questions.

I doubted it was Clive's intent, as I was sure he did not know the extent of our research, but the effect of his letter was to kick-start me back into deciphering the humpbacks' messages. I was especially interested in sussing out the epic tale shared by humpback whales all over the world. I say all over the world, but the one area I had no data on, the one area the navy hadn't sent any of the researchers I knew of, was the Arabian Sea, the place where the apparent epic took place.

The first problem I needed to solve was more mundane. We had lost the easy access to Matt's whale room. I didn't want to keep any material in my apartment, or the Witkowskis' for that matter. We had loaded everything onto one of Teddy's VAX computers. We knew this was dangerous, but we had encrypted all of our data and had coded the machine to erase everything if someone tried to access the machine without going through the correct protocols. Teddy had even modified the machine by adding an extra battery in case someone unplugged the computer without preparing the machine. He did this by cleverly hiding a battery inside the machine. If someone just unplugged the machine, the computer would have enough power to be able to make sure everything on it was immediately destroyed. However, if there was a blackout, the computer would use the UPS to shut itself down properly.

We backed the machine up occasionally, but the only place we felt we could securely keep anything was in Matt's warehouse safe, and getting to Waltham when the warehouse was open was a bother, so we didn't do that often.

My next problem was to be able to listen to Joanne's and the whales' singing. I could have done it in Teddy's office, and often did, but I felt I spent enough time there already. I found the solution watching teenagers hanging out on the Esplanade one fine summer day. I remembered kids often wore cheap-looking headphones that were attached to a small plastic box. I finally asked a group what those things were and was introduced to the Walkman. Teddy helped me transfer the songs of both Joanne and the whales themselves to cassettes. Of course the quality of sound was not nearly as good as I had become used to, but it worked well enough for my purposes. Eventually I bought two Walkmans so I could alternate between two different whale population songs. I'm not sure the kids thought I was twice as cool as they were.

My plan was to immerse myself in the sounds of the whale language, much as a musician might want to immerse himself in the sound of Mozart or Monk. In time this strategy began to pay off. The outline of the story as I had come to understand it starts with the whales relating their peaceful life in the Arabian Sea. There is no mention of different groups or of migrations. It's possible this population simply wasn't aware of other whales, but considering whales from all over the world harken back to this golden time of the whales' legend, I concluded that this was the original humpback whale population. As time went on, it appears there were friendly communications between the humpbacks and the local population of humans, likely fishermen, to the extent they did begin to understand each other.

Then at some point the communication changed — the whales felt they were being betrayed by some of the humans. It appears some whales, especially young whales, were led away from the protective pod by humans pretending to be friendly, and then slaughtered. The whales retaliated by capsizing a few fishing boats and a war began. For a while, the whales were on the losing side, their numbers decimated. Then one of the large males began approaching the city at night and making it rumble a little with his voice. According to the whale epic, it appears he was just venting his considerable anger at first, but then other whales joined him. They also began to realize some frequencies worked much better than others at causing the earth under the city to quake. This part of the legend was especially interesting to me, as it highlighted the lyrical quality of humpback language. The passage is operatic in its timing and intensity, beginning rather tentatively and softly and building to a rumbling climax. When actually narrated in a pod, all of the males join in at this point like the chorus of a Greek tragedy.

The city residents began to increase their efforts at murdering whales in revenge, so the whales needed to leave the local feeding grounds, with only some males returning at night. Eventually the whales recruited as many males as they could and something they may not have anticipated happened: the city collapsed and sank into the sea.

Gujarat is one of the most earthquake-prone areas on Earth, so it is not clear to me whether a devastating earthquake occurred while the whales were singing, one that would have destroyed the city without help from the whales. Perhaps the whales precipitated an earthquake. And perhaps it was the tuned resonance of the voices that simply shook the baked-clay brick city into the sea, as the whales believe to this day. The other result was that most of the gathered whales were also killed in this calamity. Joanne was clearly right on one point — the whales' epic is not one of victory and glory, but one of betrayal and destruction.

Understanding the purport of this universal humpback tale was only the preamble to trying to understand what they intended to do to the *Grinsby*. Were they simply venting their anger, or had the actions of the navy in using their own language to fool them aroused some deeper, more terrible angst? I wanted to notify Sonya of what I had found, but of course there was no way for me to get in touch with her. Instead, as summer melded into fall I felt my life growing darker too. I remembered what Marylin had said about Carolyn: she was strong enough to do anything that was needed, but not knowing what to do was crippling. I felt similarly crippled.

In order to take my mind off of my anxieties I began to systematically create three separate documents to explain what I had learned. The first was an explanation of the three-dimensional curved analog geometry and the base prime metric the whales use to communicate before and during their migrations, and in fact to recall past voyages as well. This was, of course, based on the work Sonya and I had been doing.

The second was a more complete description of their entire language, including a more robust translation of their universal epic than I have provided here. This was mostly Joanne DiLeonardo's notes, but I added some more details explaining how this part of their communications mesh with their geometry.

The third document was a collated recording of their songs I referenced in my first two documents, so one could listen to the sounds as one read about their meanings.

I worked on these documents for several months, feverishly if I may say so. I hadn't worked so continuously since my twenties. But, like many endeavors, the further I delved into it the more I understood, and the faster I could progress. In time, my friends the Witkowskis became concerned about my health and practically insisted I join them every evening. In fact I did catch the flu around Thanksgiving, and my neighbors were sure it was due to my maniacal pace. They nursed me back to health but would not allow me to do any work for several weeks even after I felt I had recovered.

Teddy began to exercise more control over me, which he could do as I was using his office and equipment. By mid-winter my life was again almost back to normal. One day during this period I found another cryptic note, or rather newspaper article, in my trash. We needed to drag our trash cans out to the curb by seven thirty on Monday morning to be sure it was picked up. The trash was normally picked up by nine, but on many mornings I had already left by then, and so I took my can back in when I came home. Usually I did the Witkowskis' trash as well if I got up or home first, and they did likewise. On this particular day there had been a blizzard all day, and the collector had neglected to secure the top of my trash can, so the empty barrel had filled with snow. It was cold and wet as I shoveled out the snow, so I almost missed the extra scrap of paper at the bottom. Like Clive's previous surreptitious message, this one was torn out of a newspaper with no dateline or name of the publication. It read like a paid notification from the naval post newspaper.

In Memoriam, Admiral Charles Hentoff
    A small memorial service was held at the Portsmouth Naval Chapel yesterday. In attendance were several members of Admiral Hentoff's staff, and George Hentoff, the Admiral's brother, who lives in Louisville, Kentucky. A short eulogy was given by Captain William Dickson, Admiral Hentoff's chief of staff. Captain Dickson noted Admiral Hentoff was a noted scientist as well as capable administrator and was respected by his staff for his fairness and perspicacity. Captain Dickson concluded, "He was dedicated to

protecting our country from all who would tear it down, and as
interim director of the Institute of Naval Studies on Marine Animals,
I can only hope to be as dedicated and persevering." George Hentoff
did not speak.

At first it seemed odd to me a memorial service would be held so long after someone's death, but I realized I didn't know the actual date the service took place. Perhaps Clive had just found out or decided for some reason I needed to know about it. I showed this note to Marta and Teddy, as I had all Clive's notes.

"He didn't have many people come to his service, mostly just his staff," said Teddy. "And they may have come to please this Captain Dickson, their new boss."

"I'm not sure I'd get that many," I said.

"Oh, I think you'd be surprised," Marta said.

"Indeed I would, if I were there," I said. "Anyway, this Dickson sounds like a pretty dry type himself."

"If he's only a captain, and only interim director, he might be trying to secure a permanent position. Something about that name puzzles me," said Marta.

"Me too. I think it's the initials. Didn't we see the initials WD all over Jennison's papers?" asked Teddy. The three of us stared at each other.

"I don't think this is a coincidence," I said. "I asked Clive about the initials WD. If he sent us this notice, he thinks it's something we should be aware of. And something else I had nearly forgotten — Carolyn said Harold Jennison used to refer to his aide as Lieutenant Dickhead, I think this must be the same guy." We all knew this could be momentous news, but at the time there was nothing more for us to do but pull out our instruments and play some Mozart.

A few days later, I received a message in the mail I did understand. It was a small package with the same jewelry store name and address Sonya had used when she sent me the San Diego storage room key. Inside was a small ring, and this note:

As you already have the key to your desire,
I am returning the ring you gave me.

I had never given Sonya a ring, so it was clear this was a coded message, and she was afraid of someone opening her mail. When I examined the packaging closely I thought I might have seen signs it was tampered with, but then I considered whoever did the tampering would be even more careful undoing and redoing the package than Sonya would have been in the first place. I concluded I couldn't make a conclusion. It was just one more example of playing a game where I did not know my opponent, did not know how much of the board I was seeing, did not know how much of the board my opponent was seeing. I did not even know when or if my opponent was making moves. I did know, however, that the key she referred to was the one I already had, and fortunately had saved. There was no way I could ask Jeannie to fly to California to pick up whatever Sonya had left for me, so there was nothing for me to do but fly there myself and take a taxi to the storage shed. Then I thought of Marylin.

I called her the next day from a pay-phone in Harvard Square.

"Well, hello stranger. How are you?" she asked when she heard my voice.

I hadn't told her about my accident, so I needed to spend a few quarters doing that.

"Can I come out to see you?" she said. "I want to see you in the flesh to make sure you're okay."

"I'd love that, but I have another favor to ask first."

"If I can do it, dear, you know I will."

"I need you to pick up a package for me, in San Diego."

"I hate that drive, but of course I will. It must be important. What do I do with it?"

"I don't know, I don't know what it is. It's from Sonya. I'll mail you the key and the address. Can you do this quickly?"

"Of course, I'm retired."

"I'll mail the key today and call you in a week. Then we'll figure out what we should do next."

The week passed slowly. I assumed Sonya had sent me information that might help me with my discourse on Cetacean geometry. I continued with my labors, of course, but I was concerned Sonya might throw me a curve that would force me to redo much of my work. Still, working made waiting easier than not working.

I called Marylin the next week, but she didn't answer for two days. Finally, she picked up the phone.

"Are you okay? I started calling you the day before yesterday."

"I'm fine, just arrived back here. I only received your letter yesterday morning."

I cursed the postal service but didn't voice my ire to Marylin. "What did Sonya leave us?"

"Well, she left a note, and a stack of those new plastic computer things."

"Floppies?"

"Yeah, floppies."

"What did the note say?" I asked.

Marylin read,

Dear Joseph,

I'm sorry to make this so difficult for you, but I know you'll understand. I have left the Grinsby. I gave them a formal notice and I'm sure the navy was glad to get rid of me, but I don't trust them to leave me alone. Something very wrong is going on. Did I tell you the new navy technician was fooling around with trying to communicate with a group of humpbacks we were following, and the whales responded by rattling our ship? The situation became much worse. I think the whales called in reinforcements. At times it felt like we were hit by an earthquake, but the captain obviously enjoyed the wrestling match and continued to broadcast his phony messages at the group. It was too much for me, so I have left. I plan to move to my mother country, but I wanted to hand my notes off to you just in case you want to continue trying to decipher their language. I don't blame you if you do continue, but I have come to the conclusion it's presumptuous for us to poke around with their secrets, it's almost like breaking and entering. I hope to see you again. You have been a great friend and mentor. With love, your friend,

Sonya Perez

"That's all she wrote, everything else is on the floppies. Do you want me to mail them to you?"

"Let me think about it. Thank you, I'll call you tomorrow."

I told the Witkowskis about the message. I needed their wisdom to decide what to do next.

"Where do you think her mother country is?" Marta asked.

"It's either Peru or Ecuador. Her father was from one and her mother the other. They met at the University of Texas as students, and Sonya was born in the States. Her father went back. I don't think Sonya ever knew him. Probably she's going to her mother's homeland."

"Is her mother there?" asked Teddy.

"Her mother is dead. She had a heart attack when she was pretty young, I think the result of the rheumatic fever she had when she was a teenager. She died the year before I met Sonya."

"What are you going to do now?" asked Marta.

Her question surprised me. Although I wanted their advice, I had also assumed they would encourage me to continue. "I thought I would ask Marylin to mail me Sonya's floppies, try to incorporate her ideas into what I've done. What do you think I should do?"

"On the one hand, I want to see your finished work as much as ever, Joe," said Teddy. "On the other hand, some of the pressure is off as Sonya is no longer on the ship. And after what happened to you and Gerry, and the danger Sonya feels she is in, you need to be careful."

"You think I should just quit?"

"I think you shouldn't think that way. If you continue, it's because you think it's the right thing to do," said Marta.

"And what do you think the right thing to do is?"

Teddy interjected, "I think you should get Sonya's floppies first. But be careful — you should have them mailed to Matt's warehouse."

"Good idea."

"We have something else we need to tell you, Joe," said Marta. Marta and Teddy looked uncomfortably at each other.

"You're both okay, aren't you?" I said.

"We're good, very good. We've decided to go back to Poland."

I felt like I had been kicked in the gut. "Is it safe?" I asked. It was a dumb question, and I knew it was dumb, I knew they would have thought very carefully about the move, but somehow I wanted them to reconsider.

"We think it is, safe enough to be worth the risk."

"Do you miss Poland that much?"

"That's not why we're going. We miss Poland, but we love it here too. It's a hard choice."

"Why go back, then?"

"If we could choose to be born anywhere, it would be in the United States. There is so much opportunity here, so much freedom, this is how people should live. But we were born in Poland, we feel we belong there, especially now. To teach them to live the way we have been able to live here. They have escaped from the Russian grip for now, but it will take a lot of effort to retain that freedom."

I was glum, but I understood their attitude. "When are you leaving?"

"Not until summer at the earliest, maybe next fall. If you need the VAX after that I can arrange it," Teddy said.

"How can you do that?"

"I've obtained a joint position at Northeastern and my old school, Polytechnika Szczeci ska. The State Department is trying to develop relations with ex-Iron Curtain countries, so they're paying my salary. You can continue working for me here if you want.

"Can I come see you in Poland?"

"Of course."

"It won't be the same as playing Vivaldi and Mozart every evening." I didn't want to complain, but I was feeling sorry for myself.

"No, it won't. We will miss that as well," Teddy said.

I hadn't decided what to do, but I did call Marylin the next day and instructed her to send Sonya's floppies to Matt's Waltham warehouse. I tried to resume my routine for the next few weeks. Perhaps it was because Sonya was no longer on the ship, perhaps because I'm an old man and don't have the energy to keep up a sustained effort, but I began to put less work into my treatise and more effort into my evening music.

Finally I received a call from Richie that Sonya's work arrived. I took a cab. Waltham is only about twenty minutes by train from North Station, but it takes that long to get to North Station from my place, and then Matt's warehouse is more than a half hour walk from the train depot. Some days I enjoy a mid-winter excursion, but on that day I just wanted to see what Sonya had sent me.

I was pleased with the quality of her work, nothing she offered was radically different from what I already had done, but there were several refinements and a few totally new insights into the whales' geometry. I picked up my pace again — I decided I would try to finish before Teddy left, I didn't relish the thought of spending time alone in his office.

I had forgotten about Clive's last note. I had decided if it was important Clive would explain it to me. I believe I even neglected to look for his messages for a week or two, but one day I did notice a page in the bottom of my empty trash can again. It was not a newspaper article, it looked like a portion of an intelligence memo, but all the attributions were missing. This one I didn't have any trouble understanding. It was an article on the mysterious sinking of the USS Grinsby. There was no explanation as to why the ship sank. In fact it was described as a mystery that the navy was investing an immense amount of effort to solve. My first reaction was to be thankful Sonya wasn't on the ship, my second was to put it behind me. My project on whale language was still a breathtaking venture, but it felt like normal science now, not a cat-and-mouse game with my friends' lives and my own life on the line.

Teddy spent much less time at his office that spring, so I had a taste of what it would be to spend a lot of time by myself there. I didn't like it. One day I arrived there a little early and turned the light on to see Clive Bernard sitting in Teddy's seat.

"How long have you been here?" I said.

"Why do you ask?"

"You've been here just sitting in the dark?"

"I like the dark." Clive was quiet. I don't think I had ever seen him just quiet before. It wasn't a good sign.

"Are you here to tell me why the *Grinsby* sank?"

"I don't know why it sank. Do you?"

I was surprised I knew something he didn't, and explained at some length the entire situation, including Sonya's departure.

"I'm relieved she's safe," Clive said.

"I'm surprised you didn't know that, Clive. You always know everything."

Clive smiled for the first time. "The trick to intelligence is to know more than the people you're operating against *think* you can know, to know things about their situation they don't know, to know things they don't even know they don't know. Of course, you must assume they know something about you, so you need to make sure much of what they know is wrong. But the task is never to know everything — that is impossible. And attempting to do the impossible will inevitably lead to failure."

"And what do you know about the *Grinsby* accident I don't know?" I asked.

"I know they are going to try to pin it on you. And now maybe Sonya as well."

"On me!"

"On you."

"How? Why?"

"Did you read the notices about Admiral Hentoff?"

"Of course. Did you run over him?"

Clive smiled again. "What a pleasant idea. But no, and he would be the wrong person to run over."

"Who's the right person?"

"The person who I believe had Hentoff and Jennison and Gerry and you run over: William Dickson. He's a second-rate scientist, but a first-rate manipulator. He has wormed his way into an influential position, and the first thing that happens on his watch is the navy loses a research vessel under suspicious circumstances. He needs to find a reason it's not his fault. That would be you."

"But why me?"

"Because you knew Sonya, you knew Joanne, you knew Gerry, and his two henchmen don't like you. They really don't like you."

"I barely knew Joanne."

"She visited you, that's enough. Not sure why his thugs hate you though."

"Those are the guys who broke into my apartment. I think that's Marta's fault." I told him the story about their lousy Russian and Marta's .38 Special.

"That would do it," Clive said. "I gather you were also less than cooperative in the hospital."

"They accused me of participating in a conspiracy. They didn't appreciate me denying it."

"They were right, they were sure they were right, and they were mad because they never proved it. Anyway, none of that matters to Dickson. He just needs to find a reason he won't get blamed for the loss of a navy ship."

"You know," I said, "I'll bet he's the reason they were messing with the whales anyway."

"I do not know a lot about Dickson yet. You think he was researching the humpbacks at one time?"

"I believe he was on a cruise with a biologist named Harold Jennison as a research assistant. They had a falling out, to the point that Dickson only made one cruise, and Jennison despised him."

Clive raised an eyebrow, exhibiting the ironic curiosity one would expect from an Oxford scholar. "You've done a bit of sleuthing, my dear Watson. Why did they fall out?"

"Jennison accused him of destroying or changing their data. He evidently felt Captain Dickson had decided it would ruin his career if he helped prove humpbacks were worthy of consideration, and that the navy should curtail its low frequency sonar programs."

"By the way, it's Admiral Dickson now, Rear Admiral Dickson, so whatever he has done it hasn't harmed his career. From what I gather, he is more feared than admired. His name around the navy is Ugly Eye, and it's used as much for his demeanor as his face.

"His face?"

"I guess he was burned in Vietnam, he has a scar over one of his eyes but no eyebrow."

"I've met him!" I said. I told Clive the story of his visit in my hospital room."

"Not a good sign. You're in danger, and we need to figure out a way to save you."

"Is he that afraid of public backlash?"

"There won't be any public backlash, the public will never know. That memo I sent you was part of a larger classified document that outlined the necessity of keeping the disappearance of the *Grinsby* away from the public view. But losing a secret research vessel is a very big deal inside the navy."

"So, if he doesn't pin the disaster on me, he's afraid the navy will pin it on him."

"And with good reason. In the navy, someone is always held accountable."

We sat in silence in Teddy's dingy office for several minutes. They say when you're about to die your entire life flashes before your eyes. I don't believe that's true, but when you have some time and are trying to figure out a way to save yourself, a lot of it does. I thought about my friends in Alpine, Arizona. I was surprised it hadn't occurred to me before, but I began to wonder — even if Tarik had found Sasquatch, would he ever let anyone know? Anyone, perhaps, besides his brothers. I thought about Jack's description of the scientific revolution as a slowly exploding bomb, a bomb we inhabit and are watching go off. I compared his simile to Teddy's phrase *Primordial Chord*, which he chose to use instead of *Big Bang*, because he understood a bang, or a bomb, destroys even understanding. I also thought, on a more personal scale, that I wanted to live.

Finally, Clive broke the silence. "I can get you a false ID, I can front you some funds, but I can't run a sustained witness-protection program by myself. And if I could, being in repeated contact with you would increase the risk of Dickson finding you. He is relentless, and like me, he knows it isn't knowing everything that's important. It's capitalizing on mistakes."

"Can't he be exposed?"

"Eventually he will be, but it's complicated. We believe he's implicated in murder as well, along with his two sycophants, but we can't prove any of it. If he goes down for the *Grinsby* incident, they may still be left free to wreak some damage, especially on you. They really don't like you. Situations like these can get out of hand quickly."

He was essentially telling me I was on my own. "Don't worry, Clive, I can take care of myself."

Clive's eyes narrowed, but before he said anything he relaxed his visage again. "If anyone else told me that, I'd think they were deluded, but I believe you." He stood up and searched my face again. "Anyway, like I said, I can supply some funding for your future." He hoisted a knapsack from the floor by his chair and tossed it to me. It hit me with a thud, it must have weighed ten pounds.

"What's this?

"Twenties. About 100k. It'll help you get started on your new life."

I set the bag on my table and turned back to Clive. "You came prepared."

"I'm a professional, Joey. I knew we'd really have to say good-bye this time."

As he stood up, I walked over to shake his hand. "If this is all so dangerous, how did you dare visit me?"

"Again, I wouldn't want to make a habit of it." As he spoke, Clive stuck one of his hands into his jacket pocket. For the first time I noticed he was dressed in the casual/formal uniform of a university professor — tweed jacket with elbow patches, blue jeans, loafers. He pulled out a white wig and transformed his neat crew cut into long stringy hair. He grabbed a cane I hadn't even noticed from beside his chair and stooped over, transforming himself into an old man. It seemed as if he even shrank in size. "I have an article to write on the use of verb tenses in *Beowulf*, old chap. I'd better get to it." His Oxford accent was convincing.

He hobbled out of the room looking thirty years older than he had just five minutes before, leaving me to extricate myself from my life. I had only one hope. This time I called from Coolidge Corners. "Hello Marylin. It's me again."

"Joe! How are you?" Did you get my package?"

"I'm great, better than ever, and I received the package."

"Good, I thought something might be wrong, you never call this often."

"I have another favor to ask of you."

"Sure, whatever."

"This one will take a little longer."

"Like I told you, I'm retired, I have lots of time."

"Can you pick me up and take me home?" There was a long silence. For a minute, I thought I might have made a mistake.

"Of course, dear. At your place?"

"No, let's make it the bus depot in Albany, New York."

"Wherever you want. Can you tell me why?"

"We'll have a lot of time on our trip to discuss that. Watch the roads, it's winter."

I was awakened in the middle of the night in a cold sweat by a nightmare I had of Gerry. It made me realize my plan wasn't good enough. I called Marylin back as soon as I thought polite, given that it is three hours earlier in California than Massachusetts. "Marylin, I want you to pick me up in Denver instead. I'll call later today with a date and time."

"Good for me, that's a shorter drive."

I had realized I needed another layer or two of deception. I decided to buy a plane ticket to Rapid City, with a layover in Denver. I'm not sure if the navy can track my purchase, but if they do, they will assume I'm going to visit relatives in Draper.

Then there are my cats. Since Teddy and Marta are also planning to leave the country, I've told my neighbors, Rico and Annemarie, that I will be visiting relatives for a month and asked them to care of them. They will keep them in their own apartment, and I'm sure they will treat them well. I know they will continue to keep them when I don't return. I trust that Ranger will lose his old animus toward Rico and eventually settle in.

I know I cannot not sell my condo without creating suspicion, as I not only want it to appear I'm going somewhere I'm not going, but also that I plan to come back. I thought about taking a mortgage on my condo to recoup some of its value without actually selling it, but decided that too would look fishy. I'll just have to write the whole thing off as a loss, to make it appear I plan to come back. Of course, Clive's generosity eases the pain considerably.

The travel agent made everything pretty simple, even renting me a room and a car in Rapid City. I had two days to get ready. With my plans finalized I made a last call to Marylin.

When I arrived back at my apartment, I knew I needed to write this narrative, or my treatises on the whales would not make sense.

24

I have no further insight into Captain Dickson's immediate intent, which is why I was concerned when I started this narrative that I might not have time to complete it. If Dickson had moved on me immediately, I wouldn't have had time to explain the origin of my opuses on humpback language and mathematics, and he would have gained control of all the work we have done. As I was writing this down, though, I still had to wrestle with the question of whether to make this treatise public or not. I've concluded the human race is currently too dangerous, too presumptuous, too unwise to be given access to the whales' society. However, I am a scientist too and I can't bring myself to destroy this wealth of information. Even now, I dream of visiting Alaska and getting to know some Inuit to find out more about their communications with whales.

For now I intend to become an old man who spends his days walking along California beaches and going on whale watches, an old man to be ignored and forgotten. I will hide my treatises where I hope they will not be found soon, and just hope the time is more propitious for their proper use when and if they are ever uncovered.

About the Author

Robert Leet is a structural engineer who has designed hundreds of buildings, but this is only his second novel. He lives with his wife in western Massachusetts surrounded by a wildlife sanctuary, where they attempt to keep their dog, cats, and chickens safe.

To learn more about Robert, please visit:

roberleet.com